Gangsta Jake

Gangsta Jake

The End Result of a Snitch

Nyerere Jase

Copyright: © 2006 by Nyerere Jase.

Library Congress Cataloging-in-Publication Data:
ISBN#   Softcover   0-9787958-0-6

This is a work of fiction. Names, characters, places and incidents either are the product of the author's imagination or are used fictitiously, and any resemblance to any actual persons, living or dead, events, or locales is entirely coincidental.

This book was printed in the United States of America.

To order additional copies of this book, contact:
Nyerere Jase
310-462-7442
nyererejase@yahoo.com

CONTENTS

∂

Dedication

This book is dedicated to my mother and father
who are now resting in peace.

∂

ACKNOWLEDGMENTS

First and foremost, I'd like to thank God almighty for allowing me the opportunity to make it this far in life. I've been around the block a few times and through his will, was able to overcome many obstacles.

Tak, I did it homey. I didn't believe it when you told me I had writing skills; that day we walked around the inner track at Taft. Good looking folks. Shouts out to you and all the other real soldier throughout the Federal / State systems who took their time on the chin and refused to go out like so many others who felt snitching was the easy way out. Lemuel, it's our turn to shine baby boy. I can't wait until you hit the bricks, so we can get this paper. It's been awaiting our arrival for so many years. Also thanks for helping me with the editing process. You and my boy Chris Horton did a decent job on fine tuning my story. Thank you too Rochelle and Danielle for assisting in the editing process. Without you guys my dream of putting out this novel could not have been possible. Furthermore Rochelle, thank you for having my back throughout the final stages of this project; your generosity definitely expedited the proceedings.

I also want to give a special thanks to my Jamaica partner Rohan Lemon for coming up with the title of this book. Hang in there soldier, your day to rejoin your family and friends will be here before you know it. What's cracking Dre, Sheen, Black Tone, Wood, Benzo-Ed, Zapp, Rudy Brown, Solo, Devil, Kalid, Poncho, Frankie, my celly Mike Jones, Dee-Coup, Hub, Fresno Dee, Low-key and all the other homies who shared a moment with me in A3C when I began putting this project together. Frog even though you wasn't in our unit, I also have to give you a holler for being the smoothest nigga's I ever met from Oakland. Stay down for your crown.

To all the real ones caught up in the struggle, rather it's on the streets or in someone jail-cell or dormitory; keep your heads up homies. Life ain't that bad. Remember there is always someone is a worst situation than yours. A's up to all my homeboys and homegirls from my hood. Rest-in-Peace to my nigga's that lost there lives in this bullshit ass war we've fought for so many years. Hopefully one day we all can wake up and realize who the real enemies are.

Acknowledgments

Last but the not least, I want to give it up to my little brother, Lil' Man, and my main mans, G-Rat, and Papa Gee who've been around some of those blocks with me that I referred to earlier. Lil' Man, I can't wait to see one of your screens plays show up in a movie theater or on a television screen. Stay down for your crown my brother, and don't ever give up on your dreams. Wait one second; I can't close this acknowledgement without showing love to my whole family. It's entirely too many of you to name names, so I'll just thank you all in general. Family means the world to me and without you guys my life would not be filled with so much joy. You guys touch my heart in special way, especially the youth of our family. You kids are our family future, hugs and many kisses to you all.

Always love,
Nyerere

1

Reversal

It finally happened! After doing time in the San Quentin State Penitentiary for the past twelve years for a crime I did not commit, I'm finally going to the tilt. I nearly had a heart attack when I received and opened the court order handed down by the Ninth Circuit Court of Appeals. At first, I thought one of the homies was playing a trick on me. Hell, it was April Fool's Day when my eyes read over the document that freed me. My nigga, Young Lad, who was also sentenced to die by lethal injection, had a habit of typing up fake court orders and sliding them under the homies' cells. The homey never meant any harm. He's just silly as fuck sometimes. Young Lad and I were library clerks, as well as jailhouse lawyers. Year after year, we would help guys in the prison file various motions to the court of appeals. Everyone in our cellblock had been convicted of serious crimes, mostly murder.

All of us were caught up deep in the system. In most of our cases, a snitch decided to crawl up on the witness stand and sell his soul to the wolves. Yeah, a wolf is how I would describe the prosecuting attorney on my case. The big-lipped bastard reminded me of one of those house Negroes from back in the slavery days. He stood about five feet six inches, wore a pair of thick, black glasses, and stayed in the same cheap suit every day of my trial. He and a Newton Street (Police Department) homicide detective named Pac-man knew damn well I wasn't the one who killed a little girl in a drive-by shooting. Every gangbanger in the city knew how the Los Angeles Police Department's (LAPD) gang unit task force known as CRASH (Community Resource Against Street Hoodlums) got down when it came to pulling the ultimate cross. If CRASH could not solve a murder, they were known for pinning it on a homey who fit the killer's description. The cold thing about it is, in most cases, they squeezed a snitch to lie on the witness stand and say whatever they wanted him to say in order to gain a conviction. That was my story in a nutshell. But through the grace of God, all my dealings with the racist-ass court system had finally paid off.

After sizing up the official court seal and the authenticity of the postage on the envelope, I realized Young Lad was not up to his same old tricks again. It was the real deal! My lotto number had finally hit. I would be the next prisoner to receive true justice in the California judicial system.

But fuck all that! I done gave these folks twelve years of my life behind a snitch. My dawgs and I vowed long ago to kill each other's snitches if we were ever blessed to run across any of them again in life. All the homies I've done time with were standup guys who were worthy of the favor. By hanging out with the same guys for years at a time, day in and day out, we all developed a brotherly love for one another. It didn't matter whether you were a Blood, Crip, or whatever the case may be; as long as you were a standup guy and not a snitch, then you had nothing but love coming. After reading the court order, I could not wait to hit bricks so I could look out in any way for my niggas whom I would be leaving behind.

"Young Lad! Young Lad! Wake up, nigga!" Rohan J. Lemon, a.k.a. Gangsta Jake, yelled down the tier, looking through a mirror he held in his left hand. "Nigga, I'm free! I'm the fuck out of here! We beat these bastards!"

"Cuzz, stop all that noise! Young Lad is asleep!" Dre loudly whispered back down the tier, also holding a mirror in his hand to gain a view of Gangsta Jake's smooth, round face.

Gangsta Jake was a brown-skinned brother with hazel-green eyes. He was six feet two inches, and his body stayed in tiptop shape as a result of working out and eating properly year after year.

Once Dre looked at his face through both mirrors, the giant-size smile that appeared on Gangsta Jake's face was enough to inform Dre that he was not bullshitting around. Dre immediately set his mirror on top of his flimsy pillow and jumped down from the upper bunk. Then he excitedly shook Young Lad in his bottom bunk. Young Lad woke up with a line of drool running down his mouth.

"What's up, cuzz?" he asked, peering up at Dre with a sleepy look on his face.

Young Lad was on swole with twenty-inch, cut up arms. He stood about six two and had a caramel complexion with a shy, boyish face. Behind that boyish look, however, was a cold-blooded killer. He was convicted of a walk-up shooting that left three security guards dead at the Slauson Swap Meet. Young Lad committed his crime in broad daylight, in front of a crowd of people. Dre and Gangsta Jake knew Young Lad would spend the rest of his life behind bars. The two comrades never entertained the thought of filing an appeal on Young Lad's behalf.

Gangsta Jake, on the other hand, had a lot of action on beating his charges. The whole neighborhood knew his homeboy, Ghost, actually killed the five-year-old victim of circumstance. Days after he and Zap committed the drive-by shooting at the local high school, Ghost went to the neighborhood running his mouth about it. The crowd of niggas he originally shot at escaped the drive-by with minor gunshot wounds. In essence, he had no real reason to be running around, bragging about what he had done. Had Gangsta Jake been a soft dude, he could have easily pointed the finger at Ghost and bounced out of the whole fucked-up situation. However, the thought of telling never crossed Gangsta Jake's mind. He knew he had not pulled the trigger, so he figured one day, he would eventually wiggle his way out of the tragedy that had occurred. It turned out that he was right.

"Young Lad, we did it, dawg! The Ninth Circuit reversed my case! I got you, homey! I'ma show you how a real nigga is suppose to carry it when they touch the outs. Fuck Ghost, bitch ass! That busta ain't never sent me a dime since I been down. He knows what's popping. And that mark who took the stand against me, homey, you already know what's cracking on that."

Gangsta Jake was revved up. Veins were popping out of the side of his neck from being so overwhelmed with joy, pain, and most of all—revenge. He never liked the way snitches had flooded the game. As far as he was concerned, "The game was over and the rats prevailed." That's what he would say whenever he and his real killers got together in the prison yard. Gangsta Jake was itching to get out and take down some of his comrade's accusers. He felt it was the least he could do for his fallen soldiers whom he was about to leave behind.

"I told you, homey. I knew we would pop that ass before it was over and done with," Young Lad finally yelled back down the tier as he sat on his bunk, calmly placing his shoes and socks on. "This calls for a celebration. Nigga, slide some of that green shit in your stash down here. You got plenty of that shit coming where you're about to go. And make sure when you get out, to eat some pussy for your dawg," he told his partner with a Kool-Aid smile posted up on his face. Young Lad was very excited that he and his main man's litigation finally paid off.

"Congratulations, young Blood," Crazy Mike gently blurted out after ear hustling from the next cell over. Crazy Mike had the look of a Black Panther member from back in the days. That look, consisting of a short Afro, chubby cheeks, and full beard he's held onto since his arrest in the late sixties. Crazy Mike was one of those old soldiers who had been hanging out on the row for the past thirty years. He had witnessed the row population flip a few times since his arrest. He was not with the black-on-black crimes like most of his young partners whom he was sitting on the shelf with. His thing was breaking into white folks' houses, robbing, and then killing them. He had four stays of execution, two since Gangsta Jake hit the row in the early nineties. Gangsta Jake and Young Lad personally filed the last two for Crazy Mike.

"Take advantage of your blessing, youngster," Crazy Mike told Gangsta Jake in a deep, scratchy voice. "Go out there and make something out of your life, son. You already know it ain't nothing slick about waking up in this free hotel every day of your life. Slow your roll this go-around, youngster."

"Mike, my roll was slowed when I was out there. If that rat, Lil' Papa, had not lied about me in trial, I wouldn't be here."

"Yeah, not on this case, but probably on another one. I heard how you were putting it down out there. Learn from an old fool's mistake like mine, who will never get the opportunity to see daylight again."

"I'ma be all right, Mike," Gangsta Jake said. "All I have to do is stay sucka free and keep them gold-digging hookers out of my mix."

"Yeah, I can see them all over you now, young blood. Fresh out, on huff, how could they resist you?"

"You better not go out there and trick your dick off with that bitch, Terra," Dre hollered down the tier.

Terra was Gangsta Jake's girl before he came to prison. She was tall and possessed a body like a video girl. Her perfect, round ass and juicy lips instantly attracted Gangsta Jake when he first met her at the Crenshaw Shopping Center. Terra was all the definition of a young freak. When it came to having sex, she definitely knew how to satisfy a man. Giving head on the freeway at sixty-five miles an hour is what Terra loved to do. That, along with wanting to ride the dick at least twice a day made Gangsta Jake fall head over heels for her.

Terra jumped out of the car months following Gangsta Jake's arrest. She did not have the decency to wait around and see if he would beat his charges. The last Gangsta Jake heard about her, she was balling by way of a big dope dealer out of Compton. Word on the street was, her man sold gallons of PCP for ten thousand a pop.

Gangsta Jake's big homeboy, Horsehead, sent word through his sister, Angie, on a visit, that Terra's dude was one of the best PCP cooks in the city. Horsehead told Angie how he heard Terra and her dude had matching 500 Mercedes and stayed shining every time they hit the scene. Word had it that her dude even purchased Terra a baby mansion up in Hollywood Hills. Terra was living high and mighty and never entertained the thought of getting in touch with Gangsta Jake. The way she viewed it, there was nothing he could do for her fine ass behind bars. Once she peeled off with the twenty thousand Gangsta Jake left in her care, her mission was complete.

When Terra heard about him receiving a death sentence, the only thing she done was place a collect block on her phone to avoid his calls. She would have never imagined in her wildest dreams of setting her vision on his brown skin and green eyes again. However, all that would change once he was freed from custody.

"I'm not fucking with that punk bitch!" Gangsta Jake stated while having a strange look on his face. "She dumped me like I fell off the face of the earth. It's not like I was expecting for her to place her chickenshit-ass life on hold and cater to my every demand. But goddamn, she could have at least sent a guy a dry cino every other month to shop at the commissary, some flicks of that fat ass in a g-string or something. The bitch just left a gangsta hanging."

"If you ever see her punk ass in traffic, tell her, Young Lad said to eat a dick up."

"Yeah, nigga, I'll be sure to tell her if I ever see her again." Before Half-dead (another lifer on the tier) could comment on the laughter that bounced from cell to cell, an oh so familiar sound cut directly into their celebration. By that time, Gangsta Jake had passed damn near everyone on the tier a joint of chronic to inhale and a way to get in contact with him upon his release. The clings and clangs from the three guards' keys could be heard as the guards entered the front of the tier. The aroma lingering in the air could be smelled in the immediate surroundings.

"Goddamn, Billy Bob," the guard with the two gold captain bars on his collar responded to the fresh smell of marijuana in the air, "It seems that we're just in time for the going-home party."

"I guess the word travels really fast around here, sir," the baby-faced guard in the rear of the trio commented to his captain's remarks.

Gangsta Jake's ride to freedom had arrived. He had never been so happy to see the one-times appear. He was so elated to finally be going home, he nearly burst into tears. Captain McDonald and his crew were only teasing the row full of lifers about the weed smell that permeated the air. The guards never gave a damn about weed being smoked in their jail. The way the guards viewed the situation was, the state of California had squeezed all the time they could possibly squeeze out of every single lifer on the row. The only thing worse they could have done was snatch their lives from them. Moreover, in some of their cases, the state of California forced the guards to do just that via lethal injection.

However, being legally murdered was the last thing on Gangsta Jake's mind. He was eager to be reattached with the society he left behind twelve years ago. Without any further ado, Captain McDonald gave the orders to start the release process.

"Open cell nine," Captain McDonald barked into the overhead intercom, making sure the control booth guard heard his voice loud and clear. After the command was received, cell nine was opened. As Gangsta Jake placed one foot onto the tier, the entire row began to hoop and cheer. Everyone in the prison had a great deal of love and respect for him. They admired how he remained a standup guy in spite of the homicide detectives pressing him to become a snitch. The volume of noise reached an all-time high as he began making his final stroll down the tier.

"Take care of yourself out there, my nigga," his homey, Warlock, yelled from the rear of the tier.

"Don't forget to get at mom's about that," Avalon Blue shouted to Gangsta Jake as he and the three surrounding guards walked directly past Avalon Blue's cell.

"I got you, homey," Gangsta Jake said with sorrow starting to build up inside of him. Gangsta Jake had a lot of compassion in his heart for his partners on the row. 24/7, 365 days a year had been spent with most of them since he was arrested on February 14, 1992. He never blamed the court system for locking him and his partners up and throwing away the keys. All his blame went to the snitches who, he felt, had violated all the rules of the game. When Gangsta Jake arrived in front of Young Lad and Dre's cell, he made sure to stop and say a special farewell.

"Good lookin' on all the hard work you help me put down. I could not have won this case without you, dawg. Get at me if you ever need anything. Money, documents from the courts, somebody to bring your girl up here to visit you, whatever, homey! I got your back."

He then looked Young Lad square in the eyes and stated, "You got my girl, Michelle's, number; use it. Dre, you stay down too, my nig. I got much love for all you fools," he raised his voice, realizing the whole tier's ears were in attendance.

"Don't you got somewhere to be, young Blood?" Crazy Mike interjected from the next cell over.

"I guess I do, old man," he replied with a look of joy and pain attached to his face.

"Take care of yourself, youngster. And let this be the last time you step foot in somebody's penitentiary again."

With that in mind, Gangsta Jake said his final goodbyes and kept it moving with the three guards who accompanied him.

* * *

Meanwhile, Gangsta Jake's girlfriend, Michelle, and one of her fly buddies name Robin, who both happened to be in town, were five minutes away from pulling into the San Quentin parking lot. Soon after receiving word of his reversal, Gangsta Jake saw to it that a guard at the prison called Michelle's grandmother's house, which prompted her and her friend to immediately head to the prison.

Michelle was five seven, one hundred and forty pounds, and had the sexiest walk one could imagine. Her skin tone was dark and smooth, which went perfect with her full, luscious lips and long, silky hair. Michelle was from the hood, but eventually moved to Brooklyn, New York.

She and Gangsta Jake hooked up a few years after his conviction for the little girl's murder. Gangsta Jake's cousin plugged them up during a three-way telephone conversation. His cousin, Lewis, was originally suppose to get with Michelle, but before you knew it, Gangsta Jake and Michelle were exchanging information about each another. Ever since that phone conversation, Michelle had been in Gangsta Jake's corner 100 percent.

Gangsta Jake started not to tell Michelle about the reversal. He thought about creeping up and surprising her, but did not want to wait that long to see his girl. He wanted Michelle to be the very first female he set eyes on once he was freed from custody.

"Get out the mirror, bitch. Your face ain't going to change," Robin smiled and told Michelle while making sure her own makeup was in order. Robin was also a cutie pie who had curves in all the right places. She had all the niggas crazy about her thick thighs and bedroom eyes. She and Michelle had been partners since elementary school. They both worked at the criminal court building in downtown Manhattan. Michelle and Robin also played a big role in Gangsta Jake's reversal. Their diligent research and legwork made Gangsta Jake and Young Lad's legal work a whole lot easier.

"Girl, you're silly as hell," Robin commented to Michelle in response to the middle finger Michelle gave to her.

"Robin, I'm so happy I could scream."

"You should be, fine as that nigga is. Girl, you know all those little hoodrat, homegirls of his are going to be on his jock."

"Girl, I'm not worried about them little chicken-head bitches. That nigga is in love with me. I'm the bitch who stayed down with his yellow ass for the past nine years. Running here, running there, making this and that call for him, sending him money every month. Girl, don't even go there," Michelle said while rolling her eyes back toward the road she drove down.

"Calm down, girl. I'm only teasing you. You don't have to get your blood pressure up."

"I'll beat one of them hoes to death if they ever get caught fucking around with my man."

Michelle had the look of a square, but was far from being one. Before her departure to New York ten years ago, she was into all types of drama—fighting, stealing, and selling drugs. She would even sell a shot of ass if the price was right. However, all that changed once she moved to Brooklyn. She left Los Angeles to get away from all the chaos. Robin was so impressed with how Michelle had changed up her program; she decided to move to Brooklyn as well.

*   *   *

Back at the San Quentin Correctional facility, Gangsta Jake was in the final stages of his release process.

"How are you, Mr. Lemon? You must feel like a million bucks." The warden reached his hand out to Gangsta Jake and grinned. "Congratulations, young man."

Gangsta Jake was reluctant to shake the blue-eyed, wrinkle-faced, white man's hand; however, he did not wish to give the administration any reason to slow his release process down. Therefore, he extended his muscular arm out toward the warden. "Thank you, sir. I appreciate your concern. By the way, is there any chance I'll be able to be released before the shift change? My girlfriend should be waiting for me in the parking lot, and I don't want to keep her waiting. You know, she's already been waiting for the past twelve years," he sarcastically added with a smile on his face, indicating his desire to leave.

"Oh, yes, of course, Mr. Lemon. My guards should be finished in just a few. We'll need you to sign a few more pieces of paperwork, and then you'll be on your way."

Michelle and Robin suddenly pulled into the prison parking lot, bumping "No More Drama," by Mary J. Blige. By then, Michelle had calmed all the way down and was excited about seeing her man. Two guards starting their work shift walked past the girls sitting in the car and gave them a friendly salute.

"Look, girl, he's waving at you," Robin tapped Michelle on the leg and informed her. "I see his ass, girl. I'm not speaking to that clown. Them fools had my baby locked up all this damn time for nothing. Fuck them," Michelle sharply stated as she turned her head in the opposite direction.

"Girl, you're so mean. Hey, y'all," Robin yelled out the window before the second guard made his way into the building.

*　　*　　*

Moments after the double door closed, they reopened from the force of someone exiting the building. That someone happened be to Gangsta Jake, with a huge smile attached to his face. His turn had finally arrived. He was, at last, a free man. The first thing he did was breathe in a breath of fresh air.

"Aaaaaahhhh, it's on now," he told himself as he stretched his arms out from east to west.

Robin immediately noticed his presence. "Michelle, there goes Rohan right there," she screamed out in order to gain her best friend's attention.

"Oh, my God! Oh, my God!" Michelle exclaimed as she jumped out the driver's seat and dashed toward Gangsta Jake's direction. Robin trailed behind her. When Michelle reached Gangsta Jake, her body melted into his arms like ice cream on the ground during a hot summer day. They kissed passionately for every bit of five minutes. Michelle was excited and filled with joy. In spite of Gangsta Jake being locked up for so long with a death sentence, he was the only guy who moved her in that magnitude.

Amazingly, out of the nine years Gangsta Jake and Michelle were together, she only managed to give the draws up three times. Every other time she came was with the help of Gangsta Jake via a freaky telephone conversation or letter. He had her wrapped around his pinky finger, and there was nothing she would not do to satisfy him. Robin stood inches away from the glued lovebirds, observing their every move.

"Y'all need to go get a room," she yelled out, hoping to get their attention. Once Robin was acknowledged, she spoke her mind. "I want a hug too," she requested in a friendly, but sexy manner. Robin had a lot of love for Gangsta Jake as well. The two had never met in person, but would talk whenever he called to speak to Michelle. Moments after she caught the two lovebirds' attention, Gangsta Jake turned around and called Robin over to the hugging session.

"Come here, Robin. Girl, you should already know you have nothing but love coming from me. You and Michelle helped to make this day a reality. Give me a big hug."

Robin blushed and walked into his firm, but gentle grip. Once he embraced the two sexy females, he was more than ready to depart from the location he had spent most of his life. He placed both his arms around the two girls and walked toward the 2004 Lincoln Continental Michelle rented.

Inside of it, the car smelled like perfume. Michelle and Gangsta Jake had optimistically talked for years about how they would make love on his first day out of the slammer. Due to Gangsta Jake having a death sentence, he was forbidden from obtaining conjugal visits. No conjugal visits meant he had never ventured inside Michelle's love tunnel. He was horny as a toad and just sitting between two, sweet-smelling cuties brought him to a near erection.

It had been so long since he sat unsupervised among anyone from the opposite sex, he almost did not know how to act. He had heard over and over about how loose it had gotten in the free world when it came to one guy and two females having sex with one another, that he wanted to experience it for himself.

For years at a time, Gangsta Jake would jack his meat off in the shower, thinking about all the wild sex he was missing out on, and there he sat in the mist of his vivid imagination. He wanted to see where the two best friends stood on the issue, but he did not want to cause any discomfort. Instead of him being candid about the desire that lingered within his mind, he decided to beat around the bush with the issue.

"Y'all both are looking so sexy," he told the girls as he turned and kissed Michelle, then Robin on their cheeks. "I smell that chronic; let me hit something." Michelle reached between her 38/Ds and handed her man a fifty sack of sticky, green weed.

"Now that's what I'm talking about!" he told Michelle as he placed the see-through bag up to his nostrils and inhaled. He then rolled a joint the size of an oversized toothpick.

"What are you going to do with that little bitty thing?" Michelle smiled at him and chuckled.

"Smoking anything bigger than this is only wasting weed," he said as he blazed and took two long pulls before passing it toward Michelle.

"Boy, quit playing. Robin, pass me that cigarette lighter," Michelle told her girlfriend, while pulling out of her bra a blunt the size of his fat finger.

Once the chronic was in the air, Michelle popped the "Magic Stick," by 50 Cent and Lil' Kim inside the CD player. Minutes later, Michelle's monkey was starting to get wet from the chronic and the thought of how her man would soon to be sexing her up. She looked over and gave Gangsta Jake an expression that told him, she did not want to wait the eight-hour drive it would take for them to reach their destination in Los Angeles. He noticed her actions and felt the need to capitalize on the situation. "Let's go get a room before we make it to the city," he threw out there, searching for a concurring response.

"Naw, y'all can drop me off first," Robin quickly answered.

Before she could say another word, Gangsta Jake butted in. "We're not going to be that long, Robin. Just kick back. You're rolling with us."

"No, I'm not, boy," she responded, knowing damn well she really wanted to tag along.

Michelle was not tripping; she was down with whatever Gangsta Jake had planned. When he mentioned getting a room, she never said a word. Although he did not speak about having sex with them both, Michelle and Robin could infer his intentions by the look in his eyes and how affectionate he had became after they all hugged in the prison parking lot. Michelle was not into having sex with females, but she was the type of girl who would go to any extent to please her man.

Robin, on the other hand, had freaked with a guy and girl at the same time on a couple occasions, but never revealed her secret to Michelle. As bad as she wanted to get down with Michelle and Gangsta Jake, she was too ashamed to go there; therefore, she declined.

"Rohan, I love you, boy, but not like that. Michelle and I are best friends," Robin wailed out, looking toward her girlfriend. She wanted to know what was on Michelle's mind. However, Michelle kept her in the blind by remaining focused on the highway.

After the trio drove past a few freeway off-ramps, Michelle rolled her eyes and boldly blurted out what was on her mind. "Girl, I'm about to go fuck my man." Without waiting for a response from Robin, she exited the freeway in a little hick town.

Gangsta Jake admired how aggressive Michelle had become. Before he knew it, she was rubbing his shaft as though it was being used to change gears in the car she was driving. "Damn, baby, you're working with a lot down there. I should have gotten you off the hook a long time ago. That way, I could have had some of my papa."

Hearing the word "papa" was a complete turnoff to Gangsta Jake. He hated his ex-homeboy, Lil' Papa, with a passion. Before Lil' Papa took the stand against Gangsta Jake in trial, they were not everyday running buddies, but homies who both represented the Avalon Gangsta Crips. Gangsta Jake was from the Five Tray chapter of the Avalons and Lil' Papa was from the Fortieth Street chapter.

After Gangsta Jake's trial, Lil' Papa stopped coming to the neighborhood and none of his homeboys ever heard from him again. Gangsta Jake, being the young rider that he is, was not satisfied with that alone. He figured if he wanted Lil' Papa six feet under, he would have to do it on his own. Finding Lil' Papa's (or any other snitch's) location would not be a hard task. His girl, Michelle, did work at the courthouse and had access to all confidential informants' personal information. Gangsta Jake knew that once he hit the streets, Lil' Papa's days on the earth would be limited.

"Michelle, don't ever let the word "papa" come out your mouth again. That bitch-ass nigga is the reason my life has been on hold for all these damn years! Muthafuckas like that don't deserve to live!" he yelled. Gangsta Jake was starting to get deep into his feelings and eventually checked himself before he allowed his temper to get too far out of hand. Instead of him allowing "that rat" as he put it, jack off his first day out the slammer, he simply relaxed and enjoyed his return back to society.

"My bad, y'all. I didn't mean to get so upset about that rat." Once the situation became calm, Gangsta Jake kissed Michelle on the neck as she found a parking spot at the Motel 6 next to a Waffle House.

"Robin, why don't you get us something to eat while me and Rohan check into a room. I'll leave a key for you at the front desk. Get us anything; I'm not tripping. And I know Rohan ain't either, based on all that garbage he's been eating for the past twelve years."

"Okay, I'll see you lovebirds in a little while."

Michelle drove Robin up to the front door of the Waffle House and found a parking spot adjacent to the motel room. Within a New York minute, Gangsta Jake and his girl were walking inside the room. Before he could get in good, Michelle began taken his clothes off from behind him.

"So, baby, you really did want to fuck both of us," Michelle whispered to her man as she kissed the back of his neck.

"Naw, I just wanted to fuck Robin. I wanted to make love to you. So you aren't tripping?"

"If that's what you want to do," she hunched her shoulder and said with a sort of sad look. In the same motion, she unbuckled his pants and sunk her right hand inside them. When she turned Gangsta Jake around and looked at the baldhead champ he possessed inside the Sean John jeans she purchased, all her unhappiness faded away.

"Damn, nigga, fuck what 50 Cent is talking about; you got the *real* magic stick. Go lay down, baby. I want to suck on some of this before I hop on top and ride it." Michelle's entire attitude changed.

"Slow down, baby girl. Before you do that, get naked. I want to see that body up and down. I already know it's right by looking at it in those tight jeans, but I want to see it in the raw."

She responded without hesitation. As she undressed, Gangsta Jake thought about the many times they had spoken about having sex. Instead of rushing into what had taken years to establish, he wanted to savor the moment. Michelle slowly unbuttoned her blouse and laid it on the bed. Her hard nipples pocked straight up and could be viewed through the white Victoria's Secret bra she wore.

"Take off your pants now," he told her as though he had become intoxicated with the sight of her perfectly shaped physique.

Michelle dropped her pants and proudly showcased her body as if she was a full-blooded thoroughbred. She looked like a female that had been handcrafted by a sex fiend. Her ass was round as a basketball and pretty as one that had never hit the concrete. Michelle was as bad as they came, and she did not mind setting it out for the man who she had waited so long to accompany. The few other guys that did have the pleasure to hit it had never enjoyed seeing her in that magnitude. She felt her man was the only person who truly deserved a full bar of her.

Michelle sat her ass cheeks on top of the room table, laid back, and began spreading her legs wide open. She wanted to make sure Gangsta Jake had a good view of how neatly trimmed her kitty-cat hairs were. Once that was established, she took her left index finger, slid her black g-string to one side, and slowly penetrated herself with her middle finger. She enjoyed how mesmerized Gangsta Jake was about her performance.

Looking at how freaky Michelle had become made his mouth literally water. He had never experienced anything like that in his entire life—only in his kinkiest dreams. Gangsta Jake was only the tender age of sixteen when he was charged and later sentenced to death as an adult. The boy could count all the females he banged on both hands, and one-third of them were strawberries getting him off for a ten-piece of crack. He went from sitting on death row to having a fat muffin at his disposal. Not a bad transition for a young, state-raised thug.

"Come get some of this pussy, baby; it's wet as a water faucet for you," Michelle spoke seductively as she placed her now-moist finger between her soft, full lips.

Gangsta Jake suddenly could not resist his prized possession any longer. He stood up, fully erect, and walked over to Michelle, holding his pipe in his right hand. As he came within arm's distance, she slowly went to her knees and gently cuffed him by his hairy testicles. She then placed in her mouth as much of his pipe as she could fit. He held her silky hair that rested on her back and helped guide the bobs and weaves that brought him soooo much pleasure. Michelle slowed her strokes and went straight to the crack of his head. Sticking her tongue inside his pee hole almost made him cum; however, he snatched it out before that occurred.

"What's wrong, Rohan? Don't you like it?"

"Hell, yeah, baby. I like it too much. Another minute of that and I would have came all in your mouth."

"So what's wrong with that?" she looked up and asked with a giant smile on her face.

"Naw, baby, I want my first dose to go in that," he responded and pointed at the fat muffin between her legs. He wanted to put a baby in her.

"Okay, sweetie. Let's do it then, because I got to have some of this." She licked on him a few more times before releasing him, like a good ice cream cone she did not want to put down. Once they made it over to the bed, Michelle lay flat on her back and placed within her hand every inch of his manhood. After their position was established, she guided him into her wet hole like it was the vibrator she had become so accustomed to handling. The live pulse that penetrated her felt 100 percent better than the battery-operated machine she played with year after year while the love of her life was incarcerated. She adored all eight inches of him.

"Damn, baby, this pipe feel sooo good," Michelle moaned and grunted as a tear came running down her face. "I love you, Rohan. I love you, baby. Please don't stop," she begged as she came within the first two minutes.

Gangsta Jake noticed her instant discharge and felt the need to catch up. He immediately began to deep stroke her like a madman.

"No, baby, don't cum," she quickly said. "I just came fast because I was horny and could not ah, oh . . ." she moaned with pleasurable pain. "I couldn't help it. I'm not finish, Rohan," she adamantly told Gangsta Jake as she pulled him toward her. She was far from being out of gas. The fast organism only made her craved him more.

"Let me get on top and ride it, baby."

"I don't have a problem with that, sexy." They switched positions and Michelle was now driving the car. As a result of her having so low mileage, she was tight and pleasant to be in. Gangsta Jake felt better than a kid in a candy store. He was having the time of his life. 38Ds in his mouth, tight monkey on his jock, what else could be better, he wondered. Michelle was on one. She bounced up and down on the pipe as if she was the one who had just served a lengthy sentence.

"Whose pussy is this?" he smiled and asked her while holding onto both of her breasts.

"It's yours, baby. Beat it up, daddy!" she screamed out loud, making sure not to use the word papa. "Is it what you expected?"

"Hell, yeah. Just don't cum yet," she pleaded as her body began to shiver from all the downstroking she was doing.

"Ride it faster. Go faster."

"No, I don't want you to cum yet."

"Girl, I got this. Just keep working it."

"Ohh! Ahh! Damn, this dick feel good," Michelle yelled out in a it-hurts-good scream.

"Shit!" Robin whispered to herself as she stood motionless outside the thin motel door. She had been standing there for the past five minutes, holding what had now turned into a cold meal. When she first walked up to the door, Gangsta Jake and Michelle were in full motion. The session they were having sounded so good, she did not want to disturb it. Besides, she was enjoying listening to her friend getting her sex on.

Five minutes of snooping on their lovemaking had Robin's panties wet and her plotting on a way to be a part of it. The motel manger noticed Robin with her ear on the door of room sixty-nine and decided to investigate the young woman's intentions.

"Excuse me, Miss," the old, white woman said as she crept up and scared the hell out of Robin. "What in the world are you up to? Do you know the party inside that room?" she pressed, pointing toward the room Gangsta Jake and Michelle occupied.

Robin stood in awe for a few seconds before realizing the old lady's husband had just handed her a key to the room. "Oh, yeah, my friends are in there. The old—I mean, the man inside the office gave me the key my friends inside the room left for me."

"Well, why on earth are you standing outside?" she quizzed as she held a panic button to the local police station inside her jacket pocket as though it was a concealed weapon.

"I'm sorry to be alarming you, ma'am. I just wanted to make sure they were in there." Robin verbally ran by the old lady as she stuck the key in the door and open it.

When she entered the room, the couple was in full throttle. So much, that at first glance, they did not trip on Robin entering the room, nor the old lady receiving an eyeful as the door opened and closed.

"Robin, you tripping girl!" Michelle snapped, as she threw a comforter over her naked body. "Did you see that old bitch looking at us?"

"Girl, she ain't worried about y'all. Go on and finish getting your freak on."

"Granny might want to get her groove back. Send her old ass over here," Gangsta Jake clowned as he continued to stroke his girl. Laughter filled the room as Michelle and Gangsta Jake kept the good times rolling.

"You'll give that old lady a heart attack with all that over there." Robin smiled at the two before setting the meal in her hands on the table.

Minutes later, Michelle could not hold back the volcano that erupted inside her. "Oh, baby, I can't," her voice moaned as the juices within her began to flow. Michelle closed her eyes, relaxed her body, and enjoyed her second organism with the love of her life.

Without asking, Gangsta Jake laid Michelle on her back and hit it hard until he came.

Robin sat frozen as she fantasized on being next. *All he has to do is ask for some and I'm coming out of this hot shit. Michelle ain't tripping*, Robin convinced herself. At that moment, she was pumped up and willing to get her freak on. "Damn, it's hot in here. Michelle, why do you guys have the heat up so high?"

"Bitch, ain't no heat on in here. You don't have to pretend with us. Rohan and I both knew you wanted to get your freak on. Girl, I'm not mad at your little hot ass for wanting some," Michelle said with a cute smirk on her face, cheerful from her first encounter with his love machine.

Robin was happy to at least hear her girlfriend speaking on the issue. Gangsta Jake enjoyed the exchange of words between the two girls. At that point, there was no doubt in his mind he could have both of them. However, he decided not to go that route so fast. Maybe later, but not at that moment. He had a bigger agenda ahead of him. Besides, he really did not want to upset his girl. He knew she would do anything he asked of her, but his intuition told him that Michelle did not like the idea of him running up in another woman. Once he got his nuts out of hock, he was ready to head toward the city.

2

The Meeting

Days after being released from custody, Gangsta Jake was feeling good and ready to get in traffic. Before Michelle and Robin woke up for the morning, he jumped inside Michelle's rental car and headed toward the eastside of Los Angeles. Three days of laying up, having sex with Michelle, and eating good food was satisfying enough for him. He figured it was time to stretch his wings out a little. He heard it through the grapevine that his homies were having a gang meeting at South Park. He had not seen nor heard from 99 percent of his homies since his fall in '92. Word had not yet hit the streets about his reversal, but that would soon change.

Gangsta Jake pulled out of the hotel onto Century Boulevard, drove past a neighborhood in Inglewood called the Bottoms, and came to a red light on Century and Crenshaw Boulevard. Three fine sisters walked in front of the car he was driving. The cutest one turned toward him and waved.

"Hey, cutie," he responded with the window rolled up. She was very sexy, but he was not pressed to be getting with any females outside of Michelle. His mind was focused on obtaining a bankroll, meeting up with some of his niggas who he hadn't seen in years, and finding some of the snitches who helped put him and his partners behind bars. Gangsta Jake could not rest well knowing there were snitches roaming "his town," as he liked to put it.

Instead of totally ignoring the three females, he pulled over and wrote down their information in order to hook the girls up with some of his homeboys in prison. He took ten pictures of the three girls. They did not mind the fact that he wanted to send his homies photos of them right there on the spot. To accompany the girls' photographs and hookups, he would also send a postal money order to everyone he was tight with. He promised Young Lad he would arm himself with a disposable camera for the purpose of sending some flicks of some females and that's just what he did.

Gangsta Jake understood firsthand how it felt to be stuck with a death sentence and not having family or anyone supporting him. Before he met Michelle, he experienced some hard times. No commissary, love letters, naked flicks, or nothing; he was hit like good weed when it came to outside support. Michelle was definitely a blessing to him, and he would make sure to show his appreciation by loving and spoiling her forever.

Once he conducted his business with the females, he hopped in his ride and drove Crenshaw Boulevard all the way down to Slauson. He then made a right turn on Slauson, drove past the indoor swap meet, and came to another red light on Avalon Boulevard. As he passed up the Slauson Swap Meet, he thought about his main man, Young Lad, whose conviction relied on the testimony of two of the security guards who worked for the swap meet. "Yeah, I'll be back to holla at you marks," he said to himself, as he looked over at two security guards standing next to the swap meet entrance. "Robot muthafuckas! One of yo bitch-ass homeboys got on the stand against my road dawg," he continued. "I'ma come back and kill one of you rats—watch."

Gangsta Jake was a straight lunatic. He really felt he was obligated to rid the streets of snitches. Instead of making plans to get a job, settling down, and staying out the way, he was eager to do just the opposite. No one knew if it was the PCP that he frequently smoked prior to going to jail that gave him the I-don't-give-a-fuck attitude or the fact that he came from a broken family. But the boy truly did not have it all. He was always smart, but lacked when it came to having good sense.

On Avalon Boulevard, Gangsta Jake made a left turn and drove to the liquor store on Fifty-first Street. A group of his homeboys were hanging out at least thirty deep in the liquor store parking lot, with one hundred or so more by the swimming pool across the street at the park. Lil' Boss Hog and Cool Boo noticed a strange face and immediately went on the defense.

"Say, loco, who is that fool getting out that fresh Continental?" Cool Boo asked Lil' Boss Hog while swaying back and forth from the empty forty-ounce bottle in his hand.

"I don't know, cuzz, but I'm busting if he make any wrong moves."

Gangsta Jake recognized how they were hawk-eyeing him and held up the Avalon gang sign with one hand and the three fingers representing the Five Trays with the other. After some long stares, Lil' Boss Hog realized who Gangsta Jake was.

"Gangsta Jake! Is that you, cuzz? I must be seeing a ghost. What's crackalacking, my nigga?" Lil' Boss Hog was so happy to see him that he ran over and gave him a big bear hug. Seconds later, a few more of his homies noticed the exchange and went over to embrace him as well; then, ten more, then fifteen more came. Before you knew it, every homey in the parking lot walked over and hugged Gangsta Jake.

"Cuzz, we thought you were washed up." Bull Capone, smiling, reached his fat knuckle out for a dap and told Gangsta Jake, "Cuzz, why didn't you tell us you were coming home? We could have had a house party set up for you or something."

"Hell, cuzz, I didn't really know I was coming home myself. But all that wouldn't have been necessary." Without allowing Bogart to say another word, Gangsta Jake cut him off by asking where was Ghost.

"That nigga left me on stuck and didn't send me a dime."

"We're about to have a meeting, so he should be showing up in a few."

Before Bogart could say another word, Ghost turned the corner off Fifty-first Street onto Avalon Boulevard, driving his low-rider on three-wheel motion. All eyes turned toward Ghost as he hit his switches in order to make his low-rider go back on all four wheels. He then hit the switches several more times to please his audience. His rag top '63 Impala was as clean as the Board of Health. The deep-black paint, triple-gold hundred spokes, Dayton rims, and bumping sound system must have set him back at least twenty-five thousand, Gangsta Jake thought to himself.

"This nigga got me fucked up! I'm trying to see him, homey," he told the few homeboys of his that stood next to him. With the O.G. status Gangsta Jake had throughout the hood, as well as the prison system, no one was going to challenge his pull.

Ghost, unaware of Gangsta Jake's presence, parked his low-rider as usual, pancaking it on the ground, and walked up like any other day. Once he got within arm's distance, Gangsta Jake fired on him with a hard left.

"Bitch-ass nigga, you thought I was through with money, didn't you?" Gangsta Jake caught him off guard and knocked him to the ground. "Get yo mark ass up!" he told him before running up and yanking the Rolex chain off his neck. "Nigga, give me this shit, and these car keys while you're at it."

Gangsta Jake was getting off his chest what he had pondered doing for the past twelve years. A couple of youngsters who were unfamiliar with Gangsta Jake (due to his absence) ran up in an attempt to rescue Ghost from his ass whooping. "Hold up, lil' homies," Big Joker swiftly stepped up and said to one of his trigger happy little homeboys, who clenched in his hand a brand-new 9mm he stole the night before. "Don't trip, little Crip. This is a head-up squabble among gees. That's the O.G. homey, Gangsta Jake, who just got out the pen from doing a stretch. Everything is under control."

"Let's take it to the park," Ghost told Gangsta Jake as he stood on one knee and wiped away the fresh blood from his mouth.

"Nigga, we can take it anywhere you want to take it!" Gangsta Jake pulled off his shirt and led the pack of onlookers across the street to the park. His body was cut up like bad dope. His stomach, arms, and chest were all ripped like a professional body builder. You can tell by all the muscles he had that he was as strong as an ox.

Ghost was not really trying to see him from the shoulders, but he obviously did not have a choice. Gangsta Jake had fired on him, took his Rolex, and car keys. He had to at least try and gain back some points from how he was being carried.

The one hundred or so gangbangers at the park saw a bunch of homies walking toward them and could not understand what was going on. As the two packs of thugs came closer in contact, the larger pack came to realize a fight was underway.

"Cuzz, what the fuck's going on, and who the fuck is this nigga?" Fat Daddy announced once the two crowds came in contact with one another.

Horsehead thought he recognized the other guy as being Gangsta Jake; however, due to him receiving a death sentence, he felt that that thought was out the question.

"Fool, don't worry about what the fuck is going on," he gritted his teeth at Fat Daddy's comment toward him. "This is Gangsta Jake, original Avalon Gangsta Crip, nigga! You know who the fuck I am!"

At first glance, Fat Daddy could not tell who Gangsta Jake actually was. However, after hearing his name, it all registered. He and Gangsta Jake never liked one another in the past. They had a few squabbles over the homegirl, Tray girl, which lead them to not seeing eye to eye.

Gangsta Jake felt strong and solid, like he could beat down anyone from the shoulders. He was hoping Fat Daddy stepped further out of line so he could put hands on him.

Fat Daddy was shocked to see Gangsta Jake. He wondered how he could get out of custody. He wanted to say something slick out the mouth, about whether or not he snitched to obtain his freedom, but he knew better than to make such an allegation without having the paperwork to back such a claim. Gangsta Jake was too swole and cut up to be talking shit to. Just like Ghost, Fat Daddy did not want any problems.

"Boy, you a fooooool!" Horsehead finally spoke up and smiled as he cheerfully hunched his shoulders and placed the side of his fist up to his mouth. "My little nigga is out! I'll be damn!"

Horsehead was a lightweight comedian, as well as a big homey who Gangsta Jake had a lot of respect for. Horsehead was five feet ten inches, light-skinned, and looked sort of like a horse from the neck up. The resemblance to a horse is how he got his name back in the days.

"Jake, how the fuck did you pull that one off? You a bad mothafucka boy. Nigga, it's good as fuck to see you." Horsehead placed his right arm around Gangsta Jake and pulled him off to the side.

"Man, fuck this square-ass shit. Let ya dawg take you out to get some pussy. I'm not about to sit up here and let you kill this nigga, Ghost, or jack yours off behind none of these clowns. Damn, nigga, you just got out. Don't you enjoy freedom? Can't none of them fools over there fade you. I already know your work, baby boy."

"I just don't like how a gang of these suckas have been carrying it out here, big homey."

"So what happened? Did you win your case on appeal, escape, or what?" Horsehead changed the subject, trying to calm his young homey down.

"I beat my shit on appeal, dawg. I got that money order you shot to my girl last Christmas and the message you gave my sister, Angie. But," Gangsta Jake had a look on his face that told Horsehead he wanted to get the situation he created off his chest, "but we'll talk later, folks. Let me deal with this bullshit right now."

"Okay, dawg. I'ma turn you loose, take care yo business, but don't do nothing too stupid."

Gangsta Jake gave Horsehead a quick hug and walked back toward the drama. "So what's popping, Fat Daddy? Are you looking for a squabble or something?"

"Homey, I ain't tripping on no old shit. We can leave the past in the past. I just didn't know who you were and wanted to know what was going on in the hood. Handle yo scandal, dawg. That's y'all business as far as I'm concerned." Fat Daddy bowed down and fell into the crowd of onlookers. Gangsta Jake's body looked way stronger and built up since the last time Fat Daddy saw him on the streets; just as Horsehead suggested, he wasn't trying to see him.

"Let me get my car keys and shit back," Ghost finally asked in a pleading tone.

"Fool, you owe me. I'm taking this shit. You already know what time it is. I stayed in prison twelve years behind yo soft ass. You could have at least made sure my books stayed fat."

The entire crowd remained quiet, wondering if Ghost was going to defend the rep he held.

"I should be going in a circle socking out a whole lot of you buster-ass niggas for not looking out. When was the last time some of you marks sent the homies in the pen something?" He walked up to Rabbit, a homey he had not seen or heard from since his fall in '92 and specifically said, "I'm talking to you, nigga!" He screamed in Rabbit's ear as if he was a drill sergeant giving one of his soldiers a command.

"Uhhhh, let me see." Rabbit thought about the question as he looked off into the clear blue sky.

Bink, bink, bink. Gangsta Jake stole on Rabbit three times before knocking him out cold. Seconds later, he ran over to Fat Daddy and put a two-piece on him. Then over to a couple other homies who, he heard were having money, but not reaching out to the soldiers locked up in the pen. Suddenly, Gangsta Jake's his mind snapped and he went 5150 on four more dudes in the pack. A couple of them tried to fight back, to no avail. They were no match for his strength.

About twenty-five of his homegirls stood in a huddle, making wagers on which one he would choose to sleep with first. They were all lusting over his body and infatuated with the demonstration he was putting down.

"You hook-ass niggas are out here getting all this bread, and you have real homies doing life sentences for the hood who can't even purchase a twenty cent soup from the commissary. Niggas, it's on every time I see you cowards if I haven't heard about y'all sending the homeboys some cheese. And these few thousand I took out you lames' pockets, I guarantee you, will be sent to the homies on lockdown. Bloods and Crips. Yeah, I said it. I embraced some red rags on my bid that I got way more love and respect for than some of you punks. Those are the niggas that fed me for my first few years."

"Handle that shit!" Horsehead told his young partner, happy to see another real homey back on the scene.

Ghost was not the toughest fellow from the hood, but was not a straight coward either. He wasn't about to go out without a fight. Normally, he would have had a 9mm Glock on hand, but due to CRASH sweating the neighborhood so hard, he left his gat at his house. Bad choice.

"You can't just take; just take my car and pieces like that, homeboy." Gangsta Jake had him so shook up, he was stuttering.

"What you gonna do about it then? Take them back if you want them." He clowned Ghost by holding his car keys and chain in the air. Several people, mostly females, broke out in laughter at the way he was getting his clown on at Ghost's expense.

Ghost definitely wanted his shot at getting his things back. The two squared off and fought like two wild animals. By engaging in so many scuffles, Ghost was hoping Gangsta Jake would be worn down and not able to perform at the level he did earlier. Ghost was also a big boy who had a halfway decent squabble. However, he could not fade Gangsta Jake's strength and swiftness. After sixty seconds of solid blows being exchanged, Ghost found himself in a daze. Gangsta did not give him any action. Once he dazed Ghost, he followed up with a haymaker that put him on his back. Ghost was knocked the fuck out in la la land.

Gangsta Jake was overwhelmed to finally be able to serve Ghost and the other homies who weren't contributing to the fallen soldiers. He wanted to do more then beat them down, but was not a complete fool to go out like that in front of a crowd full of people. He thought about all the time he had wasted behind a snitch and left the pack of onlookers.

Gangsta Jake told Horsehead to drive off in the rental car he pulled up in while he did the same in the '63 Impala he had just jacked Ghost for. Ghost would have loved to kill Gangsta Jake for the way he clowned him in front of everybody, but outside of doing a drive-by, he was not cut out to be a cold-blooded killer. Instead of getting himself twisted up in some drama he was not trying to be a part of, he accepted the damage and became a buster throughout the hood.

3

A Long Time Coming!

When Gangsta Jake finally made it back to Michelle and Robin two days later, he was fifteen thousand dollars richer. He walked inside the hotel room with a pocketful of big-face hundred dollar bills. Beside the ten thousand he made from Ghost's car, his homeboys passed a hat around and came up on an additional five grand for him. To show his appreciation to Michelle and Robin for sticking by his side, he loaded them in the car and headed to the Fox Hill Mall for a shopping spree.

After shopping for nearly three hours, Gangsta Jake and the girls each had three or four different outfits and the shoes to match. He purchased a pair of blue Mauri gators to wear with an all-black tailored suit, the new Jordan's to go with a Sean John sweat suit, and a few pieces of Rocaware. He was geared up for at least a few days.

He originally planned to slide up to the Western Surplus, spend a few hundred dollars on khaki suits and Chuck Taylor's, and keep his gear gangsta the way he wore it back in the day. However, he wanted to advance with time, which led him to go along with the advice of Michelle and Robin by purchasing some name-brand clothing.

To Gangsta Jake's surprise, he looked up from drinking out of a water fountain to see his ex-girlfriend, Terra. She and her boyfriend were walking past them, holding two bags full of clothes. Terra did not recognize him, but he definitely noticed her. She and her guy were looking like movie stars. She had on a pair of Chanel shoes and a Prada dress with the purse to match. The shinny Rolex on her wrist went well with her attire. Her boyfriend was also decked out with the all-gold, iced-out Rolex chain, ring, and bracelet. As he walked through the mall, all eyes were focused on his bling bling.

The more Gangsta Jake stared at Terra's boyfriend, the clearer his face became. Within a minute, he knew exactly who he was. He could not believe his eyes. After all these years, he finally ran across someone he really looked forward to seeing. Joy filled his body from excitement. He could not remember the last time he felt so euphoric about seeing anyone. He figured it would take at least a few months or so to catch up with the man who stood seven or eight yards away from him. Amazingly, Terra's boyfriend happened to be Lil' Papa, the guy who took the stand against him in trial.

Gangsta Jake knew not to go out like he did at South Park His worst fear was to be ratted on once again. In prison, he learned from reading case law after case law and personally being testified against, that it was hard to beat a snitch in court. He knew the chance of getting caught up (with all the witnesses present at the mall) was very possible if he attempted to do something to Lil' Papa on the spot. He was not ready to go back to prison now or as long as things were looking up for him. If he planned to take actions against Lil' Papa and not be apprehended, he had to come up with a solid plan.

Like the speed of light, Gangsta Jake had what he planned to do to Lil' Papa all figured out. Now that he worked it out in his mind, he had to figure out what would he tell Michelle and Robin and quickly because Terra and Lil' Papa were heading for the mall's exit.

"Say, y'all, let's go!"

"What's wrong, baby? We haven't got our food that we paid for yet. And why are you moving so fast?"

"Baby, we have to go right now! I'll explain in a second, but let's roll for now."

As the three walked toward the exit, Gangsta Jake looked around, making sure no one trailed them.

"Y'all see that guy walking with that girl?"

"Yeah," both girls responded as they placed their seat belts on.

"He's the one who took my life away from me twelve years ago. That clown got on the witness stand against me and lied!" His voiced rose as he hit the steering wheel hard enough to feel a slight vibration inside the car. The animal came out of him.

"Rohan, please don't do anything stupid," Robin nervously stated.

"Robin, this don't have nothing to do with you, so you need not worry yourself about it. What if somebody lied on you and had you all locked up behind their lying ass? This boy stayed in jail for twelve years behind him— twelve years, Robin," Michelle told Robin convincingly. She did not know exactly what he had in store, but she had his back at all cost.

Gangsta Jake followed Terra and Lil' Papa until they reached their destination in Compton. Lil' Papa had a two-bedroom condominium located on Compton

Boulevard and Wilmington. As Gangsta Jake parked the car, he reached under his seat and pulled out a .44 caliber bulldog his partner gave to him earlier at the park. Horsehead handed it to him when he seen how his young homey was carrying it in the neighborhood. He figured at the rate he was going, Gangsta Jake may need it sooner than later.

When Robin saw the gun, her heart skipped a beat. "Oh my goodness, Rohan, what are you doing with that thing?" She held her heart to make sure it would not jump out of her body. She was that afraid.

"Girl, it's crazy out here in the city. A guy has to have something to protect himself."

"What if the police pull us over and find that? We're all going to jail," Robin said out of fear.

"Hell, I'd rather be caught with it then caught slipping without it. We're cool; ain't no police pulling us over anyway."

"How do you figure that?" Robin asked with her eyes wide open, astounded at his nonchalant attitude.

"Because I'm rolling with two cuties," he smiled as he pinched Robin on her cheek.

She pouted and sat back, uninterested in what he had to say. Michelle sucked her teeth at how Robin was reacting. Anything Gangsta Jake said or did was totally agreed on by his girl.

After lounging on Lil' Papa's street for forty-five minutes, Gangsta Jake was ready to make his move. He instructed Michelle and Robin to walk up to Lil' Papa's door and ring the bell. Once someone inside opened the door, he planned on running in and handling his business. Robin was not down with the program, but after a long, back-and-forth conversation, Michelle persuaded her that everything would be okay. As the two beauties walked to the front door, Gangsta Jake trailed behind inconspicuously.

EEEKK, EEEKKK. On the third ring, a short Mexican lady opened the door with a pleasant smile. She was the housekeeper. When Gangsta Jake saw that the door was open, he took full advantage of the window of opportunity. He dashed pass Michelle, Robin, and the housekeeper, holding the .44 bulldog in his left hand. The housekeeper grabbed her heart and began screaming at the top of her lungs.

"Senor! Senor! Por favor, no me hagas dano, puedes llevarte lo que quieras!" (Sir! Sir! Please don't hurt me. Whatever you want, you can have it.)

Gangsta Jake barely paid her any attention. By the time the housekeeper caught her breath, he had already located Terra and Lil' Papa inside the shower together. Terra's heart dropped to the bottom of her feet when she looked up and saw the green-eyed gunman. Lil' Papa could not believe what he was experiencing. He would have paid any amount of money to be anywhere else at that very moment. Gangsta Jake grabbed them both by their wet hair and immediately tossed them to the floor.

"Hoe-ass nigga! You thought you would never see a gangsta again, didn't you?"

Terra nearly went into shock when she realized who the brown-skinned bandit in front of her actually was. Her first thought was, *he escaped from prison.*

"How you like me now, disrespectful ass bitch? You thought you done some slick shit when you robbed ole Gangsta Jake for his twenty gees, didn't you? It ain't no fun when the rabbit got the gun, is it?"

"Michelle! Bring that screaming ass bitch in here!" he yelled from the next room over. Michelle grabbed the poor woman by her shirt without thinking on her own. Her reaction made her appear as if she had been hypnotized.

"Here she is, baby." Robin, now scared to death, walked alongside of Michelle and the housekeeper. "What do you want me to do with her?"

Gangsta Jake tossed her a roll of duct tape he found in the kitchen drawer. "Tie her and these two up. Robin, help her," he commanded sharply.

"What?" said Robin. "Man, this ain't my cup of tea."

"Robin, let's just do it so we can get out of here," Michelle pleaded with her girlfriend.

"What the fuck are y'all waiting on?" he turned around and questioned them.

Enough time had already been wasted. Therefore, Michelle opted to restrain them on her own.

"Girl, what the fuck are you doing?" Robin asked, looking at Michelle in disbelief. "Michelle, you're tripping! This nigga is about to kill these people."

Michelle paid Robin no mind as she continued the job that she was commanded to do. Before you knew it, Terra, Lil' Papa, and the housekeeper were all duct taped. Since Robin obviously was not trying to help, Gangsta Jake assisted his girl.

"Fool, where is all the chips at? I know you and this bitch is papered up. I heard about how well y'all were living while I was suffering in a six by nine cell. I just didn't know it was yo muthafucking ass living it up with this gold-digging hoe." *Smack!* Gangsta Jake hit Lil' Papa in the head with the butt of his pistol.

"OOOOOOch!" he hollered out. Due to his hands being tied, he was force to rub his now-busted forehead on the carpet. "The money is in my safe, inside my room closet. Please don't kill me, dawg," he begged. "I have over a hundred and fifty thousand in there. You can have it all, just don't smoke me. Give me a pass, let me make it," Lil' Papa nervously plead

"Nigga, this ain't *Let's Make a Deal*, nor is it Burger King. You ain't having it your way up in here. You should've thought about all that before you got on that witness stand and told a goddamn lie on me!"

Terra felt the heat and the need to reason. "I'm sorry for taking your money, Rohan," she wept. "I can pay you back for the money I borrowed, with interest."

"Shut the fuck up, you scandalous-ass bitch! You're only sorry that I caught your ass. You don't give a damn about me, hoe.

"Michelle, cover this bitch mouth back up."

Robin could not believe what she was being a witness to. She only hoped and prayed that Gangsta Jake did not take Lil' Papa's life before her and everyone else's eyes.

After Lil' Papa mentioned the cash, Gangsta Jake dragged him and Terra to the safe in order to gain entry. Michelle and Robin stuck close by, accompanying the housekeeper, who was nervous and confused and began to sweat profusely.

"Open it up!" was the first command Gangsta Jake gave after freeing Lil' Papa's hands. With a few flicks of the wrist, the safe door opened. "Now that's what the fuck I'm talking about," Gangsta Jake told himself while removing the stacks of cash and every piece of jewelry from within.

"Can we please leave now?" Robin, scared and upset, requested.

Based on the time that had elapsed, Michelle concurred with her best friend. Without delay, Gangsta Jake walked up to Lil' Papa and placed the .44 caliber pistol up to his temple. Lil' Papa's body shook like an old mini bike. His eyes spoke the words that were trapped behind the duct tape on his mouth.

Bang! Bang! Bang! Gangsta Jake was not into giving out passes as Lil' Papa so desperately suggested. In a matter of three shots, a triple homicide had occurred. He shot Lil' Papa, Terra, and the housekeeper in the head. The way Robin reacted toward his actions, he thought about shooting her as well. Against his inner feelings, he allowed her to live. She hooped and cried as the three of them ran and jumped in the car.

"Robin, shut the hell up. I told you what that fool did to me. And that bitch." His face turned up. "That bitch robbed me, and left me for dead. I guarantee you, she won't fuck over anyone else. Them crocodile tears wasn't about to save her conniving ass. They got what they had coming, fuckem!"

"Look at me! I have blood all over my clothes," Robin complained, wishing she never came back to Los Angeles.

"Robin, take them off and change into one of your new outfits."

"You motherfuckers are crazy. Why did you kill the housekeeper? She didn't do a thing. Never mind, I don't even want to know. Michelle, I'm ready to get on a plane and take my ass back to Brooklyn. Girl, I'm scared as hell. Look at how I'm shaking. I'm not with all this shit."

Gangsta Jake did not like how Robin was continuing on about the murders. Michelle was hoping Robin would just close her mouth. She knew her man, and fully understood his feeling toward snitches and people who, he felt, took advantage of him while he was incarcerated. Robin was pushing the line, and before long, she realized it. The look in Gangsta Jake's eyes warned her to dummy up or be sorry. She caught the drift and left the issue alone.

"I'm cool, y'all. I'm sorry. Here, Michelle, do something with this bloody dress," a now aware Robin tore open one of her bags and slipped on a new outfit.

"Get off at the next exit, baby," Gangsta Jake told his girl as he peeped Robin out through the rearview mirror. "I want to get another rest spot. Those Koreans are noisy as hell at the other room. We'll double back and get our things later."

"Damn, look at all this fucking money. Y'all think we shopped up a storm earlier? We're about to paint the town up for real!" Robin, still in shock, was thinking of ways to get away from Gangsta Jake's crazy ass, contrary to his way of thinking. Rohan definitely was not the gentleman she had grown to know over the years. His telephone conversations were always smooth and charming. Every word he spoke seemed to always have a genuine meaning. She never would have imagined him turning out to be such a vicious person. There was now no doubt in her mind that the court system let a killer slip through the crack. She was convinced he had killed the little girl in the drive-by shooting that he was accused of, but she was wrong about that crime. Ghost did, in fact, kill the little girl. At any rate, she did not want to deal with him ever again is what played in her mind. She explored the possibility of Gangsta Jake killing her and decided to have a talk with God.

"Lord, I don't know what I've gotten myself into, but please, allow me to get out of it," she prayed silently with her eyes wide open. Robin did not want the others to know she was frightened.

4

Tearful Departure

"So what's up, y'all? Y'all want to have some fun or what? I got all this bread. The sky's the limit. Where do y'all want to celebrate? I'm not trying to stay in this hotel room all night. Everything on me, again," he laughed like the Joker often did whenever he got one over on Batman.

Michelle broke her silence as she lounged across the hotel bed. "Robin is acting all funny. Why don't we send her home?"

"Aw, it's like that?" Gangsta Jake said. Robin not showing any emotion.

"Oh, my bad, Robin. I'm tripping, huh? A nigga ain't been out of the pen but a minute, and I'm already off the chain. I'm sorry, girl. I know you don't need this shit in your life, you or Michelle. Y'all both got twenty thousand apiece coming. I'm sending y'all back to Brooklyn," Gangsta Jake said.

Robin's prayers were answered.

"No, baby. I'm not leaving you out here. Robin can go back, but I'm staying in the land. I love being back in Los Angeles, especially now that you're home."

"Michelle, what are you saying? What about work? What about our jobs, the apartment, your car payments, and all the other things you have going on in Brooklyn? We have responsibilities back in New York," said Robin.

"I'm tired of living out there. It's okay; the people are straight and all, but it's too damn cold in Brooklyn. Besides, my nigga is home," Michelle said as she slid under Gangsta Jake and hugged him by his waist. "My man got my back."

"Suit yourself then. Rohan, when can I leave?"

"You can leave tonight. Here's some ends for you. Robin, I hope there ain't no hard feelings between us." He looked inside her eyes, searching for the truth.

"No, I'm straight," she replied. She was a little sharper than he was. Robin knew he was examining her for signs of weakness; therefore, she kept her poker face on while tucking away the crisp bundles of fifty dollar bills he handed her.

*   *   *

The crime scene had been set up for the past twenty-four hours. Tim Goldfish, the lead detective on the triple homicide, was in the process of wrapping up his investigation. He ruled the murders as being a drug deal gone bad. When the detectives made it to the crime scene, all three bodies were found lying face down in a big puddle of blood. The white sheets over the corpses were drenched in blood when the detectives finally departed. Gangsta Jake and the girls left no concrete clues, which meant the police had their work cut out for them.

*   *   *

"I'm sure going to miss you, Robin. Thanks for taking care of my business back in Brooklyn. Girl, don't start that crying. I'll be all right."

Robin knew her best friend was in bad company. If Gangsta Jake could read minds, he would have learned of her true feelings toward him. She felt he should be locked up in the same cage he left behind. Robin no longer liked him. He was not her type of people. As the three waited on Robin's flight to board, Gangsta Jake walked off to use the restroom. This time allowed Robin a few minutes to have a one-on-one with Michelle.

"Bitch, what the fuck is your problem? That nigga is a killer. Why are you wasting your time on him?"

"I love him, Robin. Can't you understand that? I can change him."

"He's not trying to change. Didn't you see what he did at that condo? That nigga is a psycho, and you're starting to act like one too."

"Look," Michelle's left brow raised, "you don't have to worry about me and my man. I got this."

"Girl, all I'm saying is, don't throw your life in the garbage behind that no-nothing-ass nigga. He ain't headed in the right direction. Please, Michelle," she said, placing her hands in a praying position.

"Come home with me," a tear rolled down Robin's face, disturbing her black eye liner as she pleaded.

"Look at your face, girl," Michelle smiled, holding back her own emotions. "See there, you have black tears now."

"Michelle, ain't no dick worth you giving your whole life up for."

Michelle wiped Robin's eyes and nose with a piece of tissue she retrieved from her own pocket.

"Damn, girl! You only fucked him one time. Don't be stupid, Michelle. You're smarter than that." Robin looked at Michelle puppy-eyed, praying she was getting through to her. Her attempts were fruitless, though.

Gangsta Jake had a much stronger grip on Michelle than Robin could ever imagined. Hitting every G-spot in Michelle's vagina was only half the story. Gangsta Jake possessed the gift of gab. His conversations were as smooth as a baby's bottom. After nine straight years of being macked on, Michelle was basically under a spell.

As Robin turned to see if Gangsta Jake was returning, he came walking in their direction. It hurt Robin to see Michelle sprung over a guy so violent. She wanted to do more to help her, but what else could she have done—gone to the police? That thought did enter her mind, but was not entertained. She figured he would kill her and her parents if he even knew what had come into her mind. As horrible as the crimes she witnessed were, her fears of Gangsta Jake's retaliation were enough to cause her to remain silent.

Robin was so relieved when the flight attendant announced, "Flight 103 is now boarding for Brooklyn, New York," that she jumped up and nearly left her bags behind.

"Robin, slow your roll, girl. Don't you want your luggage?" Gangsta Jake asked.

"Oh, yeah."

"Let me find out you don't like money and I'll take it back if you don't want it," he joked.

Robin did not give a damn about the money. Her mind was focused on her best friend's well-being. She was very upset to be leaving Michelle behind with a lunatic like Gangsta Jake. He gave her the most uncomfortable feeling she had ever experienced. At first, he seemed to be a really nice guy, but seeing three people killed before her changed all that.

As flight 103 departed from the Los Angeles International Airport, Robin laid her head back on the headrest and tried to relax. However, all the drama she'd been through would not leave her mind. Once she played back the deadly event, big tears began running down her face. Robin was a sweet girl who would not wish death on anyone. She was the type who had so much love and compassion for people that it abused her heart to see life wasted before her eyes. It took all she had not to go to the authorities. If Gangsta Jake did not have an address on her parents, chances were, she would have spilled the beans. She loved her mom and dad so much that she was not willing to play games with their lives, no matter how many other people's lives were destroyed.

5

Da Club

"Saddam Hussein went out like a hoe. I thought he would have at least put up a fight like a soldier and take a few marines with him. He may as well have tucked his tail and left the country when Bush gave him and his sons 48 hours to do so. Then again, I don't know. I probably wouldn't have left behind all that I built either," Gangsta Jake commented while viewing the local news.

"Damn these muthafuckas are taking their time putting my rims on," he further blurted out before making his way over to the young, white guy who was installing his chrome spinner wheels. He and Michelle were in the process of having some tight rims put on the 2004 Lexus he purchased for a fat chip. He did not give a damn what it cost. He was ready to ball. Living lavish was another one of his dreams, and today would mark his first day at balling. As easy as money was coming thus far, he figured 2004 would be his year to bubble.

"How much longer will it be, Chief?" he asked the installer as he drew his left sleeve back to view the Rolex that rested on his wrist. The iced-out Rolex was one of the pieces of jewelry, among others, that were taken out of Lil' Papa's safe.

"Maybe five more minutes, sir."

"Right, Right. By the way, you don't mind if I test drive them, do you? I want to make sure they drive smooth."

"Sure, sir. I don't have a problem with that."

"How often do I rotate the tires on them?"

"Every three to five thousand miles."

"You don't say. In that case, I'll take an extra pair. Just place them in my truck, will you?"

He was rocking the young white kid to sleep. If he could avoid spending ten thousand for the rims and tires, he was all game. Once the rims were installed, he and Michelle jumped in the car and drove off with no plans to return.

"When I move, you move, just like that; when I move, you move, just like that," Gangsta Jake sang out loud to the beat while bobbing his head and burning rubber out of the parking lot.

"Boy, you so crazy! No, you didn't just run off with these rims and two pair of tires," Michelle already read his mind.

"Why pay when you don't have to? Besides, white folks owe me for slavery. I got to get some reparation off them at some point; why not now?"

"I ain't mad at you, big baller. I already knew you were going to get your money when you got out of prison, but I didn't know it would be by all means necessary. I heard that Malcom X—"

"You got damn skippy." His face lit up, then lit up even more when he looked over at the car next to him and noticed his rims reflecting off the paint job.

"Baby?" Michelle said to him.

"What?" was his response to the thought that lingered in Michelle's mind.

"Where are we going?"

"Why? Where do you want to go?"

"It doesn't matter as long as I'm with you," Michelle told him with a glowing smile on her face. Being alongside Gangsta Jake made her feel very special.

"Is the Barbary Coast Strip Club still open? When I was locked down, I heard they lost their liquor license or something like that."

"They did, but they're still open; quiet as kept they still sell liquor. Is that where you want to go? To see some dirty pussies jump up and down?" Michelle rolled her eyes.

"Look at you, girl," he smiled. "So that's what my baby looks like when she gets mad?"

"I'm not mad!" she snapped.

"Well, why are your eye brows raising like that?"

Her eyebrow going up was a telltale sign for showing her anger. If she only knew how much love he had in his heart for her, she would not be worried about him messing around. He was crazy about Michelle. The only way he would sleep with another woman was with her approval and in her presence. He considered Michelle a trooper that he needed in his corner. She had already stood by his side during his incarceration and did not frown on him for killing Lil' Papa, Terra, and the housekeeper. Michelle was the girl he planned on spending the rest of his life with.

"Michelle, you should already know that you're my numero uno. Ain't no pussy in the world worth me fucking off our relationship. I know how jealous you can be. I'm not going to play no games with you, especially without you knowing the rules of it."

"I'm not jealous."

"Yes, you are."

"Well, I guess I am a little bit. Rohan, I just love you so much, and I don't want no bitch coming out of the blue thinking she can have you. I've been through too much with you to lose out like that."

"You're locked in, girl. I don't want any of them other hoes. The most I would want from one of those big booty butt girls is a quick nut. Our relationship is way more meaningful than that."

"Why do guys feel the need to fuck this and that girl to be sexually satisfied?"

"Well, to be honest, baby, it's all about the different feels. Some females' pussies are tighter than others. Some know how to work it well. Some give bomb head—it all boils down to the feeling."

"So what if mine was not the bomb when you hit it?"

"What about it?"

"Would you have still wanted to mess with me?"

"Of course, I would have. I would be a dawg muthafucka if I shook you after what you went through with me. Niggas who dawg females out after they do all that time with them put a black eye in the game. At any rate, you don't have to worry about none of that. You got the bomb, and you're a sexy, down-for-whatever female. I saw the way you carried it when I smoked that snitch-ass nigga and his bitch."

"Yeah, I'm down with some of that gangsta shit too. Don't let all this fineness fool you."

"Check you out, trying to be all down with a guy. Oh, so I guess we're like the Bonnie & Clyde of the ghetto," Gangsta Jake said with a smile.

"I guess we are," Michelle responded.

"I wish Robin had the same attitude as you. She was acting all stupid when a guy was handling his business. I showed her nothing but love. I took her shopping, gave her twenty thousand; what else did the little bitch want from me?"

"Rohan!" She gave him a hush-your-bad-mouth look. "Baby, Robin is a sweet girl. She's just not down with people being hurt."

"Shit, what about when I was hurting behind that coward-ass nigga's testimony, or being without in prison, behind that hoe running off with my money. Some people don't realize that money is needed to live somewhat comfortably in prison."

"Well, honey, you don't have to worry about none of that drama any more."

"You damn right! Gangsta Jake is about to be the man."

"Do you plan on getting a dope sack and blowing up?"

"Fuck no! I wish I would let one of those snitches send me back to the penitentiary. I ain't even tripping on getting money right now. I'm cool on ends, thanks to that hoe-ass nigga and his bitch doing me wrong years back. As long as I stay out of prison, the money will come.

"It's a nice night this evening. Fuck the club; let's go to Venice Beach," Gangsta Jake recommended.

"No, baby, let's go to the club. I don't mind you looking at some bitches shake their asses."

"Are you sure you ain't tripping on that small shit?"

"No, I'm not tripping. I'll be good."

"We're on our way then."

When the two pulled inside the Barbary Coast parking lot, a pack of females were heading toward the club entrance. Every female in the crowd turned to look at the black Lexus and the brand-new spreewells that were twirling.

"Damn, girl, look at that nigga in that tight-ass Lex," a super fine female that resembled Gabriel Union told her girl, who looked like Halle Berry, but possessed a body like Jennifer Lopez.

"I need to be sitting where that bitch is," the Halle Berry look-alike told the others.

"Get at him, girl. He's going in the club," a short, dark-skinned cutie name Tasha in the rear of the crowd mentioned.

"I'm not going to disrespect his girl. I got more class then that."

"His girl? Ain't that a bitch!" the short, five-foot-three-inch female said to her girls. "That girl ain't nothing but a sack chaser. He don't care nothing about that girl. You know how niggas are. All they want to do is hit it and quit it. As long as he's paying, he got action at some of this. Girl, get with that nigga and charge him; forget about the girl with him. All you have to do is slide him your cell number when she's not paying any attention." Quinda, another girl in the crowd, could not resist the urge to rebut her chocolate friend's comment. Prior to the girls making it to the club, she and Quinda nearly had a fight over allegations of Tasha flirting with her boyfriend.

She was laying in the cut for Tasha to say something out of pocket so she could start some shit.

"You ain't nothing but a little hoe. All you talk about is getting over on a nigga. How do you know he's not loyal to his female? For all you know, they may be happily married."

"Bitch, you need to stay out of my business. Don't worry about what me and Já Lisa are talking about."

"Bitch! Who are you calling a bitch?"

"You, hoe!"

After Gangsta Jake parked the car, he and Michelle walked directly past the seven girls. The girls were so engrossed with the argument, they did not see him and his girl walk directly by them. Right as the couple made it to the club entrance, Quinda pulled out a box cutter and sliced Tasha across her face, who immediately disregarded the wound and ran up on Quinda, delivering several blows. She landed six hard blows that knocked Quinda up against a parked car. Blood from her face was now everywhere.

"Look at them hookers go. They definitely have some eastside in them. Michelle, I bet you ain't trying to see none of them crazy females, are you?"

"I told you not to let all this fineness fool you," she smiled. "I would punish one of these bitches if it came down to it."

"Come on, baby, let's go inside. I'm not trying to watch these hookers. They probably ain't fighting over nothing but some dick."

"Or pussy, baby. You would not believe how many girls are out here sucking on each other."

"Yeah, I heard all kinds of stories about it when I was locked down. Come on, let's go." They both walked inside the main entrance and left the girls to deal with three security guards that ran toward them.

"Salt Shaker" by the Ying Yang twins vibrated throughout the dimly lit building. Females were shaking their assets and collecting tips throughout the club. Gangsta Jake and Michelle sat down at the stage and ordered a bottle of Cristal. He was enjoying the scene, especially when three girls on stage approached him with their dance routine. The girl in the middle could have easily been a supermodel. Her tight body and well-rounded shape made Gangsta Jake reach in his pocket and pull out a knock of money.

"Damn, baby! This girl is bad to the bone!" Gangsta Jake told Michelle, full of excitement.

"You better give that hoe some ones!" Michelle screamed in his ear due to the loud music. Gangsta Jake peeled off four twenty-dollar bills and told Michelle to go get some change.

The stripper in the middle noticed how fat Gangsta Jake's bankroll was and focused all her attention toward him. When Michelle walked off, she bent over, placing her breast on his left shoulder, and asked if she could give him a lap dance later. Her tits felt so firm that he could not decline. A few minutes went by and Michelle returned with a handful of one dollar bills.

"Here, Rohan. I saw that bitch telling you something. What did she want?" Michelle asked with an attitude.

"Nothing, really. She asked if she could give me a lap dance once she got off stage."

"Is that right? I see she has my baby on trick status. Do your thing." Her jealous side started kicking in, but she held it in fairly well.

"Do you want a lap dance, baby?"

"I wish one of these hoes would come at me like that. I don't play that shit!"

"You would get one for me, wouldn't you?"

"Boy, you know I would do anything for you." He smiled at Michelle's comment. "Boy, hand me that drink because I can already read your mind."

"Nah, baby. You don't have to get one."

"Good." After two bottles of Cris, Gangsta Jake and Michelle were sauced up and having a good time. Michelle came to realize she was the finest female on the scene, and her guy did not want any girl in the club but her. The chick that spoke to Gangsta Jake about the lap dance suddenly appeared. She did not care about Michelle being present. Ole Girl was about her money.

"Excuse me, do you still want that dance?"

"Oh, yeah. I almost forgot about you." He looked at her while leaning from the alcohol. "How much?"

"For you, only ten dollars," she blushed, displaying her beautiful white teeth and femininity.

Michelle moved out the way and observed Ole Girl's techniques. Furthermore, she wanted to peep out the reaction her guy was having. Gangsta Jake had the look of a happy man. He was excited about his first lap dance, and it was written all over his face. Ole Girl danced inches away from him before turning around and resting her firm butt cheeks on his lap. When she caught a glimpse of the iced-out Rolex on his wrist, she really got loose. She stood up with her ass toward him, moved her g-string to one side, bent over in front of him, and shook her moneymaker.

"Shake it like a Polaroid. Shake it, shake it, shake it like a Polaroid," Gangsta Jake sang to the beat "Hey Ya," by Andre 3000, as Ole Girl conducted her business. She was on Gangsta Jake's jock like a basehead on crack. The size of his pipe amazed her when she reached down and grabbed ahold of it.

Michelle let Ole Girl do her thing while she grew a greater distance between the two. She knew whom he would be leaving the club with; therefore, she tried not to sweat the program. When "Stunt 101" by G-Unit came on, Ole Girl got besides herself by pulling out his shaft and placing it in her mouth. That was the straw that broke the camel's back. Michelle had a lot of patience when it came to dealing with Gangsta Jake's bullshit, but she was not going to sit back and allow this one to slide. Ole Girl definitely pressed the wrong button. Michelle tipped up beside Ole Girl and busted her in the head with a bottle of Moet.

The two bottles of alcohol and three joints of chronic had Gangsta Jake so caught up in a lustful moment, he failed to realize what he was allowing to take place. The crack of the glass bottle immediately snapped him out of his freak zone.

"Aw, shit! Damn, I'm tripping!" he told himself while pulling his sweat pants over his erected shaft.

"Trifling-ass hoe! You knew I was right across the room, and you have the audacity to clown a bitch like that!" Michelle rushed Ole Girl with the broken bottle in her hand, which prompted Ole Girl's partners to jump Michelle from several directions.

Bink. Bink. Gangsta Jake came to his girl's aid and knocked out two females wearing nothing but g-strings. "Get off my girl. You hoes got us fucked up."

Michelle and Gangsta Jake were turning out the club. For every girl he and Michelle fought off, two more seem to appear. Three male security guards finally made their way to the chaos and attempted to subdue the confusion. Two of them grabbed Gangsta Jake by the arm and tried to handcuff him. He countered their intentions by tossing them both behind the bar. The third guard backed off when he witnessed how his partners were now laid out in broken glass.

Before long, it was time for them to get in traffic. The first thing Gangsta Jake did was dash to the door and scoop Michelle up on the way out. She was in the process of fighting off two females, one of whom held a knife on her. Luckily, he was able to reach her in the nick of time because the girl with the knife had Michelle pinned to a wall.

As Michelle and Gangsta Jake made their way to the exit, two Gardena police officers rushed past them looking for the center of attraction. The couple blended into the crowd and eventually made it inside his Lexus.

"Are you okay, baby?"

Michelle did not respond. Instead, she sat in her seat huffing and puffing to catch her breath.

"My fault, baby. I should have checked that stripper before it went that far."

Michelle thought her words out carefully before commenting. When she finally gathered herself, she told Gangsta Jake that it was not his fault. She blamed the whole situation on Ole Girl. Michelle was hot as a six-shooter for the way he conducted himself, but not enough to place blame on him and take a chance on losing out on what she invested so years many into. As much as she wanted to trip, she decided to sit back and bite the bullet.

6

Serving the Law

Two months following Gangsta Jake's release from the big house, he received a letter from his partner, Young Lad, back at San Quentin.

Gangsta Jake,

What's popping, my nigga? Good lookin' on the thousand dollar money order and the flicks of the females. I can see by the flicks that you're out there having the time of your life. The females you plugged me and Dre up with are supposed to slide up here this weekend. I need you to get at them with some of that Al Green, so me and the homies will be okay for this weekend. Yeah, homeboy, ain't nothing changed on this end. Tell your girl, Michelle, I said, what's up? I already know she's out there draining you out of yo little wee-wee. I ain't mad at you, cuzz. I wish I could be out there getting milked out of mine. I sure hate that I fucked my life off over some bullshit. I didn't even have to kill them security guards, homey. If I could do it all over, I wouldn't have taken that route. I guess it ain't no use in crying over spilled milk. You just make sure to keep your wild ass out of here. My little sister told me how you carried Ghost in the hood when you first got out. She said all the homegirls were on you like they wanted to eat you alive. I told you they would be on you like a cheap suit.

Well, dawg, let me get back to doing this time. I just wanted to touch base with you. All the homies send their love. O, yeah, the courts set another execution date for Crazy Mike. I'm doing everything I can do to avoid it. He's tired, cuzz. He acts like he ain't tripping one way or another. He told me that he's worn out with doing time and dealing with the court system. I'm working with him, so he'll be all right. Yeah, homey, I'm not going to wear you down with jailhouse matters. Enjoy yourself out there and let me deal with this bullshit on this end.

Much love,
Young Lad

"Who wrote you, baby?"

"Young Lad sent me a letter to let me know what's going on in the pen."

"I'm so glad you're out, baby."

"Yeah, I am too. But I sure hate how my folks are still caught up though, especially behind all these snitches. Cowards are out here having a ball while my partners are rotting in six—by nine—cells 24/7. Where is that list I had you get from your job?"

"What list?"

"You know, the names and addresses I had you pull off your work computer some years back."

"Oh, those names and addresses. I left them back at my apartment in Brooklyn."

"In Brooklyn!?"

"Yeah, baby. I didn't know you wanted me to bring the list."

Gangsta Jake was referring to the list of confidential informants who testified against him and his partners throughout the prison system. Years ago, he instructed Michelle to dig up from her job the names and addresses of every prosecution witness he requested. Killing informants had not been something he came up with overnight. He planned long and carefully about knocking off all the snitches he could get his hand on, provided he was released from prison.

Based on the fact that Gangsta Jake had not yet had possession of the list, Lil' Papa, Terra, and their housekeeper, in essence, had a severe case of buzzard luck. His plan originally consisted of waiting a couple of months after his release to take down one of his victims. However, since he was officially ahead of schedule, he was ready to continue committing what he felt were justifiable homicides.

"Damn, baby. I got to have that list."

"Calm down, Rohan. I'll just call Robin and have her send it to me."

He did not like that idea. "Naw. For real, I'm not feeling Robin."

"Rohan, Robin is cool. I've been knowing her forever. She's too scared to tell anyone your business. I guarantee you, she will keep her mouth closed."

She better keep her trap shut, Gangsta Jake thought in the corner of his mind. *I know where she and her parents rest their heads.* Instead of him allowing Robin to forward the list, he felt the need to pay her a visit. He was aware of Robin and her people's address from corresponding over the years, but he wanted to get a visual on their location, just in case he needed to catch up with them in a hurry. He was not taking no for an answer. He and Michelle would be headed to Brooklyn, New York, in order to obtain the list and pay Robin a surprise visit.

"So, how do you want to travel, Michelle? Plane,train,automobile?"

"Let's fly. I want to hurry up and get back, so we can move into a place of our own. I'm tired of living in hotels. Even if we have to stay on the eastside for a while, we need somewhere we can call home."

"I'm not mad at you. Whatever you want to do is okay with me. But first things first. I have to get my hands on that list of names and addresses."

"Okay, honey; let me call Robin so she can be expecting us."

"No. We'll just surprise her. She don't need to know we're heading her way."

"Why not?"

"Look, Michelle, just do what I say and go along with the program, will you?"

"You're the man. Whatever you say is law with me."

"Call and make reservations for us. Make it for this weekend. That way, we can have two days to handle a few things on this end. I need to get with Horsehead in order to send Young Lad and a few of the homies a package."

* * *

Gangsta Jake pulled up to a weed-house, bounced out of his Lexus, and walked up to a black bar gate. A Jamaican with long dreadlocks saw him approaching and questioned him before he could knock on the door.

"Wha yo want, bwoy?" the dark-skinned, sleepy-eyed Jamaican asked in a deep Jamaican accent.

"How much for a couple ounces of that sticky green, rude boy?"

"Brethren wi nuh sell ounces; nothing but twenties and fifties."

"Man, you can sell me what you want to."

"What's wrong wi this bwoy?" the Jamaican turned and asked his partner, Fred, who was behind the door with him. "He acts like he no understand English. This bwoy a snitch, cop, or what?"

"Mi don't know, but he sure act like one," the other Jamaica responded with a sight chuckle, high as a skyscraper from the blunt he just smoked.

"Snitch? What the fuck did you just say? You got me twisted! Bombo clot mothafucka. Yeah, I can speak that shit too! Trick, you must be trying to get this shack shot up!"

Gangsta Jake's words were enough to alert everyone within the entire house. The first Jamaican he spoke to told the second one to wake up his young brother, who was laid out with a female on a beat-up couch. "Go for the guns and wake up Paul. This blood clot act like he wants problems."

"Fuck you! Open up this door if you want some drama! I'll run you clowns back to Jamaica. You suckas are making all this money in my neighborhood and have the nerve to be acting all arrogant and shit," Gangsta Jake shouted into the bar gate seconds away from pulling out the heat from underneath his shirt.

As he continued on with his heated conversation, an unmarked LAPD gang unit task force car drove up. The two officers were thirty minutes into their shift and looking for a little drama with some gangbangers. Seeing Gangsta Jake in an argument at the local weed-house was right up their alley. No one summoned them; they frequently drove past the weed-house on Fifty-third and San Pedro, looking for a bust.

Law enforcement constantly patrolled the block as a result of the many arrests conducted throughout the years. Shootings, robberies, and disputes among rival gang member purchasing marijuana, even the crackheads hanging out at the dope house up the street had the block hot. CRASH, regular LAPD, homicide detectives, and parole agents made their rounds through Fifty-third and San Pedro day and night. Gangsta Jake turned around to check out his surroundings and to his surprise, the police were present.

"I see we got one at the pot house," Officer Crawford told her partner, who was looking through his rearview mirror. The LAPD stayed on their toes while making their rounds through the gang and drug-infested neighborhood. "He looks fresh out of the pen. Why don't we see what's going on with him?" she continued.

"Okay. But first, watch out for this Escalade that's pulling up in our rear," Officer Arcinager advised his partner of three years as he continued to ease his foot off the brake pedal.

Crawford lightly leaned across him for the purpose of yelling out of his driver's side window. "Come back later; no dope is being sold right now!" she screamed past her partner, gaining the undivided attention of the two females inside the Escalade.

The hippie-looking sergeant had a habit of saying sarcastic things out her mouth. Her blue eyes, blond, shoulder-length hair, and narrow face were a constant reminder of the sixties. Crawford was as racist as they came. She and her partner could not stand gang members, especially ones from Five Tray, who had a reputation of shooting it out with their department. She was actually a part of the conspiracy that helped put Gangsta Jake away for his twelve-year vacation, but neither he nor her were aware of that fact.

Once the Escalade drove past the two officers, their attention turned back to Gangsta Jake. However, by then, it was too late. He had the drop on them. His regards for CRASH were the same as it was toward snitches. Gangsta Jake was one gangbanger who did not like the police and was not into dropping his pistol and running for cover.

Before the law was able to refocus its attention on him, he let off four rounds directly at them. One went into the passenger's side door, and the other three in Crawford's vest and shoulder. She and her partner retreated by ducking down and grabbing their guns.

"Shit! I'm hit," Crawford screamed out in panic.

Michelle, sitting in the passenger seat of her man's Lexus, observed the shooting and drove off to perhaps pick him up on the next block over. The

Jamaicans inside the house dove on the floor until the shooting stopped. As they were about to hop up from the floor, Gangsta Jake let off his final round into the officers' car. He did so to prevent the officers from looking up and gaining a better description of him. In the same motion, he hopped over a nearby fence and ran through the residential area.

After checking his body for bullet holes, Arcinager snatched the walkie-talkie from his belt and called for backup. "Help! Help! Officers need assistance! This is an emergency! My partner has been shot; her condition unknown! The suspect is a black male, approximately six feet two inches, two hundred and ten pounds, last seen running eastbound toward Towne Avenue! He's wearing a blue shirt and dark blue jeans."

"Ten-four. What is your ten-twenty, sir?"

"I'm located on the westbound corner of Fifty-third and San Pedro Boulevard."

"Okay, sir; a patrol car is within two minutes of your location. Also, an ambulance and air unit has been dispatched. Help is in route; please try to remain calm."

"Where are you, boy?" Michelle asked herself as she circled the block looking to aid her man.

Gangsta Jake was very familiar with the area where he took off running. Not much about his neighborhood had changed since his departure in 1992. The same old houses stood that had been there for the past eighty years. He noticed a screen door open on a one-story house and slid inside as quickly as he could.

Within three minutes, a helicopter hovered overhead and at least fifteen or so LAPD units set up a perimeter around the immediate area. Due to the severity of the call, officers poured into the rundown neighborhood from all directions. Realizing he was in the clear for the moment, Gangsta Jake leaned over a kitchen sink gasping for air, breathless due to his sudden sprint. He had no idea whose residence he entered, but he planned on staying for a while. By the aroma of soul food lingering in the air, he figured that black folks lived in the house.

Miss Avery was in the process of cooking Sunday dinner when Gangsta Jake entered her home. Moments after she advanced to answer her front door, he ran inside the back door, where her kitchen was located. Two Jehovah's Witnesses occupied her presence with the pamphlets they held up to their bosoms.

The helicopter's proximity caused Miss Avery and the two Jehovah's Witnesses to look toward the cloudy sky. Miss Avery heard the shots go off right after Gangsta Jake fired at the officers, but she did not pay them much attention. Shots fired in South-Central Los Angeles were as common as hearing airplanes go by overhead. The white officer running from her next door neighbor's backyard holding a pump shotgun made her realize the incident was too close for comfort.

"Go inside your house, now!" The officer nervously shouted, conscious of the suspect's intentions.

By now, Gangsta Jake had made his way through Miss Avery's house and had crawled inside her attic. It had been nearly twenty minutes since Michelle had seen or heard from him. His absence caused her to become a nervous wreck. Panic ran through her body for fear of what the police would do to him if they could get their hands on him. She knew how the LAPD got down, which led her to firmly believe death on the spot would be the officers' only option.

Kill now and answer questions later was the LAPD Newton Street Division's motto. Shooting fellow officers was dead serious business in their book. Michelle witnessed the looks in the officers' faces as they exited their vehicles with their guns drawn, and she did not like what she saw.

Ring ring . . . Michelle's cell phone sounded off.

"Hello."

"Baby, it's me."

"Boy, where the hell are you?"

"I'm in some old lady's attic. She lives maybe six or seven houses down from the weed spot. What does it look like out there?"

"The police are everywhere. Do not even think about coming out. They took the police lady in an ambulance. I don't know where she was shot, but she was bleeding a lot."

Gangsta Jake cracked a slight smile at the news.

"Did it seem like she was going to live?"

"Yeah, she was conscious. In spite of her bleeding, she didn't look all that bad."

"Damn! I was gunning for that hoe's head."

"Baby, I have to get your ass out of here, but I don't know how the hell I'm going to do it. A few more police cars are pulling up as we speak. Rohan, where did you get a phone from?"

"I grabbed a cordless off the kitchen counter of whoever's house I'm in. I'm about to get off this wire before the police pick up on my location. You know how these wireless phones are. I'm riding them out. I'm not moving until they move."

* * *

"Brandon, have you seen big mama's phone?" Miss Avery asked, while batting her one good eye.

"No, big mama, I haven't."

"Baby, it got to be round here somewhere. Find it for your grandmother, will you?"

"Okay, big mama, but first I want to go outside and see what the pigs are doing."

"Boy, what the hell you mean pigs? Them police ain't no damn pigs. Where did you learn all that foolishness from? Carry your ass in that front room and find me that phone before I slap the taste out of yo mouth," the ninety-year-old woman said to her thirteen-year-old great grandson.

"Yes, Grandma," young Brandon replied as he bowed his head and poked out his lips at her remarks.

"Y'all excuse my simple-minded grandson," Miss Avery informed the two Jehovah's Witnesses, who were unknowingly in the midst of a killer.

*　*　*

Gangsta Jake's mind quarreled on whether or not he should come down and make himself comfortable or remain hidden until the police left. *Doing so would be a lot of work*, he reasoned with himself. *Everyone would have to be tied up, possibly killed. I'm already out of bullets. The police may do a house-to-house search and might slip up and not find me in this attic. Yeah, I think I'm cool*, was his final decision. His mind was made up that staying put would be his best option. He was not into harming people whom he considered innocent bystanders—unless they jeopardized his freedom, of course. He gained his pleasure from seeing snitches or police (whom he considered paid informants) lying in puddles of blood.

A few hours went by and he could still hear the chopper circling overhead. He dozed off a couple of times within that period. Miss Avery and her two guests waited patiently for the officer to allow them to leave. Young Avery was ordered to his room for not finding the cordless phone, which no one else could find either. She figured he was hiding it from her and would deal with him later. Gangsta Jake called Michelle again to see what the current status was.

Ring, ring . . .

"Baby, it's me again. Where you at?"

"I'm still here, standing in the crowd. You know I'm not leaving here without you."

"That's my girl. Make sure to be there when daddy comes out."

"Baby, the police want your ass bad. They have a K-9 dog and the whole nine yards. People can not even go down that street unless they live on it."

"They ain't doing nothing but searching every yard and empty car they come across. They'll eventually get tired of searching for a ghost and break down their perimeter. A few hours more and I'll be okay. Take my word for it."

Gangsta Jake's words were correct as stated. Seven hours after the shooting occurred, the police grew hopeless and abandoned their search efforts. When Michelle gave him the green light that the coast was clear, he climbed down from the attic as smoothly as he went into it. Before Miss Avery could get off her toilet, he crept through her house and out the same door he entered. Michelle was so relieved to see him surface; a giant smile appeared on her face.

"Drive, girl," he instructed her as he hopped inside the car and ducked down out of view. Once she reached the Harbor Freeway, he sat up and became a normal passenger. "Fuck waiting two days to go to Brooklyn. We're leaving in the morning. Damn Rasta muthafuckas like to have got me caught up fucking around with them. I'll have one of my homies send Young Lad that weed he wanted. I'm ready to get my hands on that list and serve these snitches."

"Are we going to the hotel?"

"Yeah, baby. I'm ready to lay this thang down for the night. I'm tired as hell."

7

Baby Mama Drama

By the time Michelle pulled into their hotel off the 91 Freeway, Gangsta Jake was sound asleep. "Wake up, Rohan; we're here," she nudged him.

"Damn, that was quick." He stretched his tired body out toward Michelle's shoulder.

"You went right to sleep. I guess you're all out of energy."

"Why did you say it like that?" he said with a drained smile on his face.

"I ain't never too tired to hit that poo-nany, if that's what you're insinuating."

"No, no, get your rest, baby," she waved her right hand in the air. "Don't forget, I have my hand if I wanted to get off that bad."

"As long as I'm here, you don't ever have to worry about using your hand. Unless you're trying to turn a gangsta on," his eyebrows raised as he stuck the key inside the room door.

Walking into the hotel room relaxed them both. They took off their jackets before sitting on the cushy bed together. Gangsta Jake turned on the television and removed his shoes and socks.

"Do you want to take a shower with me, Michelle? We may as well get it out the way before we both fall asleep."

"Aw, you just want to see all this ass," she replied as she turned on her stomach and poked her butt up. She felt very secure about showing off her body to him. Furthermore, she was hoping to get him hard and in the mood to make passionate love to her.

They both stripped down butt naked and headed toward the shower. Michelle loved viewing Gangsta Jake in the nude. She could not get enough of his ripped up, hard body. The feeling was definitely mutual. Michelle was, by far, the prettiest girl he had ever been with in his entire life. She had a sensational smile, gorgeous body, and cute feet that any person with a foot fetish would truly admire.

Her grandmother and sister could not understand why she was so in love with a guy like Gangsta Jake. They constantly reminded her that as fine as she was, she could easily have any guy she desired. As much as they hated him, she was not trying to hear any of what they had to say. Michelle was not interested in being with a normal guy, a hip square, or anyone on that level. Her heart and mind were set on a thug; she was in love with a gangster.

As the two entered the shower, their urge to make love grew more intense. Since Michelle was the aggressor of the two when it came to making love, she placed her arms around his waist and ran her tongue over his chest. The shower water that drenched their bodies made the moment even more electrifying. The affection led to the couple kissing and rubbing their entire bodies up against one another. But the rubbing did not last long. Before you knew it, Michelle was bent over in a doggy-style position. She shut her eyes as he slowly penetrated her private parts. The moist water and her juices within made Gangsta Jake's ride to ecstasy that much more enjoyable. At Michelle's request, he slapped her on the rump and pulled her by the hair.

"Who's the man?" he demanded as he tugged harder on her shoulder-length ponytail.

"Oh, you the man, daddy! You the man!" Her voice sped up in an attempt to stay in accord with the flow they both formulated. The two carried on for nearly twenty-five minutes, until Michelle's legs began to tremble, which they both got a big laugh out of. Gangsta Jake then held Michelle in his arms long enough for her to regain her composure. Thereafter, they bathed one another and made their way to the bed.

As Gangsta Jake lay down on the soft, fluffy bed, cuddling with his queen, he could not help but to think about Young Lad, Dre, Warlock, Killer Dee, and homey after homey, who, unfortunately, were resting on a hard bunk bed in a concrete cell. He would not allow himself to forget about the pain his partners were feeling back in the penitentiary behind a stoolpigeon. He closed his eyes and visualized the ways he would go about taking the lives of the many people who had taken the stand against his homies. After having made love to a sister as fine Michelle was, one would think Gangsta Jake's thoughts would be on entertaining something a lot better than taking a chance to go back to prison. However, this was not the case with him. His hate for snitches and love for his homeboys ran deeper than the ocean.

Once morning rolled around, the couple woke up at 7 a.m. and pulled themselves together by washing their faces, getting dressed, and later headed toward the airport. Before making it to the airport, though, Gangsta Jake stopped by his older homey, Horsehead's, apartment to park his Lexus. When they arrived at Horsehead's crib, they found him dealing with a bit of a problem.

Baby mama drama was at the top of Horsehead's agenda. His oldest son's mother, Deshan, was arguing back and forth with his daughter's mom, Valencia. Valencia popped up at their apartment with two of her homegirls. Deshan had called Valencia a bitch and hoe over the telephone prior to Valencia showing up. She figured Valencia would come looking for some drama, but not as fast as she did. To Deshan's surprise, Valencia rounded up her crew and was in route toward her apartment before either one could hang up their cell phones.

Deshan was expecting three of her homegirls to show up as well, but she also knew how slow they could be, especially in the morning. At any rate, Valencia and her girls were on deck and ready to rumble. They all had Vaseline on their faces and no visible jewelry. Valencia made sure no one had on earrings and chains before hopping in her car. The only jewelry they wore was in their tongues or navels. Valencia even made sure her sister, Veronica, removed the ring in her nipple.

Horsehead's presence between the girls prevented them from having their way with Deshan's cute, round face. She was not trying to injure that pretty face of hers; therefore, she stayed behind Horsehead as she verbally assaulted the other girls. "I don't know why you and your hood rat-ass homegirls are at my place starting shit. My man ain't trying to fuck with your busted ass. Hoe, don't nobody want you!"

"That ain't what your man said last night when he was begging to get my pussy." All three of Valencia's girls broke out into laughter.

"You a damn liar," Horsehead defended himself, in spite of knowing what she said was the truth. When he looked behind him and saw Gangsta Jake pulling in his driveway, he determined it was time to remedy the situation. He did not want it to appear that Valencia and her girls were dominating his domain.

Horsehead turned toward Deshan and ordered her inside their apartment immediately. Once she abided with his demand, he pulled from his back pocket an all-black Saturday night special. With the .38 in hand, he shouted for the girls to leave. "Y'all better get the fuck away from my spot before I shoot one of you hoes." He twisted his face up while walking in the girls' direction. His actions caused them to scatter and run in separate directions.

"Horsehead!" Gangsta Jake yelled at his big homeboy before coming face-to-face with him. "Hold up, big homey. When I first got out, you checked me about tripping on that buster, Ghost, at the park, and you're about to let these females get you off your square like this?"

All four girls were now hiding behind several parked cars and an old ice-cream truck. Horsehead winked one eye at Gangsta Jake and quickly explained that all he was doing was scaring them off. "Nigga, I'm some dumb, not plum dumb," he whispered to his young partner as he continued with his performance. *Pow! Pow! Pow!* He let off three rounds in the air and slammed his left palm up against the ice-cream truck Valencia and her friend, Tomeka, hid behind.

"Boy, don't do nothing stupid. You know I have to raise your child!" Valencia screamed out, as serious as a heart attack. She knew he played a lot, but was not sure if he was at that moment.

"I'm giving you and your chicken-head friends thirty seconds to jump in that bucket y'all pulled up in and get the hell away from me and my family. Valencia, I'm cool on you. You don't know how to keep your mouth shut and don't come calling my house and showing up at my door with this bullshit. I'm too old for these kiddy-ass games you're playing."

Out of nowhere, Deshan's three homegirls, Cho-Cho, green-eyed Jackie, and Tiffany, pulled up in a dark blue, 1978 Oldsmobile Cutlass. They were straight off the eastside and held reputations for not only beating down crews of females, but guys as well.

"Aw, damn!" Horsehead pouted to himself with a look of distress. "As soon as I halfway get this shit under control, here comes some more shit in the game. Man! I might really have to shoot one of these crazy-ass broads."

Once Deshan peeped outside her front room window and discovered that her homegirls were finally on deck, she ran out with her sweatshirt and tennis shoes on. She was ready to defend her space. She did not appreciate how Valencia and her girls came to her home, disrespecting her and her man.

Horsehead knew at that point there were too many females to control single-handedly. He looked over at Gangsta Jake and gave him a "help me out of this shit" face. Gangsta Jake, however, was ready to park his Lexus and just get dropped off at the airport. Therefore, he reluctantly helped out by keeping the packs of disgruntled girls separate. After a few minutes, he determined the best solution was to let Valencia and Deshan get the situation off their chest by having a head-up fight.

"Ain't nobody jumping in, either. And if anybody do . . ." Gangsta Jake gritted his teeth on both packs of females with a cold look in his eyes. They knew the rep he held and understood how serious he was about what he was saying. "That's on my hood. I'll have some of my homegirls stump a mudhole in whoever gets out of line. As a matter of fact, I won't even wait that long. Y'all see my girl sitting in that car over there? She's fine, but I guarantee you, she got some vicious hands. Let one of you hoes get out of line and I'm siccing her on whoever."

"Yeah, right," green-eyed Jackie said underneath her breath. Michelle recognized him pointing in her direction and without anyone else noticing, began cracking her knuckles. A few other girls in the pack looked over at Michelle and were hoping he would have involved her in their business. They figured as soft as she appeared, beating her down would be easy. Michelle looked like she did not have a fighting bone in her body, but as Gangsta Jake and she both knew, that was far from the truth.

"Yeah, right? What does that mean? Are you trying to see my girl or what?"

"I don't give a fuck! I'm not running from no fight." She called his bluff.

Horsehead suddenly stepped in and defused the situation before it got further out of control. "Hold up, baby boy. Let's just let Valencia and Deshan get down. All that other stuff is too much extra. Besides, don't you have something else on your agenda?"

Gangsta Jake thought about it and realized that what Horsehead was saying was the truth. In order to move forward with his set schedule, he basically ignored what she had to say. He then walked up to Jackie and told her, "Girl, consider this your lucky day. If I didn't have a plane to catch, yo ass would be grass."

"Whatever," she rolled her eyes at him. Gangsta Jake kind of liked her attitude, which is why he really did not press the situation.

As Michelle sat in Gangsta Jake's Lexus observing the scene, the two girls went at it with a vengeance. They never liked one another, and it clearly showed by the way they were exchanging blows. Valencia swung at Deshan, missed her, and hit her hand up against a parked car. Deshan took advantage of the situation by ramming into Valencia's body and taking her to the ground. A real live catfight was in full swing. Hair was being pulled, clothes ripped off—the whole nine yards. Both crews of females stood by and cheered on their friend. Each side was hoping to gain bragging rights at the victory of their homegirl.

Before long, Gangsta Jake grew tired of the entertainment and separated the two females. He had better things to do than sit up and watch the girls go at one another. The fight turned out to be a draw, which temporarily satisfied both crews of females. Valencia and her girls eventually departed from Horsehead's apartment with plans of catching up with Deshan in the future.

"Good lookin', baby boy, I don't know what I would have done without you. Deshan! I let you and Valencia get y'all scrap on! If she calls back over here, just hang up on her, damn it!" Horsehead shouted at Deshan, relieved to finally have some order back in his domain.

"But—"

"But, my ass! Just do what the fuck I said!"

Deshan was not trying to hear him talk crazy to her, which prompted her to head toward her bedroom and slam the door behind her.

"My bad, baby boy, for exposing you to all that drama. You know how it is with these hook—"

Before he could get the word "hooker" out of his mouth, Michelle cut him short by defending Valencia and all other females.

"Boy, don't even go there! You don't have no business calling that girl out her name. I heard how you be out there sticking your thing in anything that move. If anything, you're a hoe. You're the one that's the hooker. Guys are so fast to disrespect a female by calling them out their names, and they're the ones who stay trying to bone something."

"Hold up! Pump your brakes, Michelle! Damn, little homey, she gets to talk to your O.G. like that?" he turned toward Gangsta Jake and asked.

"Michelle, Michelle, come on now. Let that go, baby," he said, calmly walking over to his girl. Outside of being a cold killer, when it came to Michelle, he tried his best to be the perfect gentleman.

"Baby, I understand everything you're saying, but now is not the time. Let's not diss my nigga house like this. He just went through enough by dealing with his babies' mamas. Okay, boo?"

She wanted to say more. However, the peck he planted on her lips and the smoothness in his voice settled her emotions.

"I guess so. I just don't like to hear that type of talk."

"Baby, we have a plane to catch, so let's turn the page on this scene, okay? Now give daddy another kiss."

"What's up with this Romeo and Juliet shit?" Horsehead recognized that Gangsta Jake was not going against his girl, so he felt he may as well throw a joke out to curb the negative vibes. By him being the oldest of the three, he realized it was time to resolve the situation and move forward. Besides, he appreciated the fact that Gangsta Jake pulled up and was able to help cut short the headache he created by seeing Valencia on the side.

8

Too Close for Comfort

"So what's up, young homey? What brings you over this early? Do you have a jack-move up or something? My chips are getting kind of low. Taking care of all these damn kids keeps me broke."

"I'm heading to Brooklyn, cuzz, and I need to park my ride over here for a few days."

"You know that ain't no problem. What's going on in New York? Y'all trying to get married or something?"

"Naw, nothing like that. I just need to check some traps on that end."

"Boy, you're doing big thangs. You must have a few bricks of that cocaine you're trying to get off."

"Hell, naw! I'll be damn if I let one of these snitches sell me out to the feds in order to get some time off their asses. You already know these rats done put a black eye in the game by telling on everything moving. I just have to take care of some business. Damn, big homey! What are you doing, writing a book or something?"

"Naw, Naw. I'm just concerned about your wild ass."

"I'll be all right. But anyway, my flight leaves in two hours. Good lookin' on parking my car for me."

"Parking it? Did I hear you right? Homey, you know I have to hit a few corners in it. It's okay if I drive it while you're gone, isn't it?"

"That's not what I had in mind, but I'm not tripping. Get your ball on. Just don't be fucking in my ride. Get you a room if it comes down to it. Me and my girl are the only ones that got action on putting it down like that in here."

"Rohan," Michelle said while blushing, "don't be telling our business."

"Girl, it ain't no secret. I know fine as you are, the little homey stay running up in you every chance he gets."

"Hey! Hey! Slow your roll, big homey. This conversation is getting way too personal."

Twenty minutes after driving away from Horsehead's apartment, the three drove up to terminal one at the Los Angeles International Airport. The Department of Justice had recently issued a code red throughout the nation, which had security at its peak. Al Qaeda was threatening to blow up U.S. and British targets. FBI agents, airport security with bomb-sniffing dogs, and military personnel could be seen throughout the terminal. The country was in a panic, and it was obvious by the stressful looks on the public faces.

Thinking about the pistol on the floor mat of Gangsta Jake's car suddenly reminded Horsehead that it was time to leave. He had been running the street long enough to understand that guns, criminals, and the police presence were a bad combination. After unloading the luggage onto the curbside, he would soon be making his way off the airport property.

"Say, youngsta, this scene ain't my cup of tea. I'm about to get some distance between all these white folks with badges. I'm already in violation by coming in contact with the police. It would make my parole agent's day to send me back to the pen behind some bullshit like this. Chirp me when you get back in town, and I'll come scoop y'all up. Better yet, catch a cab to my pad. I can't fade being around all these police. They give me the creeps."

"All right, my nigga. Make sure to take care of my ride. You already know I don't have any insurance on it."

"I got your back, young rider. Y'all have a good trip. And Michelle, don't be so mean to me the next time."

"Boy, don't start with me again," she snapped.

"All right, all right, relax, little mama," he placed both of his open palms at her. "I don't want no beef with you. A's up, my nigga; I'm out."

At that moment, Horsehead was not trying to hear her voice any longer. He was hoping his little homey would have placed his girl in check. *It ain't no way I would allow any one of my females to get that far out of pocket with my folks*, he mumbled inside his mind as he drove off. Nonetheless, by having much love and respect for Michelle (mostly based on the fact that she stayed down with Gangsta Jake for so many years in prison), he was able to put up with her drama. Her loyalty alone superseded any bad feelings he may have had for her.

As the couple stood in line waiting to purchase their tickets, Gangsta Jake observed two plainclothes police looking at them. He remained calm while the line moved forward. At the counter, he reached inside his pants pocket and pulled out a wad of hundred dollar bills. The half ounce of marijuana in his possession was secured in a location that only a body x-ray would be able to detect. He was not worried about them finding that. However, the triple homicide and the attempted murder on the police did circulate through his head as he tried to look relaxed.

•

"Sir, would you like a window or an aisle seat?"

Gangsta Jake remained quiet as he pondered on possible ways to evade being apprehended. But all his thoughts were to no avail.

"Excuse me, sir. Sir, excuse me. Hellooooo?" the clerk said as she began to wave her hand near his face. Gangsta Jake did not pay her any mind as he continued to space out. Michelle, out of embarrassment, was forced to tap him on his right arm.

"Oh, I'm sorry, Miss. What was the question?" Gangsta Jake said, feeling the jitters. He was not at all concerned with the threat of terror. His worries were set on all the police around him. He did not like the fact that they were armed and he was not. He felt naked without his piece. His mind was made up that he would not be going back to prison without a gun battle first. Apparently he failed to factor in the possibility of being inside an airport unarmed, with police everywhere.

"Where would you like to sit, sir? By the window or aisle?"

"Make it a window. As a matter of fact, here, Michelle, deal with her." He passed Michelle twelve big-face hundred dollar bills before turning to look back at the officers, who had disappeared.

"Sir, is everything fine?" the tall, thirty-something-year-old white woman asked.

"Yeah, yeah, I'm okay. I'm just a little stressed out behind all these terrorist threats."

"Yes, they can become a bit nerve-racking. But you do not have to worry too much about the threats; we are currently on high alert status."

Little did she know, the high alert was the main cause of his concern.

When Michelle received their tickets, the two made their way toward the boarding gate. The two undercovers' disappearance made Gangsta Jake feel a lot better. He summed it up that they may not have been police after all. Against his better judgment, he blanked them from his mind.

"Baby, it's going to be nice to shake L.A. for a minute. When I was locked down, I use to dream of traveling."

"Honey, you're going to love Brooklyn. I hated to leave it all behind, but you know," she began to blush like a little girl, "I couldn't leave my Boo out here all by himself."

"Aw, ain't that cute. Give me a hug, mommy."

As the couple hugged near a gift shop, two agents posing as a couple intercepted them. They were the same two who scoped them out at the ticket counter earlier.

"Excuse me. DEA. Do you mine if we have a word with you two?" a white, blue-eyed man who stood five feet nine inches announced with the voice of authority. He was in his mid-thirties. His female partner was only twenty-two.

She was also white and could have passed for Jody Foster back in her younger days. Her partner startled Gangsta Jake and Michelle, but not to the point of panic. Michelle was well schooled when it came to dealing with the police. She had been grilled by the law on several occasions due to all the drama her two younger brothers stayed in.

Gangsta Jake kept his cool. He did not know what they wanted, but the crime he committed did come to both their minds.

Damn! I'm popped. These mothafuckas got me! played in his mind when the agents confronted them. But as a few seconds elapsed, he came to realize that whatever the agents wanted could not have been too detrimental. If so, he would already be face down on the ground, with handcuffs attached to his body.

"What's the problem?" Michelle spoke up.

"We noticed you purchased your plane tickets with cash. We have reason to believe you are transporting drugs."

"Do you mind if we conduct a search of your bags?" the female agent eventually joined in on the investigation.

"Why do you believe we're transporting drugs? Is it the fact that we're black? Hell, no, you can't search our bags. Go and search those white people's bags." She pointed at three white teenagers walking along the side of their parents. Michelle was now creating a scene.

"Calm down, Miss. Drugs are the only thing we will be checking for. We are certainly not trying to cause any problems. We're only doing our jobs," the female quietly mentioned to Michelle, wishing her partner would have never decided to interfere with the black couple.

Gangsta Jake experienced total composure after understanding the agents' rationale for invading their space. Something as minor as a pat search was so common for him, he was actually relieved that that was the core of their interference. A murder investigation, on the other hand, would have been a whole different story. Out of respect for Michelle, he attempted to avoid any further embarrassment.

"Officer, there must be some type of mistake," he let the male DEA agent know while staring him square in the eyes. He knew Michelle was handling the situation wrong, so he stepped in once he believed the coast was clear.

"Honey, I'll take care of this." He turned to his girl and gave her a wink only she could observe. "Dang! They act like we're the damn terrorists," she released out of her system before letting Gangsta Jake take over the conversation.

"Pardon my wife. She's been under a great deal of stress lately. We're mourning the lost of her dad and younger brother, who were both serving our country over in IRAQ," he smoothly lied.

Michelle's dad and brother were both safe at home less then five miles away. She saw where he was heading with his story and played right along. Crocodile tears began rolling down Michelle's face as Gangsta Jake went deep into his fabricated tale. He kept in touch with local and worldly events, so any story he gave could be verified by the news.

"They both were killed in a firefight that lasted eight hours in the heart of Saddam's hometown, Tikrit. We received news of the tragedy only twenty-four hours ago. My wife and I are headed to New York to meet up with the rest of the family. We're both multi-platinum producers who chose to make our purchases with cash. We have no reason to be in possession of drugs. We're both successful people," he hunched his shoulders and turned both palms in the air, indicating a bit of arrogance.

His story seemed so plausible, the DEA believed every word he said. Before long, the two agents let their guards down and were nearly in tears themselves. They both served in the military and felt personally affected by their loss.

"Sir, ma'am, we're very, very sorry to have inconvenienced you nice folks. You're free to go. And by the way," the male agent spoke on behalf of the two, "we wish you both the best of luck and our condolences go out to you and your families."

The female agent looked at Michelle with shame written all over her face. "Miss, I'd also like to apologize for the way I conducted myself. Please forgive me for being so shallow minded."

Michelle did not say a word. Gangsta Jake, fully confident that the two agents were now wooed to sleep, decided to put extras on top of the performance he'd already presented. "We're both law-abiding citizens who pay taxes. I've also had the privilege of serving in our forces during operation Desert Storm. Just a minute, let me find my identification in my carryon." He reached over in order to go through the bag resting on his shoulder. His clean-cut and freshly trimmed mustache gave him the look of a square. Unless you were familiar with his character, you would not have imagined what type of person stood behind his charm.

"No, no. That will not be necessary, sir. We've already taken up too much of your time as it is."

"Okay, then. You officers have a great day. As a matter of fact, I feel safer knowing that you guys are nearby," he jokingly said as he walked away, holding Michelle by the hand.

"Suckas!" he boastfully whispered to Michelle as he drew farther away from the agents.

"Boy, you are so crazy. You should have been an actor. You really have a lot of talent, baby," she flattered him, smiling from ear-to-ear. "I knew for sure we were busted. At first, I was so nervous. I thought maybe that bitch could smell the weed in my panties. It seemed like she was sniffing, trying to inhale something. This chronic is so loud."

"Chronic! I didn't know you had some bud."

"I wanted to surprise you once you ran out."

"Baby, I appreciate you wanting to surprise me and all, but that ain't cool. That shit have to be properly stashed if you're going to bring it through an airport."

"Properly stashed? Damn, you act like you stuck yours up the crack of your ass or something." Michelle thought for a second about how he used to hide balloons of weed she gave him during their visits back in the penitentiary. "OOOOOH, you did stick it in your—" she smiled and pointed at him.

"Shhhhh. What are you trying to do? Get me x-rayed? Keep that under your hat. Come on, girl. They just announced our flight is boarding. These white folks got me shaking in my boots. I'm not fucking around with this hot-ass airport on the way back. They must have a green light to hassle any young person that's not white."

9

Surprise!

"Please fasten your seat belts. Flight 803 will be making its final decent to JFK International Airport. Allow me to thank you for choosing American Airlines for your flight. The weather is a beautiful eighty-five degrees in downtown Brooklyn."

"Rohan," Michelle bumped him. "Wake up, baby. We're about to land in Brooklyn. Here, let me buckle your seat belt." He was still half asleep.

"Huh?"

"We're here. We're about to land. Wake up."

"Okay, shit. Damn, what time is it?"

"My watch says five o'clock, but you know we're three hours ahead of L.A. time. Five, six, it's eight o'clock."

"It seems like we've been in the air all day."

"Well, we're here now, so you don't have to complain any longer. Robin is going to be so surprised to see me. I miss my girl."

"Yeah, I bet you do. I hope she don't try to act all funny because I came out here with you."

"Boy, that girl ain't thinking about you."

"Good!"

"Baby, I'm only playing with you. Don't get mad at me."

"I'm not mad at you."

"How long are we going to be out here, Rohan?"

"Not long, Michelle. I'm trying to get back as soon as possible, but I guess we can stay for a couple of days."

"That's cool."

Eventually, Gangsta Jake and Michelle drove away from the airport in pursuit of what could be a useful tool in his killing spree. They rented a 2004 Mustang to get around town in. Realizing he was so close to possessing the desired list, Gangsta Jake reclined in his seat with a smile attached to his face.

"Yeah, it won't be long now, sexy, before I can pop one of them snitches right in his forehead for selling my niggas out."

"Baby, you're serious, huh? You really hate informants, don't you?"

"You got damn right! I can't stand them coward muthafuckas. I wish I could line up every person who's told on someone in life and gun their asses down with a AK-47 assault rifle. I like how they carried it back in the days when it came to handling these rats. You snitched, you died—bottom line! It wasn't how it's being carried nowadays.

"These days, guys get on the witness stand, sell their homies out, and often go right back to their hoods like ain't shit happened. Not all of them get away with it, but some do. I have three homies in the Feds right now, who were told on by a fourth homey who caught a case with them. The clown who told ended up serving only three years. Everyone else got broke off time ranging from eight all the way to twenty-one years. Two of them took deals and only one went to trial.

"The cold thing about it is, he had a lot of homies fooled, like he was the one who was told on, when his bitch-ass knew damn well he told on the homies. If the one homey had not gone to trial, that clown probably would have never been exposed. He was hoping everybody would have taken a deal; that way, the prosecutor wouldn't have been obligated to fully disclose the evidence against them in trial. When people plead out, the prosecutors don't go through all that paperwork trip, but since one homey did, they had to. That's when the truth came out."

"Are you sure they did not tell on him?"

"Did you not hear what I just sat up here and explained? The homey who went to trial sent all sorts of court documents to the streets on that bitch-ass nigga, showing who the real impostor was. Grand Jury statements, FBI interviews, and even testimony from the witness stand at trial."

"What type of case did they have?"

"They were all charged with armed bank robbery."

"The one who went to trial, how much time did he get? He did lose his case, didn't he?"

"Yeah, he did. They broke him off fourteen years behind that rat."

"Why didn't anything happen to him?"

"I guess it was because nobody could; then again, I don't know. Don't get me to start making up excuses for the homies for not handling their business. I can't call it. That shit definitely wouldn't have happened if I was on the street. I haven't heard nothing about that lame since I been out, but if I ever run into him, it's on. Remind me to check up on that clown."

"Whatever you do, just be careful, baby. I don't want to see you back in trouble."

"It's all good. I know how to bob and weave when it comes to staying out the way."

"So, honey, where do you want to stay while we're out here? I know you don't want to stay at Robin's."

"Let's get a nice room somewhere."

"I guess we could stay near Manhattan. Maybe at the Ramada Inn. The rooms over there are not that bad."

"Michelle, can you get me a pistol while we're here?"

"I have a twenty-two at my apartment. Would that be okay?"

"Yeah that will work. I feel naked without having my heat by my side. The deuce-deuce will hold me for the couple days we're here."

*   *   *

Unbeknownst to Robin, Michelle and Gangsta Jake were in town and would be headed her way once they checked into their room. It had been a little over three months since Robin last saw the two. She basically had gotten over seeing the trio being killed before her very eyes. By it being the weekend, her plans consisted of spending the day at home with a guy she and Michelle knew from work.

His name was Rick Johnson. Rick stood six feet tall, had dark skin, and a round face. He wore a military-style haircut. Rick was one of those pretty chocolate brothers who normally only dated white women. He was employed as a court bailiff for the past four years. Robin loved dating men in creased-up uniforms, especially guys like Rick with eighteen-inch arms.

She and Rick were hanging out at her and Michelle's old apartment. The two were laughing their heads off, watching the *Queens of Comedy* on DVD. They had only dated three times, but Robin felt very comfortable in his presence. Robin and Rick were kicked back with their shoes off, eating pizza and drinking beer when suddenly, Robin heard something strange going on at her front door. The odd thing was, whoever was at her door was not ringing the bell like any other visitor. That person was unlocking locks from top to bottom. The unannounced visitor startled her to the extent that she turned toward Rick, looking for him to protect her.

"Rick!" she nervously whispered. "I have no idea who the hell that is coming inside my apartment."

The fear on Robin's face instantaneously shifted Rick into his police mode. "Just lay on the floor and do not move!" he softly told her as he made his way over to his jacket on the coat rack. By the time he grabbed his .40 caliber Smith

& Wesson, the last lock opened up. The person in the hallway pushed the door open and stepped in with a large box in hand.

"Freeze, motherfucker!" Rick screamed out in a deadly tone, with his gun fully extended.

Michelle, scared as hell, dropped the box and placed her hands in the air as she screamed back in return. Her scream resembled the voice of a person who found themselves in a near-death situation. Gangsta Jake was in the process of obtaining something from the car and had not yet made it up the two flights of stairs. Robin, now realizing who the intruder was, jumped up with the speed of light and called Rick off of her.

"Rick! Rick! It's Michelle from work. Don't shoot!" All three of their hearts raced like a crackhead who had just taken a fat blast. "Michelle, you scared the hell out of us, bitch!"

Michelle held her heart with both hands. "Scared y'all? Look at me—I'm still shaking."

"Girl, why didn't you tell me you were coming into town? Come here and give me a hug. It's so good to see you. I'm so happy you came home and left that nothing-ass nigga behind."

Michelle broke her hug in order to fill Robin in. "For your information, I didn't leave my man. Rohan is here with me now."

Robin's heart could have hit the ground when Gangsta Jake walked from behind the bar door five seconds after her rude statement. She was praying like hell he was not standing outside long enough to hear their conversation. The last thing she wanted was for him to know her true feelings toward him. She fully understood that that could turn into a deadly affair.

"Rick, you bastard," Michelle playfully said to him once her fears subsided.

"I'm so sorry, Michelle. You had us shook up pretty good."

"I'm not mad at you, Rick. So I see you and my girl finally hooked up."

"Yeah, I guess you can say that. She's really a special person."

"Oh, Rick, I'm sorry. This is my husband, Rohan."

"Husband!?" Robin asked in shock.

"Well, not officially, but eventually." Gangsta Jake smiled at his girl's remark.

"Rick." He offered his hand to Gangsta Jake in a courteous manner. His Southern background was being displayed by his kindness.

"Yeah, Rohan. Pleased to meet you, my man," he replied to Rick's introduction moments before reaching his hand out for a shake. Gangsta Jake acknowledged the fact that he was in the presence of a square, more importantly, an officer of the court; therefore, he made sure to stay balanced by being on his best behavior.

"Robin, how have you been, girl? It's a pleasure to see you again. Michelle and I decided to pay you a visit, to make sure you were okay."

Yeah, right, went through Robin's mind.

"I see that you've taken good care of yourself. This is some beautiful furniture you have in here."

Robin was not feeling him at all, but she did not want to give him any reason to draw any suspicion of her true feelings toward him. She simply went along with whatever would seem to keep him on his square. She was so happy to learn he did not hear her initial remarks that she was able to muster up a civil conversation. Well, at least, she *believed* he did not hear her.

"Hi, Rohan. Thanks for being concerned. Come in and have a seat. Did you guys drive all the way out here or what?" Robin said, walking over to her refrigerator.

"No, we took a flight," Michelle answered.

"Can I get you guys something to eat or drink?"

"Naw, we just ate," Gangsta Jake answered the question for both of them. *This bitch might be trying to poison you, baby boy,* he thought to himself. "Thanks for asking though," was his followup with a straight and sincere look on his face. The negative side of his mind kicked in before declining her offer.

"So, how long do you guys plan on staying in Brooklyn?" *Please, do not say forever,* went through her brain. She had a few personal thoughts of her own.

"Only a couple of days. Michelle and I are planning on renting a house when we make it back to Los Angeles."

Thank God. If Gangsta Jake could only hear her thoughts.

"Girl, you hooked the spot up. I might want to come back now."

"Come on, I'd love to have you back."

"I'm only playing, Robin. I like living back in L.A., but I sure miss you though, bitch," she smiled. "My bad on dropping in on you guys like this. It seems like you two were having so much fun. *The Queens of Comedy,*" Michelle read, picking up the DVD case. "Forget this, Robin. Y'all need to be watching some porno in here."

Rick blushed in embarrassment.

"Michelle, hush your mouth, girl. You know I don't watch that stuff."

"Well, look, Robin, me and Rohan are about to paint the town. We'll leave you lovebirds for now."

"Michelle, give me a call before you guys make it back tonight."

"Oh, we rented a room so we're cool. I'll still give you a call before I turn in for the night, though."

"It was nice meeting you, my brother. Take care of my little sister. Robin is a sweetheart."

"For sure. She's in good company. And I even have a gun," Rick joked, displaying his sense of humor.

Square-ass nigga, you need to let me have that gun, Gangsta Jake thought to himself as he laughed along with what he felt was a corny joke.

"Take care of yourself out there, Michelle. You know how it is on these streets." She really wanted to say, *Keep your eyes on Rohan's wild ass before he gets the two of you killed.*

"I'll see you, Robin. Don't do anything I wouldn't do."

"I'll see you later, girlfriend; and Rick, it was nice seeing you again."

"Likewise, Michelle. You guys enjoy your stay here."

10

The List

Halfway down the hallway, Gangsta Jake reminded Michelle about the gun he asked for earlier. He would love to have held onto the fat .40 caliber Rick pulled on Michelle, but knew that it was out the question. He knew that he was a smooth and manipulating talker, and for a second, pondered the thought of trying to talk Rick out of it for a couple of days. However, his better judgment would not allow him to go out like that.

"Oh, yeah, I almost forgot about the twenty-two. You know how forgetful I can be."

"Don't worry; I wasn't going to let you forget."

"Can it wait until tomorrow?"

"No. I got to have some iron up under me, Michelle. You know how I am."

"Okay, baby. Let's go down to the basement and get it."

*　　*　　*

Robin could not believe who had just walked in and out of her apartment. The creator of her worst nightmare was in town. She had previously prayed that her last days of seeing him were back in Los Angeles. Unfortunately, she was wrong. Robin sat quietly on her couch as she gathered her thoughts.

Rohan ain't stupid. He knows I did not approve of what he did to those people back in L.A. I wonder if he came out here to kill me. I sure hope that bastard did not hear me talking about him.

"Robin, are you okay? Robin? Robin!" Rick's voice rose due to Robin's failure to respond. She was in a daze.

"Oh, my bad, Rick. I'm sorry. I was thinking about something. I'm straight."

"Would you like some time alone? We can finish the tape another day."

"No, don't be silly. I'm fine. Cut it back on." Robin wanted all the company she could gather while Gangsta Jake was in town. As he and Michelle made their way down to her basement, Robin's mind was focused on the person who caused her a great deal of discomfort.

*   *   *.

"Grab the box at the top of that shelf, honey."

"That one?" Gangsta Jake pointed.

"No. The one next to the grey box at the top."

"Damn, you have a lot of junk in here."

"It's not all mine. Some is Robin's. Sit it right there, Rohan. Thank you. Okay, let me see what we have here . . ." Michelle opened the larger box and searched through the contents.

"Here's the bullets." With that, her conversation paused as she dug deeper inside the box. "And here's the gun."

"Where did you get this little pea shooter from?"

"I can't tell you all my secrets. You ain't the only one who has connections, big baller."

After busting open two more boxes, Michelle found the list of confidential informants' names and addresses Gangsta Jake so desperately desired. She decided to find the list while she was in the process of searching. Once Michelle discovered it, she looked over to find Gangsta Jake playing with her gun. Instead of giving him the list, she tucked it in her pocket and decided to hand it over before returning to Los Angeles. She figured if he placed his hands on the list too fast, their trip to Brooklyn may come to an end.

"Come on, Rohan, let's get out of here."

"Where's the list?"

"I'll find it for you in the morning." A look came over Michelle's face that he had never witnessed before.

"You're lying. I can see it all over your face." He grinned at Michelle. "You already have it, don't you?"

She smiled but did not say a word. Her eyes and facial expression told it all. "I'll give it to you, but you have to promise that after I do so, we can still stay for two days."

"Is that what you're worried about?"

"Yeah. I know how you can be."

"And how is that?"

"So demanding at times."

"Don't worry about that, beautiful. We can always come back to Brooklyn at a later time."

"See? That's exactly what I'm talking about," Michelle pouted like a little schoolgirl.

"I'm only teasing you, big head. We'll be here for a couple of days, so you can stop poking your lips out."

Her glow suddenly returned when she was certain they could stay for a couple of days.

"Okay. Here's the list." When he reached for it, she snatched her hand back and ran to the other side of the room, giggling.

"Oh, I see. You want to play games," he said before running toward her and gently diving on her back. They wrestled and rolled around the storage room like two big kids. He prevailed, of course.

"Get your big butt off me. Here, boy, take the list." He accepted the list with gratitude.

"Thank you, baby. Now give daddy some of that tongue."

"I love you, Rohan," she looked him square in the eyes while speaking, still laying on the floor beneath him.

"Likewise," he assured her as he lifted her from below.

His focus then turned to the folded up paper he now possessed. Excitement and rage filled his mind and body as he unfolded the document. His dream, year after year, of obtaining what he now held in his hand had finally come true.

"Yes!" he squeezed his fist as though he hit a buzzer beater shot for a championship basketball game. The devil reentered his body as his eyes scanned the list of confidential informants who were no longer confidential. All he could picture were people on the witness stand—and murder! He wanted to kill something! He wanted to place a bullet in someone's forehead.

"Coward muthafuckas! Bitches couldn't even hold their water!" He was furious.

"Baby, don't get so upset." Michelle recognized how heated he had become and tried to calm him down. "It's going to be okay, honey. Don't allow them rats to get you like that."

His hatred toward snitches was starting to rub off on her.

"I know I shouldn't let them hoes get me so worked up, but I can't help the way I feel. I can't stand the fact that I have folks doing the rest of their lives behind these bustas. Some of my people, just like me, did not actually commit a crime. The police crossed people into telling lies on them." He glanced at the list. "You see this mark's name right here?"

"Yeah," Michelle responded with great concern.

"I didn't even know he sold my nigga, Baby Cal out from rolling sixties. His name was in the air for telling, but somehow, he convinced his homeboys that he was solid. And look at this clown right here," he pointed at the list again. "He got down on my dawg, Killer Dee, from my hood."

"You know all them people on that list?"

"Nah, but I know all the homies these snitches sold out to the wolves. I don't need to know them, but they will know who Gangsta Jake is before the dust settles."

"Everybody on that list was responsible for helping the DA give your homeboys life sentences?"

"All of them didn't deal with the district attorney. Some sold their souls to the assistant United States attorneys, which are federal prosecutors. I know a lot of real dudes who are doing time in Federal Prison behind these marks too!" He popped the paper with his fingertips.

"I have homies doing time in Terminal Island, Lompoc, Leavenworth, Florence, all the way to Ray Brook, which is right out here in New York, all behind these suckas on this list. All my niggas didn't receive life sentences, but at least 85 percent of them did. I'm going after the big fish first, the ones who assisted with the life sentences. Then I'll deal with the ones who done lesser damage.

"Come on, let's get out of here. I'll deal with this business later. I know you're dying to show me Brooklyn."

11

A Night on the Town

While driving down 105th and Broadway, Michelle came up with a two-day agenda for the time they were on the East Coast. First, they would swing by their hotel to freshen up, then get a bite to eat at JR's restaurant, and later head to a nightclub called Tunnel's on the westside.

"Baby, we're going to have so much fun. I can't wait for everyone to get an eyeful of my man. Honey, there's some nice people in Brooklyn. I wish my girl, Robin, could go out with us. She and I go way back. That's my girl."

"Where did you say that club was located?" he asked, hoping to erase Robin's name from their conversation.

"Oh, it's right over that bridge," Michelle pointed at the Brooklyn Bridge, which could be seen from the street they were traveling down. "Those lights all the way over there is Manhattan."

"Word is bond."

"Word is bond! When did you start talking like that?"

"Ain't that how y'all talk on this end?" he smiled before pulling out a sack of sticky green from his right tennis shoe. "Where's the rolling papers?"

"Look in my Gucci bag in the backseat. As a matter of fact, why don't you roll up a blunt instead of using a Zig-Zag. I have a cigar in the ashtray."

"A blunt! I'm cool on that blunt shit. With the amount of weed it will take to roll a blunt, I can roll ten of the joints I smoke. I may roll one back in L.A. where this chronic is plentiful, but not way out here in Brooklyn. I only have a little left, and I'm damn sure not trying to run out of this sticky shit."

The sizes of his joints were small, but he felt the full effect. Once the chronic kicked in, Rohan began cracking jokes on nearly everyone they drove by on the streets. Tears were running out of Michelle's eyes when she pulled inside their hotel parking lot. She knew he was comical, but never imagined him being so funny.

"I know you're trying to bounce to the club, but I'm trying to bounce inside that pee hole, as my pops used to say," Gangsta Jake whispered in his girl's ear while opening up the room door and hugging her from behind. Her fat ass felt so good pressed up against the front and center part of his pants, that his shaft was starting to get an erection.

Michelle felt his bulge and decided to mess with his head. "You're sticking it in wrong. You have to stick it in the other way."

"What?" he said.

"The key to the door is what I was referring to."

"Oh, okay. Damn, I'm tripping. I think I smoked too much. Let me make sure I stick it in the right hole. Oops, I mean, the right way. See there, I got your freaky self back."

Gangsta Jake was so high from the weed he smoked, he could not open their hotel door without a helping hand. To get him refocused, Michelle reached her hand behind her butt and grabbed him by the shaft.

"Give me this key before we end up standing here all night."

By the time they made it inside the room, Gangsta Jake had became hard as a barbeque bone. Within two minutes of foreplay, he was digging Michelle out. He put it down so well, she changed her mind about going to the club. All she wanted to do was lay up ass-hole naked and sleep the night away. Gangsta Jake wasn't having it, though. He was the one who eventually woke her up and spoke on going out. He wanted to see what Brooklyn was all about. At his request, they hopped out of bed, got dressed, and made their way to the club.

"This music is bumping like a muthafucka!" he screamed inside Michelle's ear.

The club was packed from wall-to-wall with some of the cutest females from New York. It took nearly an hour to get inside. Gangsta Jake could not believe how fine the women were on the East Coast. Dark skin, light skin, big booties, tight bodies, Whites, Blacks, Latinos, all different flavors were on deck at Tunnel's.

Missy Elliot's cut, "Work It," vibrated in every nook and cranny of the club. The disc jockey was on one with his turntables, mixing, scratching, and filling requests. He went from "Work It," to Mobb Deep's joint, "Got It Twisted." Their cut was fresh off the press, and the club was feeling it.

"Party over here, fuck you over there," the DJ announced over the microphone, hyping the dance floor up. When he mixed "Hypnotize" by Biggie Smalls into "Got It Twisted," the partygoers turned the volume of noise up. They loved Biggie. Everyone danced and cheered to "Hypnotize" like it was a new cut.

"Come on, baby, let's dance," Michelle yelled in Gangsta Jake's ear.

He had not danced in public in years, but that did not stop him from shaking a leg. Back in the penitentiary, Gangsta Jake would win all the crip-walking contests against his homies. He had rhythm and did not mind showing off his skills to Michelle, or to Brooklyn's club scene.

"Go baby go baby go, go baby go baby go." Once Michelle saw how good he danced, she became so excited that people nearby noticed and began cheering him on with her. Gangsta Jake enjoyed the attention. The music combined with the crowd, gin, and weed in his system had him feeling good and full of himself. The boy was living one!

Dancing freely among a crowd that big is something he played in his mind over and over again back when he was doing time. He was thrilled about his moment of fame, and at that instant, no one could tell him shit. When "Gangsta Party" by Tupac and Snoop Dog came on, he began to crip walk in the middle of the dance floor, drawing a couple of hundred people around him. The DJ then mixed "Ain't Nothing but a Gee Thang" behind "Gangsta Party," which prompted Gangsta Jake to hold up the Avalon gang sign with his left hand, dig into his pocket, and pull out a blue bandana. He then waved the blue rag in the air as he put down some crip walk moves no one had ever seen in their lives.

"No, that nigga didn't," a cute female also from Los Angeles told her girlfriend with an innocent smirk on her face. She could tell by the way he was dancing that he was a straight gangbanger out of her town. She'd been around enough gangbangers to realize he was not from New York.

Her name was Nancy Kelley. Nancy was a five-foot-eight-inch female who took very good care of herself. Her dangerous curves and smooth, brown skin made Nancy one of most attractive females in the club. Gangsta Jake dancing alone gave her all the reason to believe he was at the club by himself; well, at least, without a female companion. His bold attitude and gangsta mentality instantly caught her attention. She liked what she saw.

Nancy was a professional dancer who had appeared in several big stars' videos. Her girlfriend, Terri, and sister, Suzette, talked her into joining him on the dance floor. By Gangsta Jake being her flavor, it did not take much to convince Nancy. She gave Terri her purse and made her way to the dance floor. When Gangsta Jake saw Nancy dancing toward him, he held his hand out and allowed her to join him.

The party was off the chain as the two hopped and glided across the dance floor. They were having a ball representing Los Angeles to the fullest. Just to show off, Nancy stretched her right hand over her head, before twisting two middle fingers displaying a West Coast sign. Seeing the letter W on Nancy's slim fingers let Gangsta Jake know she was from the West Coast as well. The club was popping and Nancy and Gangsta Jake dancing was the center of attraction.

Michelle could not believe how open he had become. The last time he came that close to any other female was back at the Barbary Coast Strip Club. As long as Nancy did not go as far as Ole Girl did, everything was going to be okay. Michelle loved how much fun he was having. Whenever he was happy, she was as well. Once "What's My Name?" by Sly Boogie mixed in and out to another song, Gangsta Jake closed the circle around him by making his way over to Michelle. Nancy carried on for a minute with the crowd that closed around her.

"Ladies and gentlemen, give it up to the two for displaying so much raw talent. They have more moves than a chess game," the DJ announced over the loud speakers as he cranked up the volume to Usher's "Confession."

Everyone on the dance floor clapped before continuing on with their partying. Gangsta Jake left Nancy hanging on the dance floor while some square-looking brother made an attempt to dance with her, but she was cool on him. Her mind was set on finding out who that fine-ass nigga she bust a sweat with was. Michelle and Gangsta Jake danced a couple more songs as Nancy and her crew stood idle, sipping on Long Island Iced Tea.

"Girl, that green-eyed nigga got it going on, and I'm trying to hook up with his fine ass."

"I think the girl he's dancing with is with him. When you guys were dancing, she was all excited," Suzette told her sister.

"Well, that's too bad for him, because I'm too cute to be getting into it with a female over her man."

"Especially a gangbanger," Terri added her two cents in.

Nancy made the right choice. Michelle did not play around when it came to females flirting with her dude. She was not looking for any problems, but if some occurred, Michelle was fully prepared to deal with them. Gangsta Jake made sure Michelle smuggled her twenty-two inside the club. Getting passed security was not a problem for her. At his request, she placed the gun in her panties, and with a little charm along with a one hundred dollar bill, she and Gangsta Jake were in. He could not remember the last time he had so much fun. After a few hours, the couple grew tired and made their way back to their hotel.

12

The Other Side of a Gemini

Ring . . . ring . . . ring . . . ring . . . ring . . . "Michelle, get up and answer your cell phone!" Gangsta Jake yelled from the shower.

"Baby, I'm tired," is all she moaned from underneath a fluffy comforter. Michelle had a hangover out of this world. Too many mixed drinks had her head spinning the following morning.

Ring . . . ring . . . ring . . . ring . . . ring . . . He eventually jumped out of the shower, wet and ass-hole naked to find Michelle's phone. "Damn, girl! Get your lazy butt up. Hello!" Gangsta Jake answered in a upset voice.

"Is Michelle awake yet?" Robin asked in a low, sweet tone.

"What happened to speaking first? I know your mama raised you better than that."

"I'm sorry. Good morning, Rohan. Is Michelle, I mean, are you guys okay?" Her concerns were actually in reference to Michelle only, and he sensed it.

"What do you mean, okay?" He plexed on her and caught an attitude. The other half of him surfaced. Michelle had always teased Gangsta Jake about his split personality, but in spite of being a Gemini, he denied having one.

"Check this out, Robin. I'm not about to be playing games with you any longer. For your information, don't think for one second that I'm some stupid-ass nigga who don't know how you feel about me."

"Rohan, what are you talking about—"

He cut her off from speaking the words at the top of her mind. "Listen, little bitch!" He looked over at Michelle, who had dozed back off underneath the comforter. His voice lowered as he thought out his next few sentences. "I hope you haven't told anyone about what went down in L.A. I told you what them selfish bastards did to me, so I don't know what your problem is."

"Rohan, I don't have any problems with you. Whatever you did is your business. I know how the game goes. I'm not into running my mouth about other people's affairs."

"I heard that little slick shit you told Michelle when we first came to town. Talking about 'I'm glad you left that no-good nigga.' You lucky I didn't do something to you behind saying that dumb-ass shit!" His face frowned up, while a hot flash came upon Robin's entire body. She was caught off guard with the threat he sprung on her.

"Look here, Robin. Let my name taste like shit in your mouth. I thought we could be cool based on Michelle and the fact that you did help with my defense while I was in prison. But, Robin, you've been acting real shady."

She was practically speechless. "But . . . but . . ." tears rolled down Robin's frightened face; her voice shook and was uneven, "Rohan, I—"

He interjected once again. "I drove past your parents' house yesterday; don't give me a reason to swing back through there."

She understood exactly what he was referring to.

"Another thing, you better act like we never had this conversation. And if I find out you mentioned it to anybody, you and your folks can cancel Christmas."

Click! Robin sat on the edge of her bed, listening to what had turned into a dial tone. She could not stop crying or imagining Gangsta Jake killing her and her parents.

"God, please do not let this fool do any harm to me and my family," she cried out loud as tears continued flowing down her face. "I don't know why this boy is stressing me like this. Lord, please protect me from him," she cried out while dropping down to her knees. Robin had become hysterical.

Gangsta Jake hopped back in the shower and continued jacking himself off. Masturbation had been a part of his program during his entire stay in prison. Since Michelle was out of commission and he was horny as a toad, he did what he had grown accustomed to doing. As much as he denied it, Gangsta Jake had become institutionalized. If it wasn't for him being so in love with Michelle, he probably would have been back in prison with his buddies. He had been home for a few months and owed it all to Michelle. She was one of the main reasons he strived so hard not to be caught after committing crimes. On the other hand, no matter how bad he wanted to be there with her, he refused to use that as a deterrent to avoid the promise he made to Young Lad and his other homies on lockdown. Killing snitches is what he vowed to do. And as long as he was capable of doing so, that is what he planned on doing.

Five hours after Gangsta Jake hung up on Robin, Michelle rose from her sleep. She stretched her arms out and yawned before placing a pleasant, well-rested smile on her face.

"Hi, Boo. Can I have a kiss?" Her breath was stale from the smell of alcohol the night before.

"Ugh, you stink, girl." She knew he was only teasing her.

"All that's jacked up. Forget you, nigga."

"I'm just messing with you. Give me one, beautiful. Damn, you're even cute in the morning."

He not only walked over and gave her a big, wet kiss, but also spread her legs wide open and tapped that ass with the quickness. He had to have it at least twice a day. Thereafter, he reached over and grabbed a joint from the ashtray, took three long drags, exhaled, and laid under Michelle's perfectly round butt. The two fit together like a glove.

"Here, baby, hit this." He attempted to place the pinhead in her mouth.

"I'm cool. You know I don't like them that small. It's too little to smoke."

"Girl, hit the shit! It ain't gonna kill you to save weed!"

"Okay, Mr. Demanding. Whatever you say."

"I talked to your scary friend earlier."

"Who? Robin?"

"Who else?"

"I should have known. Were you nice to her? Rohan, please don't tell me you were mean to Robin," Michelle searched his eyes for the real answer. "She's my girl."

He had a too-late-for-that look on his face.

"Rohan, what did you tell her?" By being aware of all the love she had for Robin, he was reluctant to reveal the truth. But, of course, he did. Besides, he and Michelle vowed to never hold secrets or grudges from one another.

"I put her ass in check! I heard what the fuck she said at her apartment yesterday. Girl, you just don't know," he shook his head from side to side. "I'm seconds away from cutting you off from her," he added.

"What! Why?"

"For not hollering at me about what she said. That shit was bogus! You know we're not supposed to hold back anything from one another."

"Baby, I know. I'm sorry." They had never engaged in an argument, so Michelle did not know how he would react. She was not afraid to the point of fearing for her life; she knew him better than that. But receiving an ass whooping did cross her mind.

"Baby, I just didn't want to get you upset. Robin did not mean nothing by saying that anyway."

Gangsta Jake stood up from the bed with a upside-down smile. Once he placed his boxers on, he turned back around and looked Michelle square in the center of her face. He didn't like the way she continuously defended Robin.

"I know that's your girl and all, but . . ." he paused and placed Michelle in suspense for a few seconds, "but, I don't want you dealing with Robin any longer from this day forward. It's over between the two of you!" he told Michelle with a voice of authority. "It's a wrap. A done deal."

Michelle battled with her emotions as she pleaded her case. As much as she tried to maintain her composure, the thought of being forced to abandon her best friend did not sit well with her. A tear rolled down her left eye, then her right. She was heartbroken, but Gangsta Jake did not care. He was extremely upset at her betrayal.

"As a matter of fact, we're getting the fuck out of Brooklyn today!"

"Dang, baby, why are you tripping? I told you I was sorry. That ain't nothing but the Gemini in you that has you acting like that. Rohan, please don't stop me from seeing my friend. Our families are tight, Rohan. Her mother raised me when my mom died. Please, Rohan, please, let us remain friends."

As time went on, her tears were starting to have an effect on his decision. She eventually wore him down with her constant weeping and bedroom eyes. He was ready to reason, but not without a firm scolding.

"Goddamn, Michelle! Shut the hell up." His order only made her cry harder. When she recognized a downshift in his attitude, her emotional display grew more intense. She enjoyed the undivided attention and the effect her sobbing was having on him.

"Look, Michelle!" he firmly stated with his finger pointed at her face. "I'ma give you one more chance, and one more chance only to be cool with Robin, as long as you're black," his face twitched as he gently poked her with his index finger. "Don't you ever get out of line like that again."

He was still extremely upset, but was willing to work with her based on how tight the two girls were. The fact that Robin helped him gain his freedom also had an impact on his decision. Michelle's boos and hoos came to an end when she realized her battle was easily won with tears. At least remaining friends with Robin was possible. Without allowing her a second to celebrate within her own mind, Gangsta Jake reached back and slapped her with half his might. He then repeated the same process a couple more times.

"Don't you ever hold nothing back from me again!" he screamed out with aggression.

"I'm sorry, baby. I won't do it again, daddy." She grabbed her face and was very upset. Michelle was shocked, but not at all surprised. She was well aware that Gangsta Jake did not take disloyalty lightly. Principles he stood on would be enforced with violence if violated. Not even Michelle could escape his wrath if she went against the grain.

When Gangsta Jake was a youngster, being disciplined by his big homies for misbehaving was a part of his upbringing. After an ass beating from his O.G.s, they would hug him and no love was lost. His intention was not to hurt her, but to show her there would be repercussions for disobeying his program. Let him and his homies tell it, it was only done out of love.

Michelle did not see it as such. She viewed it as a bunch of bullshit. After Gangsta Jake slapped her up, she came back with a series of swings and punches of her own. Her first blow caught him in the lip and busted it. He responded by pushing her to the ground and placing his fingertips up to his lip.

"Ain't this a bitch!" he told himself while viewing the blood on the tip of his two middle fingers. He was stunned. He didn't think she had it in her to take back off on him, but he was wrong.

"Nigga, I ain't no fucking punching bag. I'm suppose to be yo bitch, and this is the way you treat me? That's fucked up!" She wept. "I didn't do all that time with you in prison for you to come home and beat my ass. I'm not no damn masochist. I don't get no thrill out of getting my ass slapped around. I'm not having this shit, Rohan!"

Gangsta Jake walked over to the restroom mirror as Michelle continued to rant. "I'll be damn! This girl done bust my shit," he whispered to himself while looking at Michelle through the mirror. By this time, someone had summoned the NYPD due to all the commotion in their room.

Boom! Boom! Boom! Boom! "Open up this door!" a tall, jet-black officer demanded as his white partner stood inches away, gripping the gun inside his holster.

"Who the hell is it?" Michelle yelled toward the door, surprised that someone was banging on it in the first place.

"NYPD! Open up!"

"Fuck!" Gangsta Jake softly stated as he looked over at Michelle.

"Just a moment! I have to get dressed!" Michelle stared back at Gangsta Jake with a look of confusion.

He immediately ran toward the table to retrieve Michelle's gun that sat in plain view, then went over to a bag of weed that lay next to a pack of zig-zags. As fast as he could, Gangsta Jake stuffed the contraband beneath the mattress and dashed over toward Michelle.

"We'll deal with this later," he hissed to her. "Let's just get these white folks out of our business for now."

"Rohan, all I want to do is leave. I need some time alone, to think."

"Think?" he questioned with his face turned up. "Think about what?"

"I don't like the way you carried me. That shit hurt my feelings." Tears continued to flow down her face.

"Pull yourself together!" His lips tightened, therefore his voice was heard only from inside the room. "We've been through too much together for you to be going out like this."

Boom! Boom! Boom! Boom! "Open up, ma'am! We don't have all day."

"I'm coming!"

"Rohan, I'm not going to let them do nothing to you, but right about now, I just want to be alone. I might go over to Robin's apartment for a while to clear my head. I need to let these people in before they kick this door down."

After the small delay, she finally opened the door as the tall, black officer so adamantly commanded. The two officers walked inside the room with the hotel manager in the rear. Michelle stood at the door in one of Gangsta Jake's white tee shirts, while he pretended to be using the toilet.

"What's the problem, Miss?" the white officer with a New York accent spoke up. His partner scanned the room, making sure they were not in harm's way. "We received a call of some type of disturbance coming out of this room. Is everything okay?" he continued.

"Yes, I'm fine." Her tears came to an end when the police entered her room, but they could tell by the puffiness in her eyes that she had been crying. They both sensed a problem.

"'What happened to your face? Who hit you?" the black officer asked with a look of great concern.

"I got into it with my man over him getting some female pregnant. His sorry ass had the nerve to fuck her nasty ass without using a condom." She began crying again. Being around Gangsta Jake and hearing his tall tales to those in authority trained her to be a great liar.

"Did he hit you and bruise your face like that?" the white officer looked her in the eyes and asked. He was ready to get to the bottom of the situation and move forward with his shift. He had hot donuts and coffee in his patrol car that he was eager to get back to. Gangsta Jake sat on the toilet behind the closed door, with his neck and body stretched out. He wanted to hear every word that was being said.

"No, he did not hit me. The girl he got pregnant and one of her friends jumped me."

"Where did that take place? According to other guests, loud noises were coming out of this room. Were you girls fighting in here?"

"No."

The black officer made a few steps toward the restroom and asked if anyone was inside it. His intuition told him someone was. As he advanced toward the door, Gangsta Jake flushed the toilet so the officer would not be startled. All attention then focused on whoever was in the restroom. If Michelle planned on getting the police out of their mix, she knew it was time to start lying again.

"That's my boyfriend's scandalous ass."

The hotel manager tilted his head and looked at Michelle over the rims of his round glasses. "If he's so scandalous, what is he doing here, young woman?" the short, Arab man sarcastically asked with a wise-guy attitude.

"Look, Mohamad, Abo, Swami, or whatever your name is. This ain't got nothing to do with you. You need to get you some business!"

"Young woman, I have everything to do with what is going on in my business. I assure you—" Michelle cut him off by making him talk to the hand she placed in front of his face.

"Could y'all please tell him to shut up."

"I will not shut up."

"Fuck you then!"

"Screw you! Officers, I want her removed from my business at once!"

Gangsta Jake contemplated on making the four-story jump from the restroom window. The fall was too far to avoid serious injuries; therefore, he opened the restroom door before the police did. When he walked out, Michelle and the Arab were engrossed in a heated conversation. The towel Gangsta Jake dried his hands off with somewhat subsided his nervousness. By him sucking in his bottom lip, the officers did not notice the cut in it. Well, at least, not until he was asked a few questions.

"Step over there," the white officer pointed toward the bed where the gun and weed sat below. The officer did not pull his gun out, but did unbuckle his holster and grab ahold of it. Their focus turned from Michelle (and the manager who thought he was the owner) to Gangsta Jake. The shape of his body alone was enough to gain their undivided attention.

"Is anyone else in there?" the black NYPD asked Gangsta Jake, also cuffing his hand around his firearm.

"No, sir."

They both felt intimidated by his masculinity. He kept his body in tip-top shape by doing twelve-hundred pushups, eight-hundred crunches, and five-hundred burpies five days a week. He was in the best shape of his life, and the two officers were not taking any chances with him.

"How long have you been out of prison, bud? Do you have any identification?" the white officer quizzed him.

By Gangsta Jake being inches away from the gun, his preference was to grab it, shoot the police up, and flee the scene. He was quick to pull a pistol and pop it if necessary. However, he knew damn well the desires lingering in his head were mathematically impossible, if he planned on living to see another day. Without giving it much thought, he realized he had no choice but to shoot from another barrel: his mouth piece.

"First of all, I have never been to jail in my entire life."

"What happened to your lip, sir?" the white officer asked once he began to speak.

He could only hide his injury for so long. "If you do not mind, sir, I would like to answer one question at a time. As I was saying, I have never been incarcerated in my entire life. If you are stereotyping me based on my killer body, I understand your rationale, and your apology is fully accepted. I'm a man with a sense of humor, which means I certainly can take a joke." He cracked a half smile.

"But on a serious note," his face straightened out as he focused on the character he was portraying, "I've been a professional body builder for the past twelve years, and unfortunately, I've had to deal with this form of discrimination on several occasions. Sure, I have identification. It's right over there in my suit coat pocket." He began walking toward the suit coat, but was cut short.

"Just stay put while my partner retrieves it for you. As a matter of fact, why don't you place your hands over your head for me."

"Excuse me, sir. Why am I being treated as a common criminal? I know my rights as a tax-paying citizen."

"Yeah, right! Just keep your hands over your head where I can see them, bud. And I don't want no fucking shit out of you, either. Keep talking and I'll have you in handcuffs."

Gangsta Jake did not want any problems. He was too far away from home to be getting into it with the police and hauled off to jail. Besides, the bunko driver's license and social security card that he paid one thousand dollars for was good as long as he was not arrested and fingerprinted. Once at the station, a thorough background check would be conducted. He was not a fugitive, but did not want the police knowing his true identity. To accompany his one thousand dollar spread were ten fake credit cards, all in the same name. American Express, Gold Visa, Master Charge, you name it. According to his wallet, he was like MC Hammer claimed to be, "Too legit to quit."

"So, what did you say happened to your lip, Mr. ahh . . ." the officer raised Gangsta Jake's fake driver's license up to the light. "Let's see here, Mr. Kenny Wilson. What actually happened again, sir?"

"I did it," Michelle interjected. "This is my boyfriend. The one I was telling you guys about. He disrespected me, so I hit him." She gave Gangsta Jake a shitty look that only he knew the truth behind.

"So, let me get this straight. Here is your wallet, Mr. Wilson. You can put your hands down, sir."

After seeing his credentials, they treated him with some respect. "Where was I? Oh, yeah, Miss, you found out that he banged some female and got her pregnant, then . . ." he paused and rolled his eyes as if he had more important things to do. "According to you, of course, somehow you ran across another young lady and her girlfriend who jumped you. After that, you and your boyfriend—this is your boyfriend, correct?" the officer pointed his finger at Michelle.

"Yes, it is, or, at least, it was." Her eyes rolled away from Gangsta Jake. He did not know if her last statement was apart of her script or her true sentiments. Nevertheless, she was doing a great job, and he was not going to disturb her unless he deemed it necessary.

"After that, you guys came to this room and ultimately had an altercation. Oh, yeah, Miss, and last, but definitely not least, you punched him in the mouth?"

"That's exactly what happened," Gangsta Jake spoke up and concurred with the officer's assessment.

"Is that right?" The white cop held the bottom of his chin and thought for a few seconds. When he looked over at his partner, his partner had already read his mind. The two worked with one another long enough to pick up on each other's thoughts.

"Miss, turn around and place your hands over your head." Michelle's heart began beating like a drum. The police were not tripping on Gangsta Jake anymore. Michelle became their center of attention. Her own statements winded up getting her handcuffed and on her way to the station. The hotel manager cracked a smile. He felt relieved to see some action being taken against her.

"Officers, officers, please allow me a minute to speak to you," Gangsta Jake cut in. "Sir, may I have one moment of your time to perhaps rectify this situation?" The white officer continued to cuff her hands.

"What can you possible say to correct what's already happened? She hit you, so she's going to jail." The black officer sat back and let his partner take control.

"Sir, would it be possible to speak to you alone, without the presence of this gentleman?" he pointed at the hotel manager.

"You have sixty seconds," the black officer spoke up.

"Sir, could you please step outside the room."

The manager was not feeling the request, but did comply with the officers.

"Officers, I don't know any other way to say this, but truthfully, this girl truly does not deserve to go to jail. First of all, her brother and dad just died in the Iraq war." That caught both officers' attention. "Second, I, the love of her life, turned around and got some other female pregnant. And on top of all that, she was evicted from her home just two days ago. That's the reason she's living out of this room," he told the officers with a straight face. "She's the sweetest girl in the world. Granted, she did hit me, but I'm the one who created this entire situation. She clearly acted on emotions."

"So, you're telling me that you do not wish to press any charges?" the black officer asked the person who he believed to be Kenny Wilson. He felt her pain. He actually did not want to arrest Michelle in the first place, but was doing so based on his partner's decision.

"I'll tell you what. Sit down for a moment, Miss, and let me and my partner discuss the issue." They walked to the far side of the room and talked for a couple of minutes while Michelle sat on the bed, handcuffed. She did not speak a word as the two cops decided her fate.

"All right. Here's what we're going to do. First of all, whose name is this room rented in?" the white officer asked the two of them.

"Mine, sir," Gangsta Jake responded."

"Okay. Since you're not interested in filing charges, we have decided to cut her loose. Miss, consider this your lucky day," he said, pointing at Michelle as he instructed her to stand up in order to be uncuffed. "You can thank my partner for you being freed. My vote was for you to be arrested."

"Thank you, officer. I appreciate you not arresting me."

"Don't worry about it. Make sure you keep your hands to yourself, Miss. By the way, sorry to hear about your family." Michelle had nearly forgotten about Gangsta Jake feeding him that story.

"Oh, yes. Thanks for your concern."

The officer continued, "We're going to let you go on the condition that you leave from here for now. Just long enough for things to cool down with the two of you."

That was right up Michelle's alley. She was trying to get away from Gangsta Jake for a little while anyway. Michelle had to show that she was still upset about the way he slapped her up. She grabbed her purse and headed to her old apartment. Gangsta Jake was so relieved to get the police out of his face, he did not oppose their request.

13

Licking Her Wounds

"Girl, I told you that nigga was no good for you."

"Robin, don't even start that. You're the reason why I got my ass kicked in the first place—protecting you. Please keep his name out of your mouth."

"Damn, Michelle! That nigga sure do have you in check. You and I are supposed to be able to talk about whatever we want among ourselves. Girl, don't let him take our bond away from us," Robin rolled her eyes.

"Robin, I hear what you're saying, but I don't hear what you're saying. I honestly can't hide anything from him. He knows me like a book. He knows what's on my mind before I speak it. Rohan might be wild, but he ain't stupid by far. Normally, he's the sweetest person in the world, but sometimes he can be so mean. I love him to death, Robin, but I'm not with getting my ass beat."

"Michelle, why don't you take a break from being with him or leave him all together?"

Michelle looked the other way, as if she was giving Robin's statement some serious consideration. When Robin saw her reaction, she made all attempts at severing Michelle's relationship with him.

"Girl, you can easily move back in here with me. The lady who took your position at work is constantly messing people's paperwork up. They would let her go in a heartbeat to rehire you. My rent and utilities are paid up for the next two months, so you don't have to worry about paying bills for a while. For real, Michelle, you never have to worry about paying bills with me. You can stay for free, as far as that matters. And you already know I purchased a new car, so you can drive it whenever you want to. Girl, I just want you back home with me where life can be safer for you," Robin urged her.

Michelle stared at her best friend with tears forming at the bottom of her eyes. She was overwhelmed with gratitude. Michelle appreciated the way Robin was willing to bend over backwards to help her. However, as much as she tried to convince her, there was something inside of Michelle that would not let go. She loved Gangsta Jake's dirty drawers.

"Robin, thanks, girl." Michelle hugged her as they sat on the couch, tears now running down both of their faces. "I really appreciate your help and all, but I can't leave him. I love his ass too much. Girl, I know you're not trying to hear this, but I'm sprung on that nigga. He and I have been through too much for me to let it all go like that."

"Michelle, you should know better than to continue a relationship with a guy who put his hands on you. If he does it once, he'll do it again. Girl, that nigga frightens me. He gives me the creeps. I find myself constantly worried about you. What type of future can you expect by being with him?"

Robin was hitting the nail on the head. She gave Michelle a lot to think about during their three-hour conversation. All she spoke was the real, but not enough to modify Michelle's decision about being with Gangsta Jake. Michelle's nose was too wide open to leave him, so much so that she was tired of the conversation.

"Robin, let's change the subject because I'm already in violation for sitting up here speaking about him. Forget about me and Rohan. What's up with you and Rick's chocolate ass?" The two smiled and finally shared a much needed laugh together.

"The nigga stays in the mirror a little bit too much, but beside that, he's all good. I'm really feeling him."

"Have you given him some yet?"

"Girl, hush your mouth. You know what's up with my three-month rule. He is a nice kisser though. And Michelle," Robin's eyes filled up with excitement, "that nigga got a big dick."

"Now how in the hell do you know all that, if you haven't given him any?"

"I rubbed it when we were kissing."

"You dick-teasing bitch, you," Michelle smiled. "What were you trying to do, get yourself raped?"

"He's too square for all that. Furthermore, I run this pussy. Ain't nothing going up in this unless I approve of it. Don't forget, I have a black belt." She held up a karate pose in laughter.

"I heard that, girlfriend," Michelle gave Robin a high five as she sat next to her.

Knock! Knock! Knock! "Speaking of Rick, that may be him right there." Robin jumped off the couch and walked over to the door. When she looked through the peep hole and discovered the person on the other side was not Rick, but, in fact, her worst nightmare, she refused to open it.

Gangsta Jake was sliding through to pick up Michelle and head back to a place that he was familiar with. He enjoyed the time spent in Brooklyn, but was ready to return to Los Angeles. His mind was set on going back to Cali and knocking off one of the rats who appeared on the list he now possessed. Instead of opening the door, Robin backed away from it and informed Michelle who it was.

"I'm going to bed," Robin let her friend know with a nervous facial expression.

"Robin, you are so scary, girl. You need to stop acting like that."

She was certainly not putting on an act. Gangsta Jake had Robin worried and confused. The mere sight of him automatically caused her to become traumatized. Robin was so afraid, she refused to tell Michelle how he had threatened to kill her and her parents. All she did was pray that somehow, her problem would fade away.

Michelle was only out of Gangsta Jake's presence for a few hours, and in spite of getting slapped around, she missed him already. Let the truth be told, she kind of enjoyed being spanked by him. Of course, her pride would never allow that fact to be revealed.

When she opened the door, Gangsta Jake strolled in with a Billy D. Williams smile attached to his face. Michelle's true feelings toward his presence were waiting under the surface of her skin. However, her stubbornness helped to reserve her emotions.

"So, what's up, sexy?" he asked Michelle with charm in his eyes. "Oh, I see you still have your poker face on."

Michelle remained silent, while Robin locked her bedroom door and placed her ear up to it.

"This nigga got his damn nerve," Robin spoke silently to herself. "Gonna threaten my parents' lives, slapped my girl, and then come to my place like nothing has happened. I hope somebody kills his ass. I bet you end up going back to prison, no-good-ass nigga. Yeah, I said it," she softly mumbled from behind the locked door.

"We're leaving tonight, Michelle. Fuck the airplane. I already made reservations for us to travel by bus. All our luggage is packed away in the rental car. Since we're not going back through the airport, I figured we can take this little pea shooter you have here." He offered the gun to Michelle, but she declined to accept it. She wanted to play the stubborn role for a little while longer; however, he was not in the mood to play along with her little game.

"Check this out, Michelle. I don't have time to play these reindeer-ass games with you right now. I'ma about to get in traffic. If you're rolling, let's roll. If not, I'll holla!"

He did not want to depart from Brooklyn without the love of his life. But in order to not look soft, his plans consisted of doing just that. Gangsta Jake turned around and walked back toward the door he came through. As he made his way through the door and down the two flight of stairs, Michelle came running behind him.

"Rohan, wait!" she screamed from the top of the two flights of stairs. "Let me at least say goodbye to Robin!" He was so happy to hear her sexy voice, he made an about-face and walked back up the stairs.

"Girl, why you playing with me? You know damn well you ain't trying to leave all this behind." He reached his left hand down and grabbed ahold of his crotch. Without realizing it, the corners of Michelle's mouth turned up and a bright smile appeared on her face. His funny attitude is one of the reasons she could not resist him. "Come here and give daddy a hug."

14

Shit Happens

Twenty-four hours into the bus ride, their bus pulled into a Denver, Colorado, bus station for a two-hour layover. At that point, Gangsta Jake was down to his last joint of chronic and was not trying to run out.

"See there, Michelle. Messing around with you and those damn blunts got us about to be dry on weed."

"I'm sorry, Boo. You should have stuck to your guns and waited until we made it back to L.A. before you rolled one."

"Some of my homeboys used to serve dope out here, so I know there's a ghetto somewhere in town that sells weed."

"Boy, can't you wait until we make it to L.A.?"

"I can, but I'm not trying to. You know how much I need my medication. Michelle, I been smoking bud every day since I was in the sixth grade."

"So, what are you trying to do? Jump in a cab and ask the driver to take you to a weed house?"

"Well, not actually, but kinda sort of. We have two hours to play with. Would you rather sit here and do nothing?"

"Not really. I never been to Denver before, so I guess it would be kind of nice to see what it looks like out here. Let me use the ladies' room first."

While Michelle freshened up from the long bus ride, Gangsta Jake mingled around the lobby area. As she walked away, three local gang members saw Gangsta Jake from a distance and headed his way. He fit the description of a rival gang member who committed a drive-by shooting on their neighborhood two days before. The three wanted to make sure he was not the one who violated their territory.

Psycho led the two other gangbangers. He was a five-foot-nine-inch, one hundred and ninety-pound, jet-black brother who walked with a slight limp.

His homeboys, Slime and ET, walked on both sides of him as if they were his personal security guards. Psycho was known to be one of the most notorious gangbangers the state of Colorado had ever seen. Drive-bys, walk-ups, kidnaps—you name it. The three had just returned from one of their homeboy's funeral. They were at the bus station to pick up Psycho's mother from work.

Psycho wore a long sleeve, blue khaki shirt, black jeans, and a pair of blue, high-top All Stars. Slime and ET both had on black khakis with two different colored "Charley Brown" striped shirts. ET's was two-tone brown and Slim's was two-tone blue. The blue rag wrapped Aunt Jemima-style around Psycho's head notified Gangsta Jake that the three were some type of Crips. All three were in their early twenties.

"Say, cuzz, what set that is?" Psycho boldly asked Gangsta Jake with a mean, hard stare. The black 9mm underneath Slime's shirt gave Psycho all the courage he needed to go up against Gangsta Jake's muscular body.

"Cuzz, you look like this fool who blasted on me and my homeboys the other night."

Slime took one step back and nearly pulled out his gun. The two Denver cops walking nearby slowed his motions. Gangsta Jake peeped his reaction and was aware that Slime was strapped with some type of weapon. Michelle's gun was with her in the restroom, so he felt somewhat defenseless.

"Cuzz, it couldn't have been me because I never been to Denver in my life. I'm only passing through. If it wasn't for this layover, I wouldn't be standing here talking to y'all." Gangsta Jake did not like the idea of being the recipient of an interrogation, but he respected Psycho and his homies for holding down their town.

"Homey, I'm all the way from Los Angeles, which means, I don't have no beef with y'all."

"Los Angeles!" Psycho's mentality changed from aggressive to friendly. He had much love for Crips from the Mecca of gangbanging. If it wasn't for L.A. Crips coming to Denver and starting up his neighborhood, he probably would not have had the reputation he obtained.

"Cuzz, what set you from out there?"

"Five Tray Avalon," Gangsta Jake let him know as he flashed his three middle fingers on them.

"Is that right?" Psycho's face lit up with happiness. "Cuzz, your homies used to come out here and sell dope. Big and Lil' Joker, Lil' Man, Lunatic, Crazy Ni, Maniac, and Snoopy Slim."

"Snoopy Slim is now resting in peace."

"No shit!"

The two Denver police doubled back to see what was going on. "You boys aren't causing any trouble are you, Timothy?" They were very familiar with

Psycho based on all the shit he stayed in. By Slime having the pistol handy, he laid in the cut and maintained his cool.

"Naw!" His facial expression changed back to his hard look. "I'm here to pick up my mom. Why are y'all fucking with us? We ain't breaking no laws."

"You better watch your mouth, boy!" The white officer pointed his walkie-talkie at Psycho as he began to turn red in the face.

"Man, I ain't pressed to hear all that. We ain't breaking no laws, so why are we being harassed?"

"Oh, we haven't begun to harass you yet," his white partner spoke up.

ET placed his arms around Psycho's right shoulder and walked him over to the side by himself. As he did so, Psycho continued to look back and talk trash to the officer.

"Psych! Psych! Listen to me for a second, homey."

"What's up, cuzz?" His eyebrows rose from being disgruntled. "ET, fuck them cowards. I wanna bust one of them pussies in their mouth."

"Why don't you cee cool, loco? Nigga, don't forget that Slime is strapped, and you got an ounce of cut up rocks in your pocket."

"Damn, homey!" Psycho's voice became a light whisper. "I did forget about this zip of dope in my pocket. Good lookin', dawg. I got it from here, cuzz. Let me go over there and smooth this thang out so we can get away from these Po-Pos." Psycho spun around and walked back toward the crowd. By then, Michelle was returning from the ladies' room and was puzzled about what was occurring.

"Baby, what's going on? Is everything okay?" She looked at the police, the three gangbangers, and figured Gangsta Jake was having some type of altercation. The officers' presence reminded her of the gun in her possession.

"Michelle, everything is cool," he let her know. Psycho kept his mouth shut as Gangsta Jake continued. One of the officers stared at Psycho and contemplated taking him to jail.

"Michelle, these are my cousins out of Denver," he waved his right hand toward the three in a humble manner, pretending to faze the police out. As their conversation continued, the police decided to go about their business.

"My bad, loco. I didn't mean to have the Po-Pos all in our business. Cuzz, what did you say your name was?"

"Gangsta. Gangsta Jake. And what's yours?"

"Psycho Tim." I'm from Harlem Thirties. These are my homeboys, Slime and ET."

"What's up, cuzz?" They all shook hands with Gangsta Jake. Michelle stood in the circle of guys and waited to be introduced.

"This is my girl, Michelle."

"What's up, y'all?" She was happy the situation turned out the way it did.

"Well, cuzz, I'm about to get out of here. My mom should be walking up in a minute. She works for this bus station. Stay up, my nigga. If you ever come through Denver again, look me up. Everybody knows me as Psycho." As he and his crew walked away, they were stopped by Gangsta Jake at the end of the terminal.

"Psych!" Gangsta Jake yelled out until he finally caught up to the three.

"Gangsta. What's up, dawg?"

"Say, cuzz, I was just wondering. Could you hook me up with some bud while I'm out here in Denver?"

"Homey, that ain't no problem. I don't smoke, but I know who got it."

"Is that right?" Gangsta Jake commented, happy with the answer he received. "Well, I have a couple of hours to work with, so plug me up."

"That's the least I can do for one of my allies. Let me pick moms up, drop her off at the house, and swing back to scoop you and your girl up. I stay close by, so I'll be back in about fifteen minutes."

Eighteen minutes later, Psycho came rushing through the terminal door. It only took him a half minute to locate Gangsta Jake and Michelle hanging out at a video game.

"Here comes that boy," Michelle tapped Gangsta Jake on his arm and told him. He was deeply engrossed in a game of Ms. Pac Man when Psycho approached him.

"I see you made it back, dawg."

"I got a little caught up in traffic, but I'm back on deck."

"Here I come. Let me just finish this game."

"Baby, we only have an hour and a half before our bus leaves."

"Yeah, you're right. Fuck this game. Let's slide," he said, looking at Psycho.

Slime and ET accompanied Psycho, who drove a dark blue 1977 Cutlass with a pair of chrome Dayton wires.

"Slime, let cuzz and his girl sit in the front seat," Psycho told his longtime friend. Slime was not feeling his request, but did comply without protest.

The five cruised through downtown Denver and within ten minutes, drove across Colorado Boulevard. They took Colorado Boulevard down to Martin Luther King and made a right turn heading toward Park Hill.

"This is Crenshaw Mafia Gang (CMG) neighborhood, so keep yo eyes open for some of them red rags."

"You bullshitting. They have CMGs all the way out here in Denver? Hell, I didn't know they had a street called Crenshaw out here."

"They don't, but some Bloods from CMG came out here back in the eighties and turned these dudes into CMGs," Psycho revealed to Gangsta Jake.

"I wonder, was that Tako and them? I know a few CMG's from the pen. Lil' Bee told me they was going out to Denver, turning little niggas out. I thought he was just fucking around with me."

"Look, there go two right there," Slime said with excitement as he pointed at a youngster wearing a red Chicago Bull hat with a red, long sleeve tee shirt. His partner had on a red L.A. Clipper's shirt, black jeans, with a red rag hanging out his back pocket. Both of them were teenagers. Slime was charged up at the sight of two rival gang members.

"Double back, loco. I'm 'bout to serve both of them."

Twisting caps back was right up Psycho's alley. He drove to the next block over and eventually made his way back toward his rivals. Slime pulled out his 9mm, made sure the safety was off, and focused his mind on murdering his opposition. He was really putting extras on the situation to impress Gangsta Jake. Nonetheless, he and his little crew were hyped and looking forward to creating a crime scene.

"Say, cuzz!" Gangsta Jake finally spoke up as Psycho rapidly approached their targets. "Y'all need to handle this type of business on y'all own." Psycho was so caught up in the moment, he totally ignored Gangsta Jake. The adrenalin running through his body had him pumped up and tuned out to everything around him, but his targets.

"This ain't going to take long, Crip," Slime told Gangsta Jake from the backseat.

"Nigga, hold the fuck up!" Gangsta Jake pressed the back of his extended arm up against Psycho's chest. Gangsta Jake became enraged at the thought of being a part of a crime he had outgrown years ago. The look in his eyes and base in his voice detoured Psycho's fast approach toward the two young gang members. Rather than executing their original plan, Psycho drove directly past the two.

"Damn, Blood! Did you bee them fools in that butluss that just drove by?"

"Hell, yeah! That was some of them Harlem Thirties," the baby-faced gang member responded to his homeboy's question.

"Let's hit a corner, before they double back on us."

"What's wrong, my nigga? Did you see the law or something?" Psycho asked as he quickly scanned the area, looking for the police.

"Fool! I just met you niggas. I'm not about to let y'all send me back to death row behind no bullshit! I just did twelve years of my life behind somebody else's bullshit! You clowns got me fucked up!"

Huh? went through all their minds. They were all puzzled about why Gangsta Jake switched on them in defense of saving their arch enemies' lives. The seven or eight years' age difference and his hard-core demeanor gave Gangsta Jake a green light to speak without being challenged. The Denver gang members came to realize they were not dealing with a buster. If they were not willing to turn a gun on him like they started to do back at the bus station, they determined the best thing to do was to kick back and take notes on his style; well, at least Psycho and ET did.

"Furthermore, I don't have no animosity with them youngsters or no other Bloods, as far as that matters. My beef is with snitches! Them two little red rags ain't never done nothing to me. Besides, I don't know you little niggas that well anyway to be putting 187s down with. Y'all might be snitches as far as I know," he boldly announced.

The change in Gangsta Jake's attitude caused Michelle to reach inside her handbag. She grabbed hold of her pistol without pulling it out. She was so quiet, no one paid her any attention.

"Cuzz, you may be older than us and all, but you're out of line for saying that," Slime's face frowned up, which led Michelle to pay very close attention to him.

"Nigga, I said y'all *might* be snitches. I never said y'all *were* snitches. But anyway, you right about that. I was out of line. My bad, cuzz," Gangsta Jake realized he was wrong and broke down what he stated.

"You muthafucking right, it's your bad. You got the Harlems fucked up."

"Little nigga, you better kick back! I done told you it was my bad."

Slime turned his head toward Psycho. He was looking for the okay signal to pull out his pistol and start capping on Gangsta Jake. He did not appreciate the statement he made, or the fact that he had to sit in the backseat in order to let two strangers take his normal spot. But by Psycho having so much respect for Crips from Los Angeles, he refused to give Slime the go-ahead.

"Let that shit ride, Slime. He did say it was his bad," Psycho told him.

"Lil' fool, you don't have to keep looking at me like you want a fade. Where I'm from, we fight among each other all the time and after the fact, there ain't no love lost. We can get down if you want to."

"Nigga, I ain't fighting with yo big ass." The only fighting Slime wanted to do was with a gun.

"I'll tell you what, cuzz. I'll put one hand behind my back and fight you." Everyone in the car broke out laughing, but Slime.

"Nigga, that shit ain't funny."

"I can't tell. Everybody else is cracking up," Ganstga Jake sarcastically told Slime.

Psycho finally pulled up to a brick house on 29th and Jasmine. "This is the weed house, cuzz. What are you trying to buy? They sell dubs and dimes."

"Ten sacks? They must got stress weed."

"Yeah, pretty much. This ain't California where they sell that sticky green."

"I ain't mad at them. Here, homey. I'm sure fifty dollars worth will hold me until I make it home. Psycho, I know you don't smoke, so I'm sure you're cool. ET, Slime, do y'all want a couple sacks on me?" Slime was still bitter, so he did not say a word. ET, on the other hand, did.

"Hell, yeah, I'll take a sack or two. Good lookin', loco."

"Here, Psycho, take this extra dub. Get ET two dime sacks too."

Before Psycho bailed out of the car and into the weed house, he ordered Slime to give ET the gun. He was aware that Slime was still upset and did not want him flying off the handle and shooting someone he considered a guest. When Psycho departed from the vehicle, Gangsta Jake decided to light his last joint.

"Give me a light, Michelle." Without saying a single word, she dug inside her top pocket and flicked the lighter for him.

"Gangsta Jake, your girl sure don't say much. I almost forgot she was here," said ET.

Michelle did not forget about him or his two homeboys. Had Slime drawn his gun on Gangsta Jake, he would have literally felt her presence with the concealed weapon she held in her hand.

"Yeah, she likes to lay low. Here, cuzz, hit some of this sticky green straight out of South Central Los Scandalous."

"Damn, this shit smell bomb. I'm glad you broke it out," ET commented before smelling the tip of the joint and moments after taking a puff.

Slime had never smelled weed that strong and wanted to hit some as well. After ET hit the chronic and spoke on how good it was, Slime reached his fingertips out, indicating his desire to take a hit. When Gangsta Jake saw him reaching for the joint through the rearview mirror, it made Gangsta Jake crack a smile. Slime noticed him looking at him and stopped reaching for it.

"Go on and hit it, cuzz! You don't have to act funny with me. We're both Crips, loc. We're entitled to make small mistakes with one another."

Slime was not trying to hear what Gangsta Jake had to say. He reclined in his seat and remained quiet. When Psycho hopped in the car and handed over the weed, he could feel tension in the air. Gangsta Jake was getting fed up with Slime and his stubbornness.

"Good lookin' on plugging me with the weed. Here you go, ET."

"Right on, big homey."

"That's small shit. Don't trip, loco."

"You still have a little time left. Do you want to swing by a food spot and get a little something to eat? You like pig ears? They sell pig ear sandwiches on the Five Points near the bus station."

"Pig ears? I'm cool on that; besides, this little nigga's attitude ain't sitting well with me. Cuzz acts like he's on his period or something."

"Period! Whatever, cuzz." Slime's face, lips, and nose twitched simultaneously. "Psych, fuck this nigga cuzz. I don't know why you treating this fool with so much love. You know them L.A. ass niggas don't give a fuck about us anyway. They act like Crips around the world are suppose to bow down to their asses. Let's hurry up and take this buster back to where we found him."

Slime said one too many words when he referred to a real gangsta as a buster—which is the ultimate disrespect to gangbanging. Without worrying about the consequences of his actions, Gangsta Jake drew back his right hand and bitch-slapped Slime, who sat in the backseat. Slime fell backwards and began hollering like a hoe who had just been bitch-slapped by a gorilla pimp.

"Who's a buster now, you little bitch ass nigga? You better learn some respect for your O.G.s."

"Fool, I ain't new at this cripping. I'm a muthafucking Gee," Gangsta Jake said before tightening up his chest muscles. Once the drama unfolded, both doors swung open on Psycho's Cutlass as everyone swiftly exited the vehicle. The slap to Slime's face pumped the blood up in Gangsta Jake's body. Slime was also hyped and not at all afraid of his much larger opponent. He possessed more heart than Gangsta Jake believed he had. The slap caught Psycho and ET off guard. They both had grown a respectable liking for Gangsta Jake and really did not know how to respond to him taking fight on their homeboy. Surely they were not going to sit back and allow a stranger to get away with an assault on one of their own. That would cause for an automatic ass whooping by their homies once they returned back to their neighborhood.

Slime ran over to ET and demanded he give up the 9mm on his hip. His mind was made up to pump some hot slugs in Gangsta Jake for bitch-slapping him. He insisted he was nobody's coward and was willing to prove it. ET's heart was not with passing the gun off to Slime, but according to his code of honor, he was obligated to do so. After contemplating for five seconds on whether or not he should place Gangsta Jake's life in harm's way, ET reached for the gun in an attempt to hand it over to his comrade. His delay in judgment was a costly mistake. Michelle, who was locked in on the gunman since her initial meeting at the bus station, brought her piece out of her purse with the hammer cocked, aimed, and ready to fire.

"Freeze, mothafucka! Don't move!"

The three Denver Crips nearly mistook her for being a cop. Psycho froze, ET did the same, and Slime—Slime had too much pride to comply as his homeboys did. He grabbed the gun from ET's hand.

Pop! Pop! Pop! Pop! Surprising even herself, Michelle got off four shots. She had never shot anyone in her life, but that suddenly changed. She shot Slime like her life depended on it, which it did. Two bullets landed in his arm, and the other two in his head. ET's mouth dropped toward the ground as he placed his hand over his jaws. Gangsta Jake quickly rushed over to Michelle, very happy with her response.

"Here, baby!" she screamed as she gave him her murder weapon. Michelle was scared, but also excited that she was able to assist her man. The reality of killing someone had not yet kicked in. Her six shooter now only held two more bullets. Gangsta Jake raised the barrel of the gun and aimed it straight at ET's chest. ET stood motionless three feet away from his gun, which now sat next to Slime's curled up body. Gangsta Jake ordered ET to back away from the gun long enough to reach down and pick it up. With more firepower came more control over the situation. Now that the threat of ET or Psycho grabbing Slime's gun and retaliating was eliminated, Gangsta Jake was ready to shake the spot. He swung one gun toward ET and the other toward Psycho.

"Michelle, get behind the driver's seat!" Gangsta Jake ordered.

Psycho and ET were scared to death. Gangsta Jake had total control over whether they had a future or not. He could have ordered the two to do triple backflips and they would have tried to oblige him. However, seeing ET and Psycho dead was not his desire, or Slime, as far as that mattered. If he could have turned back the hands of time and changed what had already occurred, he would have. But that, obviously, was not going to happen.

Slime was out for the count, lying in the street with holes in his head and body. As the flow of thick blood filled the cracks in the street, a young woman in her early teens walked around the corner and began screaming at the top of her lungs. Her screams caused Gangsta Jake to run to the car and jump inside the passenger door. For reasons only God knows, or the Devil, in Gangsta Jake's case, he allowed the unknown woman, Psycho Tim, and ET to survive after seeing what they had witnessed.

"Punch it, Michelle!"

Sweat poured down her forehead as she burned rubber away from the episode. When she looked through the rearview mirror and saw Slime laid out face down on the concrete, it dawned on her the impact of her actions.

"Damn, baby! Do you think he's dead?" She already knew the answer to her own question.

"It don't matter," was the encouragement he provided.

"He was about to shoot us. It was self-defense. I had to kill him."

"Baby, don't trip. We're cool. Just relax."

"Where are we going? What do you want me to do?" Michelle was discombobulating.

"Make a right turn right here. I don't know where the fuck we are, but we have to get the fuck out of this hot-ass car." When they reached Colorado Boulevard, he told Michelle to pull inside a self-serve car wash.

Once there, Gangsta Jake began searching through the glove compartment of the vehicle. He was in search of a way to contact Psycho. He happened to find a phone number to Psycho's mother's house. Next they saw three Denver police cars rushing to the murder scene as they sat inside the hand car wash stall.

"Hello."

"Hello, Miss. Do you have a son named Psycho?"

"Yes. His real name is Tim. Is everything okay with Timothy?"

"Oh, yes. Everything is fine. I'm a friend of his. I haven't heard from him in a while and was wondering if you could give me a way to contact him."

"Well, I guess I can give you his cell number."

"That would be perfect. Thank you, Miss."

After receiving the number, Gangsta Jake called Psycho right away. He answered his cell phone on the first ring.

"Who is this?" Psycho held the flip phone up to his ear. The police were sectioning off the crime scene with yellow tape, looking for possible witnesses and evidence.

"Say, cuzz, this is Gangsta Jake."

"Who?"

"Gangsta Jake. I just left you."

Psycho could not believe who had got in contact with him so fast. "Cuzz, yo bitch killed my homey. I thought we were cool."

"Psycho, that shit was never supposed to happen. You seen how it all went down. Cuzz was about to have my head. The way I look at it, it was either him or me; one of us had it coming."

"That shit was bogus. She didn't have to blast my nigga like that. I'm standing up here looking at my homey laid out as we speak." Psycho paused for a moment and let out a tear he was holding back.

"Psych, as much as I would like to bring Slime back, there ain't nothing I can do about it." Michelle looked in Gangsta Jake's face, trying to figure out what was being said on the other end.

"Homey, I ain't no snitch or nothing, so I'm damn sure not going to go to the police. But something got to happen behind yo bitch doing that bullshit. It's on with you and your bitch. You're the one who started that shit when you slapped cuzz for what he felt. The homey really wasn't out of line for coming at you the way he did. Nigga, you know how this shit goes. You don't go around accusing people of being no snitch. I should have let the homey pop you when he was sizing you up."

"I'm trying to come at you correct, based on all that's taken place and the fact that I took a liking to you and ET. But don't fuck that off over being in your feelings. I know you're hot about what happened to your dawg and all, but look at the big picture." The cab Gangsta Jake requested Michelle to summons pulled up at the gas station down the street from the car wash.

"I'm leaving your car at a location not far away from where you are. ET's pistol is under the floor mat with no bullets in it." Gangsta Jake dug into his pants pocket, pulled out a knot of hundred dollar bills, and pilled off twenty-five of them. "I'm also tucking a little something under the mat. Make sure cuzz have a decent funeral." He then walked over to the cab, covered the phone with his hand, and instructed the driver to take him to a rental car place. Psycho was still on the phone.

"How in the hell am I suppose to find my car?"

Gangsta Jake let him know where his ride was located once he had a mile or so distance between him and the car.

"Like I said, Psycho. That shit was a fluke. You see I gave you and ET a pass. If I wanted to be scandalous, I could have dropped both of y'all. I had you both at my mercy."

"Nigga, fuck that bullshit—" Psycho cut him short.

"Homey, check this out. I'm not about to sit up here and go back and forth with you all day. Hopefully, as time goes by, you can see my point of view. I got to roll. I'm out."

He pressed the off button and that was the last he heard from Psycho. His plans now consisted of driving the rental car back to Los Angeles, picking up their luggage at the bus station in downtown L.A., and dropping off the rental car at a rental location near the airport. His plan went accordingly. Within twenty hours, he and Michelle were safely back in Los Angeles.

15

Officially on Schedule

Three weeks later, Gangsta Jake was headed toward the eastside of Los Angeles, sipping on a tall can of Old English 800. Michelle stayed back at their new apartment located in Inglewood. Enough time had elapsed. Gangsta Jake was ready to execute one of his victims. Before his plan could be carried out, he needed to obtain another vehicle. The Lexus he purchased was too flashy for the type of work he planned on doing.

Upon arriving on the eastside, he turned a few corners in his neighborhood and found himself pulling up on a pack of his homeboys.

"Gangsta! What's up, homeboy?" Lil' Too Cool said as he walked away from the crowd of ten and went to the passenger side of Gangsta Jake's Lexus. The nine other gang members' eyes were glued on his shining Lexus. Most of them were youngsters who had only heard about Gangsta Jake by other homies' war stories.

"Damn, that nigga ride is tight as fuck," Cap Peeler told Boo Bop, who stood next to him. Cap Peeler and Boo Bop were in their teens, but already had a few murders under their belts.

"Jump in Lil' Too Cool. I need you to roll somewhere with me."

Doc Rob strolled over and talked to Gangsta Jake before he and Too Cool pulled off in traffic.

"Say, baby boy, I can see you're doing okay for yourself."

"Yeah, I'm hanging in their O.G. What's popping with you?"

"Well, you know a guy is just trying to stay alive. We're throwing a house party next weekend. If you ain't doing nothing, swing through and hang out with the homies."

"Yeah, I might slide through. Let me get out of here for now, though. I have to take care of some business."

"You all right, Lil' homey. You need me to do something for you?"

"Naw, I'm straight."

"Okay, then. Hey, Lil' homey, shoot yo big homey a little something before you smash out. I just lost all the ends I had on me in the dice game over there." Doc Rob pointed to the crowd of guys and a couple of females who were kneeling down, shooting craps on the sidewalk.

Gangsta Jake dug in his pocket, pulled out a wad of money, and gave his O.G. three one hundred dollar bills. "Is this enough to hold you, big homey?"

"Well, you know what they say, beggars can't be choosey."

"It ain't like that, cuzz. You need some more or what?"

"Yeah, they're shooting long money over there. Slide me a few more, baby boy."

He gave Doc Rob the money he requested and then drove off with Lil' Too Cool. When a crowd of his homeboys waved to him from a short distance, Gangsta Jake held up the Avalon gang sign with his left hand out the window, bumped his horn three times, and drove off, headed down Avalon Boulevard.

"So, what you got up, cuzz?"

"I need you to go up to this rental car place with me so I can rent a car."

"You got a robbery up for us? I'm overdue to hit a major lick. Cuzz, shit is tight on this end."

"Naw. I just need you to drive the rental car to my grandma's house on Fifty-second Street. You can hold something if you're doing that bad."

"Good lookin', loco. This will definitely keep somebody from getting robbed tonight," he smiled and said as he stuffed the three one hundred dollar bills in his pocket."

"Your grandmom still live on Fifty-second Street?"

"Yeah," Gangsta Jake answered.

"I thought she moved out the hood."

"Naw, she's still on deck."

"Sorry about what happened to your mom when you were locked down in 1998."

"Yeah, that hurt the hell out of yo boy."

"What did she die from?"

"Cancer."

"That shit ain't no joke."

"I know. That's one of the reasons I take care of myself so well. But anyway, enough about that. Here, light this up." Lil' Too Cool fired up the pinhead of chronic as Gangsta Jake entered the fast lane of the Harbor Freeway.

*   *   *

On the other side of town, Michelle relaxed in the tub after hours of nonstop working on her new apartment. The bubble and hot milky bath nearly put her to sleep. Killing Slime and seeing his body laying in the street was no longer a reoccurring thought playing in her head. Gangsta Jake's words convinced her that she had done the right thing to protect them both. He was now confident that if the situation arose again, she would not hesitate to use deadly force to protect their lives or the principles he stood on.

A black, two-door, 2004 Crown Victoria was the car Gangsta Jake rented. The dark-tinted windows were what sold him on renting the vehicle. As he drove the rental down Vermont Boulevard, he double-checked the list to confirm the address at the top of his head.

His first victim would be one of the security guards who testified on his main man, Young Lad. Two male guards and a young woman by the name of Tiffany Jones sealed Young Lad's conviction. Four days of testimony from the three was enough to satisfy the jury that Young Lad was guilty as charged. The two guards' testimonies went without challenge. Their candid, step-by-step display of the crime scene was clear, concise, and unequivocally worthy of belief. Tiffany's statement, on the other hand, was not so credible. In fact, her being a witness was the only favorable evidence Young Lad's attorney had to rebut the prosecution's case.

During cross examination, Young Lad's attorney revealed that Tiffany had all the reasons to lie on his client. Not long before Young Lad gunned down the security guards, he and Tiffany had a sexual relationship. Before long, she became sprung on the dick and wanted more than just a booty call. Young Lad, however, was not feeling Tiffany like that. The sex was cool, but not enough to create a real relationship. Eventually, he tried to end his involvement with her altogether. That only fueled her desire to be a part of his life.

As time progressed, Young Lad developed a meaningful relationship with Tiffany's arch enemy, Socorra. Not only did he hook up with Socorra, but they also had twin girls together. That development caused Tiffany to become as hot as a forest fire. By doing so, she pledged to pay him back if it was the last thing she did. Not long after her vow, she definitely reimbursed him by testifying to the murders he committed, in spite of not actually being a witness to them.

Once the shooting occurred, every bystander ran in several directions and later refused to cooperate with authorities. Young Lad ran out a side door and could not be identified based on the events unfolding so fast. Fortunately, as far as the detectives handling the case were concerned, a video surveillance camera took some identifiable photos of the shooter, which were broadcast on the local news. When Tiffany viewed Young Lad's photo on the news, she not only made a positive identification of him, but also claimed to be an eyewitness to the crime.

Gangsta Jake drove by Tiffany's house on a few occasions since his return from Brooklyn. Luckily for her, she was unable to be found. Rumor had it she was in and out of town working as a flight attendant. Gangsta Jake figured her luck would run out sooner or later, and therefore decided to track down Young Lad's other accusers. That landed him in the backyard of Terry Armstrong, also known by his security buddies as Pistol Pete.

The time was 9:45 p.m. and Pistol Pete was in preparation of grooming himself for a night on the town. He had put in an honest forty hours of work for the week and looked forward to having a good time at the Century Club. When Gangsta Jake peeped through his bedroom window, he noticed that Pistol Pete had a .45 and a 9mm sitting on a nightstand; along with a 12 gauge on a gun rack in the very next room.

"Damn! This busta got heat on deck," Gangsta Jake told himself, as he hunched over and continued to scope his victim through a bedroom window.

Pistol Pete stroked the sides of his fresh haircut a few times, splashed on some fly cologne, grabbed his car keys along with his gun, and headed toward the door. As he swung the door open, Gangsta Jake suddenly appeared with a .44 Bulldog in his face.

"Nigga, back the fuck up!" was Gangsta Jake's first demand. The element of surprise gave Gangsta Jake all the advantage he needed. Pistol Pete's heart began pounding a mile a minute. Everything was going down so fast he didn't have a chance to draw his gun. Doing so would have only been suicide.

"Young brother, what's the problem?" Pistol Pete asked nervously as he thought about gaining the opportunity to pull out his concealed weapon. His eyes then opened wide as Gangsta Jake backed him up with the barrel of his .44 lodged in his chest.

Seeing Pistol Pete scared shitless was a thrill to Gangsta Jake, so much that he wanted to see more. He cocked the hammer of his gun and told the forty-five-year-old, light-skinned black man to get on his knees. As sweat rolled down Pistol Pete's forehead, he started begging for his life.

"Cry like a bitch, then!" Gangsta Jake told his victim as he held his .44 in his left hand and slapped him with his right.

"Damn," Pistol Pete screamed out while tucking his head toward the ground, "why am I being treated like this? What do you want from me? Money or what?"

Money? he thought. "Hell, yeah! Where is it?" Gangsta Jake pressed. "Before we do that, let me get this pistol off you, slick. Yeah, I know you're strapped like The Lone Ranger in this muthafucka. I been peeping you and this spot out for the past two hours. Now let's get to those ends you spook on," he told his victim after disarming him of his 9mm.

As Pistol Pete walked down his short hallway with the gun planted in his back, he prayed his assailant was only interested in robbing him of his cash and valuables. He calculated that he could replace the thirteen thousand dollars and few pieces of jewelry he'd accumulated over the years. His life, on the other hand, was worth more than any amount of money. Once it was gone—it was gone. When they arrived in the master bedroom, Pistol Pete showed Gangsta Jake where his money and jewelry were located.

"Here you go, man. This is all I'm worth. I pray, I mean, I hope it's enough for you."

"What if it ain't?" Gangsta Jake sarcastically asked him.

"I beg your pardon?"

"Lay on the bed, face down. I'm not trying to hear all that square-ass shit. Say your prayers while you have a chance."

Pistol Pete turned back to look at Gangsta Jake with fear and confusion in his eyes. "What? What the hell do you want from me, man?" He was frustrated with and very fearful of the guy who held the key to his existence.

"Clown, I know you may have forgot about a guy you testified on back in the days name Lemuel Jackson."

Pistol Pete thought about it for a second. His job required him to give testimony on many people who violated the laws within the facilities he had worked for, so at first, he could not recall the name. However, after pondering Young Lad's birth name for a few seconds, the day when he sat on the witness stand and gave a detailed analysis of how he witnessed his co-workers being chopped down by a hail of bullets came to mind.

"Yeah, muthafucka. Lemuel Jackson, also known as Young Lad." Spit sprayed out of Gangsta Jake's mouth and onto Pistol Pete's forehead. He became overwhelmed with the realization that he had accomplished tracking down one of his partner's accusers.

"Yeah. Yeah, I do remember Lemuel Jackson," Pistol Pete said before becoming extremely nervous, more so than before. He now realized the gunman may have entered his home to take more than his money. *Oh my God!* he thought to himself. *He's here to retaliate against me for testifying against his buddy. He's about to kill me! I have to do something before it's too late!* His blood pressure spiked due to his heart pounding out of his chest.

"Just so you'll know," Gangsta Jake told him with his gun hanging over his head, "Young Lad was sentenced to the death penalty behind your soft ass; and as you can see, I'm hot about it!"

"Man, I'm sorry about the whole situation. I was only doing my job. Three of my guys died on that day as well."

"I don't give a damn! They probably were fucking with people like they always do. You and I both know how you fools carry it at the swap meet. Guarding those Koreans' shit like it belongs to y'all. I don't have no pity for you lames!" Gangsta Jake's eyes bulged out in rage.

Out of desperation, Pistol Pete spun back around and attempted to grab the gun from his assailant's hand. He understood he was seconds away from becoming a victim of a homicide. His efforts were courageous, but only prolonged his intruder's intentions. Gangsta Jake was determined to fulfill his agenda. He had made Young Lad a promise, and intended to deliver.

When Pistol Pete reached for the gun, Gangsta Jake pulled it back and with the other hand violently gripped him around the neck. Once he overpowered his victim, he poked his .44 in his right ear and pulled the trigger three times. With the blink of an eye, Pistol Pete's brains were splattered all over the immediate area. His body wiggled for five seconds, long enough for his entire life to flash before him. Gangsta Jake looked at Pistol Pete's body for a few seconds, turned around, and suddenly gained some distance between him and the corpse. The three shots caused one of the next door neighbors to notify the authorities.

When the LAPD arrived on the scene, they discovered Pistol Pete's slain body and summoned the homicide detectives. The detectives roped off the scene with yellow tape, gathered a few pieces of evidence, and within five hours, went about other duties. The evidence the detectives came up with was useless without a suspect to match with it. No fingerprints, no witness, no conviction is the last thing Detective Burns told his fellow homicide detectives as he departed from a briefing with other detectives.

*　　*　　*

"Baby, where have you been? I've tried to call you for the past two hours," Michelle said. He checked his cell phone to discover it was turned off.

"I didn't realize my damn phone was off. My bad, Michelle. I had to take care of some real business."

Michelle went to hug him and became scared at the sight of his attire. "Rohan!" She stepped back and covered her mouth in amazement. "Are you okay, baby? Did someone shoot or stab you? Why is there blood all over your shirt? What happened?"

"Relax, baby, I'm not hurt. I'm cool as a fan. I actually couldn't be better." He smiled and popped his collar with his right thumb and index finger.

Michelle could tell by the look in his face that someone on his list was dead, and he was responsible for it. Gangsta Jake dug inside his jacket pocket, pulled out the list of names and addresses along with an ink pen, and drew a line through number eighteen on his list.

"Yeah, that's one less snitch in the world," he told Michelle before crip walking to a song playing in the next room.

"Boy, you so crazy. You never cease to amaze me," she blushed. "Take off those clothes so I can wash that blood out of them."

"Naw, I ain't crazy. I'm just a soldier who can't stand snitches. Here, baby." He stripped down to his boxers and handed Michelle his bloodstained clothes.

"Rohan, no one saw you, did they?"

"Hell, no. I'm a professional at what I do."

"What makes you such a professional?" she asked, starting to worry about him getting caught up over committing crimes she felt he did not have to do.

"Girl, I'm not about to get into all that, but trust me, I know what the hell I'm doing."

"Okay, you don't have to get an attitude with me. I'm only asking out of concern," her eyes rolled.

"Aw, it ain't like that, precious," he flashed his pearly white teeth at her. "Come here, sexy." They hugged in the middle of their apartment.

"Rohan, I'm sorry for getting all into what you do. I understand you being loyal to your homeboys who are doing time behind those guys, females, or whoever. But, I don't want to lose you. Killing people is serious business. The police do not take that shit lightly."

"I feel what you're saying, Michelle, but—"

"Wait. Let me finish, Rohan. What I'm trying to say is, if you're that stubborn to where you feel you have to handle your business . . ." she paused as he turned his lip up. "Shut up, boy, 'cause you have no idea what I'm about to say."

"I don't care what you're about to say, because no matter what, I'll be damn if I stop putting in work on rats. I'm sorry. That's my mission."

"Are you finished? Can I say what I have to say without being interrupted again?"

"Go ahead, Michelle; speak your piece."

"What I'm trying to say is, if you have to do it, take me with you. That way, I can at least watch your back and lessen your chances on getting caught."

"Say what?" He could not believe his ears. "Baby, I don't know about that one."

"You know I ain't no punk bitch. We've already been over that. I'm a big girl. I can handle myself. Rohan, I'm not taking no for an answer."

Michelle was stubborn as a bull when her mind was set on something. Gangsta Jake's first thought was that she would only be in his way if she tagged along. However, out of his own personal selfishness to complete his mission, he was satisfied that her assistance might be able to aid him in the killing spree he had in mind. He determined her beauty and charm could be an asset. Eighty percent of the people on his list were men who would have to be gay to turn down a conversation or sexual invitation from her, he further thought to himself.

"You know what, Michelle?" he slightly smiled, bopped his head twice, and looked her square in the eyes. "I like that idea, and I truly believe we can work good as a team, but listen to me very carefully. I don't want you," he pointed his index finger at the center of her face, "for one second, to rule out the fact that we both could be caught. We're definitely going to be taking penitentiary and death sentence chances, Michelle," Gangsta Jake studied her very closely, searching to see if she still thought assisting him is what she wanted to do. He credited himself on detecting the truth. After a few seconds, Michelle's sincere look only gave him half the confidence he was looking for. "Are you *sure* you're trying to get involved with what I have in store?"

"Rohan, get at me when you're ready to get busy because as of right now, there isn't any use in talking about it."

"Is that right?" He backed away from her and threw his hands in the air as if he had no say-so in the matter. The smile attached to his face informed Michelle that he was pleased to have her aboard his mission.

"Don't be acting like you don't want a down bitch by your side," she seductively batted her eyes at him. "You should be over here on your knees, eating me out for my willingness to be on the front line with you."

"Gangsta don't eat pussy."

"Yeah, right! I know a lot of gangstas who eat it."

"I never said gangstas don't eat pussy, because I'm sure they do. What I did say was, Gangsta Jake don't eat it. If God wanted me to eat pussy, he would have made my tongue out of a spoon."

"Rohan, you are such a comedian," Michelle giggled while thinking about the commitment she made in the back of her head.

The two laughed for a minute before Gangsta Jake took off in pursuit of a hot shower. Killing Pistol Pete had him feeling cheerful and in a very good mood; especially now that his girl was willing to participate in his killing spree. From that point on, he felt everything would go as smooth as it had been.

Michelle, on the other hand, was somewhat down with his program, but not all that enthused with being an accessory to multiple murders. In fact, up until the moment when she knocked off Slime back in Denver, she did not believe she was capable of taking a human life. Michelle nearly backed out of her proposal. However, against her better judgment, her pride would not allow her to do so. She, undoubtedly, bit off more than she could chew, but at that point, it did not matter. At any cost, Michelle would prove to her man that she was not a punk bitch.

16

Unusual Events

Gangsta Jake wasted no time in assessing the level of heart his girl possessed. If she was faking about committing a crime as hideous as murder, it would soon be revealed.

The very next week, he and Michelle were fresh on the trail of the other guard who testified on Young Lad. Since Young Lad helped Gangsta Jake gain his freedom from prison, Gangsta Jake made sure Young Lad's accusers would be the first to die, following his own accusers, of course.

"Baby, I don't know what this clown looks like, so I need you to get a description of him."

"Rohan, how the hell am I supposed to do that? What about the address I gave you? You don't think we can find him over there?"

"Naw, he moved from that location."

"How do you know?"

"Because I swung through there yesterday and the house was boarded up. His ex-neighbor told me the place has been abandoned for a couple of years."

Gangsta Jake pulled inside the Slauson Swap Meet parking lot and parked his rental car. Flashy cars which belonged to mostly blacks filled the large parking area. People were walking back and forth to their vehicles with bags full of cheap clothing, tennis shoes, and all sorts of accessories purchased from the many Korean shopping booths inside the large building. Security guards could be seen throughout the facility. Gangsta Jake instructed Michelle to walk up to one of the guards and ask for James Elway, who was the other guard that helped put Young Lad away forever.

As Michelle approached three guards, she noticed a black strip of tape stuck across each of their badges. The tape was clearly in recognition of one of their fallen soldiers. Then Michelle came close enough to eavesdrop on their conversation without cutting into it. She was shocked to hear what they were discussing. One guard was telling his partners exactly what Gangsta Jake previously described to her about what he did to Pistol Pete. The guard breaking down the scene happened to be Pistol Pete's first cousin. Following the murder, homicide detectives called him to identify his cousin's body.

"Man, it was horrible. I nearly threw up everything in my stomach," the light-skinned, almost-white brother explained to his co-workers. His slim, six-foot-four-inch lanky frame seemed to have been better suited for a basketball player. "I can't believe those fuckers asked me to identify my cousin in that condition. His fucking brains and blood were blown all over the place." A short guard standing inches away from Michelle turned his nose up in disgust.

"Hey, man, I'm really sorry about what happened." He knew his friend was taking it hard. "It's only been a week. Are you sure you're ready to handle work so soon?"

"Yeah, I'm cool. Besides, sitting at home would only make me more depressed."

"Do the police have any leads on who may be responsible?" the short guard questioned his partner.

Michelle tilted her head toward the three, hoping to receive an earful of information.

"There was one person who did see the back of a male suspect fleeing the shooting. Nothing concrete through."

Michelle was relieved to hear that bit of news.

"Hey, guys, I have a meeting with Mr. Kim in a few minutes," the third guard who stood listening to his two co-workers said while looking at his wristwatch. He and Pistol Pete were very close and had actually been the longest working employees at the security firm. Their longevity landed them the number one and two positions at the firm.

"If you guys need me for anything, you know where I'll be . . . and Armstrong," he looked Pistol Pete's cousin square in the eye like a concerned drill sergeant, "take a few days off if you need to."

"That won't be necessary, Lieutenant Elway. I'll be fine."

Michelle's heart skipped double time when she heard Elway's name roll off the tongue of his co-worker. She immediately walked over to Gangsta Jake, who stood a short distant away, and reported what she heard. She let him know Pistol Pete's cousin was also on hand and possessed the same last name as Pistol Pete.

"Baby, that means Elway may not be the same person we're looking for. He may be a relative of his."

"Which one is Elway?"

"He's the white guy with the glasses on."

"The one who just walked off?"

"Yeah, baby, that's him."

"Walk right back over there and ask one of the two remaining guards if James Elway is on hand."

Michelle did not waste one second. At Gangsta Jake's request, she spun her body around and walked directly toward the two remaining guards. "Excuse me, gentlemen. My name is Yvette Tucker, and I'm looking for James Elway. Have you guys seen him?"

"Yes, he just went to a meeting. You probably will have to wait until it's over. As a matter of fact, let me hustle down there and see if I can catch him before it begins."

"No, no. Don't worry about it. I have a little shopping to do anyway. I'll just wait until he returns or catch him at a later date."

"Are you sure?"

"Yes, I'm sure. Thank you. You've been helpful," Michelle said to Armstrong as she strolled off and merged into the crowded shopping center.

Gangsta Jake felt a sense of relief to know the identity of the other guard who, he believed, sold his homeboy out. Too many of James Elway's partners were on hand to make an attempt on his life, but once the time was right, Gangsta Jake would see if Michelle was as down for the cause as she claimed to be.

Two hours later, the two were parked down the street from James Elway's residence. Gangsta Jake scoped the scene and determined the best thing for him to do was just sit back and observe the murder from a distance.

"Michelle, by us following him here, we already know he's inside the house. Are you ready to handle this business?"

She took in a deep breath and answered, "Yeah, what do you want me to do?"

"Here, take this gun." He handed her his .44 Bulldog. The way James Elway's house was set up, he had no way of laying in the cut and running in once Michelle got Elway to open the door. With Elway's job and training as a security guard, Gangsta Jake did not want to take the risk of creeping up from such a long distance. Michelle would have to complete the mission alone.

"Baby, this shit is going to be a piece of cake. Here's what I want you to do. Put the gun inside your handbag and walk up to his door. Once you make it to the door, ring the bell and wait for him to come. When you hear the door opening, grip the gun inside your bag without pulling it out. Once he opens it all the way, pull out the gun and shoot him in the center of his face. That's it; that's all."

"Baby, how will I get him to open the door? What will I tell him? What if he doesn't want to open it up? What if a female or someone else comes to the door?" she nervously asked, wishing she never volunteered her services.

Michelle was full of questions and wanted answers. She did not like the swift, clear-cut plan Gangsta Jake came up with. When she informed him of her willingness to participate in his missions, she did not realize her duties would actually include pulling the trigger. Michelle was under the impression that, at most, all she would have to do is gain him access with her super tight body or charm. Nonetheless, she was on deck, pistol in bag, and moments away from hesitantly stepping out of the car.

When Gangsta Jake noticed her shift in demeanor, he immediate caught an attitude and snatched her handbag. "Man, why you bullshitting with me? I knew you were faking! Michelle, you know how serious I take this shit!"

"What's wrong, baby? Why are you tripping? Give me my bag back. I'm not faking."

"I can't tell! Look at you," he waved his hand free from the steering wheel at her. "You look scared to death. You're shaking like a mini bike."

"Rohan, you act like you can't understand this is my first time doing something like this."

"Michelle, you already passed basic training when you killed the dude in Denver."

"Yeah, but that was different. Me killing him was in self-defense."

"I'm not here to convince you to do something you're not trying to do. You were the one who came at me with the idea."

He stuck the car keys inside the ignition and fired it up with disappointment written all over his face. Michelle felt personally responsible for his frustration and responded by grabbing his hand, the one he used to place the car in gear.

"Stop, baby! Cut the car off and give me a few minutes. I'll be right back. I think, I know how I can do this."

Gangsta Jake slowly turned his head toward her with a mean stare that did not take long to reverse into a smile. "Well, goddamn it, that's what the fuck I'm talking about," he cheerfully and energetically stated.

Warmth filled Michelle's entire body from seeing her man in such a good mood. She could not believe how happy he had become. Without saying another word, she leaned over, gave him a wet kiss, and exited the vehicle with her adrenalin flowing. The walk from the car to James Elway's door was an anxious one; however, she managed to do it with a calm look on her face.

Dark, Versace sunglasses and a blue Von Dutch cap somewhat obscured her sexy, chocolate face. Her ruby-red lipstick, black mascara, and well manicured fingernails gave her the look of a model as opposed to a killer. Arriving at the door of Elway's house, she rang the doorbell three times.

When he looked through his peephole and caught a glimpse of Michelle, the first thing that came to his mind was, *Who is she?* and *how can I get to know her better?* Not once did he imagine the beautiful stranger being his worst nightmare. Thinking this must be his lucky day, he mumbled to himself, "Hold on, cutie," as he opened the door.

"What the fuck is going—" were the last five words James Elway ever spoke. Michelle got off three shots aimed at his face. By him ducking for cover, only one hit its actual target. The other two caught him in the neck and collar bone. He hit the floor and fought for his life by gasping for air. Fast as she could, Michelle made her way back to Gangsta Jake, who anxiously awaited her arrival.

James Elway's twenty-one-year-old nephew was in the process of parking his car when he witnessed Michelle moving very fast toward the waiting car. He had not yet figured out what had occurred, but would soon find out that his uncle had become a victim of a brutal crime.

"Baby, I did it. I did it," Michelle told Gangsta Jake with nervousness and excitement in her voice. He placed the car in gear and drove off, combing the immediate area with wide eyes.

"Sit back, Michelle. Calm down."

"Baby, did you see that white boy looking at me as I walked away?" she asked while he pressed his foot up against the gas pedal.

"Naw, I didn't see nobody. Are you sure someone was looking at you, because I was peeping in all directions."

"Yeah, I'm sure. He was in the process of parking his car."

"Shit! I have to double back and serve him then."

"Double back? No, baby. Let's just go."

"Fuck that! If that clown was hawk-eyeing us, I can't let him live to give the police a description."

Gangsta Jake drove around the corner and made his way back to the crime scene. By that time, James Elway's nephew had already discovered his uncle lying in blood. The first thing his nephew did was scream for assistance.

"Help! Help! Somebody, please, help me, please!" he cried in panic.

An old couple two houses down heard his cries and ran outside to aid him. When the couple noticed the injured person on the ground, they both dashed to their telephone in order to call 911. Other neighbors sat in their vehicles and doorways, watching in disbelief.

When Gangsta Jake came around the corner and observed the scene from a distance, he could not believe how many people surfaced so fast. "Damn! Check out all these fucking people."

The nephew looked up and saw Gangsta Jake and Michelle cruising by the scene.

"Look!" he pointed. "That's the car the shooter got in." Frightened people began to hide behind any shelter they could find.

"That fool just pointed at us. Baby, please, get us the fuck out of here. Don't do nothing stupid."

Gangsta Jake, realizing he had been spotted, went along with his girl's suggestion. Since the car windows had such a dark tint on them, no one was able to make a positive identification of the people inside it. He briefly contemplated rolling the windows down and shooting at anything that moved, but understood that would amount to nothing.

"Yeah, let's get the hell out. I only hope that clown can't identify you."

"I had on my hat and sunglasses so he could not have seen me all that good."

"At any rate, it's definitely time to change this car up."

"Luckily, no one was close enough to write down the license plate number," Michelle said with confidence. She was aware that people were close by, but realized they were not close enough to jot down the plates.

"Yeah, baby girl, you did good. As long as we get the hell away from here, we'll be cool."

*   *   *

When the ambulance arrived, James Elway was barely clinging to life. He was not conscious, but still alive and possibly could give an accurate description of the person who shot him. Two detectives walked through a group of people, hoping to locate possible witnesses. One of their co-workers, Detective Winston, was already in the process of obtaining statements from the victim's nephew. Unbeknownst to Gangsta Jake and Michelle, James Elway was still alive and might be able to positively identify Michelle.

"I'm pretty sure the person I saw leaving my uncle's house was a female."

A female? the young homicide detective thought to himself. "How tall was she?" he asked, amazed that a woman was capable of doing something so horrific.

"Approximately five feet seven inches."

"What about weight, sir?" the detective also asked as he scribbled down the measurements on a pad inside the palm of his hand.

"After she left from my uncle's door, she hopped inside a black, two-door car with tinted windows."

"Did you happen to see the license plate?"

"Yes, I saw the back plate, but I was too far away to read the number. The plates were definitely from California. After the driver picked her up, they came back for some reason."

"At that time, did you have the opportunity to look at the driver's face?"

"I'm sorry, but I didn't."

"Can you think of any reason someone would want your uncle dead?"

"Well, I can't personally think of any reason, but he does work as a security guard for a swap meet. Maybe someone from his job wanted him dead. My uncle has told me stories about disgruntled customers looking to start trouble.

Come to think of it . . ." he paused and thought about a story his uncle told him years ago, "three of my uncle's co-workers were killed by this one crazy guy. Maybe, somehow, he got out of prison and felt the need to get back at my uncle. Uncle James did testify against him. But, naw, that can't be possible; that man was sentenced to death."

Detective Freeman made a mental note of Elway's nephew's assessment and wrapped up his investigation. "Okay, Mr. Elway, I'm very sorry about what happened to your uncle. If you have any questions, concerns, or perhaps remember useful information about this terrible crime, please give me a call. Here's a number where you can contact me." The detective gave him a card and went about his business.

After wrapping up the crime scene, Detective Freeman and another detective by the name of Mark Hardiman paid James Elway a visit for a possible description of the shooter. When the detectives arrived at the hospital, they found the victim was in surgery with hopes of his survival slim to none. While the detectives waited for the outcome, two of Elway's co-workers rushed inside the waiting room, hoping to hear some good news.

"Please, tell me James Elway is going to make it," Randy Simpson, a co-worker of James Elway, quizzed a short, white woman who sat at the reception booth.

"Pardon me," the young nurse replied, unfamiliar with the patient he spoke about. "I'm sorry, sir. We just changed shifts maybe two minutes ago. If you'll give me a few minutes, I'll be able to better assist you."

"What do you mean a few minutes? My friend may be fucking dead in a few minutes. I don't have a few minutes, Miss. I need to know his condition, now!" he demanded.

"Whoa, wait a damn minute," she placed her hand up in the air and rolled her blue eyes toward the other direction as if she wanted him to talk to her hand. The nurse was a white girl but hung out with nothing but black folks. She wasn't accepting this rudeness under any circumstances.

"I can see by your security guard uniform that you're into law enforcement, but you ain't running nothing up in here," the twenty-five-year-old nurse said before popping her chewing gum twice.

The two nearby detectives recognized the situation growing out of control and one of them intervened. "Excuse me, sir. Please allow me to intervene. My name is Detective Hardiman, and this is my partner, Detective Freeman. I couldn't help but overhear you asking about James Elway. We're both detectives with the LAPD, and we've been assigned to investigate the shooting of your friend."

"How is he?" Randy questioned him, turning his attention away from the nurse at the reception desk.

"Well, the last I was told, he's in surgery and the doctors are doing all they can. We're pulling for his recovery. I can see by your uniform you also work with him." Detective Hardiman's investigative mind began churning.

"Yes, I do. Lieutenant Elway and I both work as security guards over at the Slauson Swap Meet. The weird thing about Elway being gunned down at his home is . . ." Elways's co-worker pondered, trying to make a connection, "we had another co-worker killed at his house just a week or so ago. I don't know if the two shootings are related, but thinking about it brings chills to my bones." Hearing the news raised the eyebrows of Detective Hardiman.

*   *   *

Gangsta Jake and Michelle were working on their second bottle of champagne. They were celebrating the shooting of James Elway. Little did they know he was still alive and potentially able to identify Michelle as the shooter.

"Here's a toast to all the real ones that kept their mouths closed and stayed down like real men." The couple bumped their glasses of champagne together.

"I told you I could do it, Rohan." Michelle gave him a sexy smile, tipsy from the warm alcohol circulating throughout her body.

"I see my girl do have some gangsta in her. Come here and give daddy a kiss." They kissed for a couple of minutes, but were cut short when Gangsta Jake caught an earful of what a local news reporter was reporting on the radio in the next room.

"Michelle, did you hear that?"

"No. What did he say?"

"He said that a security guard was hanging onto his life after being gunned down at his home in the 1100 block of Vermont."

"That's the guy I shot," she responded, becoming very nervous at hearing the developments. "Shit, what the fuck am I going to do? He saw my face. The police probably know who I am by now."

"Ssshhh. Be quiet for a minute. Let's hear the rest."

"Thus far, no suspects have been taken into custody. Investigators are hoping to obtain more information about the shooter if and when Mr. Elway regains consciousness. As of now, he's in critical condition."

"Let's go!" was Gangsta Jake's first response to hearing the news that Elway was still alive.

"Go where?" she asked, confused about his next move.

"We're on our way to the hospital. I can't let that lame live!"

At first, Michelle could not believe what she was hearing. That is, until it dawned on her who made the statement. She realized there was no use in protesting. Gangsta Jake was as stubborn as she was when it came to whatever the situation may be. Furthermore, by Michelle being the shooter, she also wanted to make sure Elway did not pull through.

Forty-five minutes after hearing the news bulletin, the two changed clothes and were in the lobby area of the hospital. The shooting occurred over twelve hours ago, which meant everyone pretty much went their separate ways. Elway's parents were the only two who stayed behind. They encouraged all of Elway's friends to go home and get some rest and assured them that they would call each and every one of them once his condition changed. While his parents lounged in the waiting room, Elway laid in a coma.

It did not take Gangsta Jake long to locate Elway's room, or get fitted into the long, white, doctor's jacket and rubber gloves he stole from a supply closet. Once in position, he instructed Michelle to park his new rental car in front of the emergency room door and wait on him to exit the building.

Looking inside his victim's room, he saw James Elway laying flat on his back with tubes running out his body. The machine he was attached to was his only source of life. Without it, he was history. Seconds after Gangsta Jake entered the room, he grabbed Elway by his throat and began choking him. The man's body wiggled for a few seconds, then lay lifeless from the killer's death grip.

Beeeeeeeeeeeeep went the machine that monitored the heartbeat of his latest victim. Unsatisfied with the loud single beeps, Gangsta Jake quickly yanked the cord out the wall. Because Elway was weak and still unconscious when his attacker entered the room, he never had a chance to defend himself.

As Gangsta Jake wrapped up his business, detectives Hardiman and Freeman were on their way up to pay James Elway a visit. They were hoping by now he had regained consciousness and would be able to help in their investigation. Halfway up the stairs that led to Elway's room, Detective Hardiman realized he needed to obtain something left behind in his vehicle.

"Hey, Bill, I freaking left the report in the vehicle. I need Dr. Hamilton's signature. You go ahead, and I'll be right there."

"Sure, Mark. I'll see you in a few minutes."

Gangsta Jake was moments away from exiting the room when he looked through the door crack and saw Detective Freemen walking straight for it. He did not know who the detective was, but did recognized the police badge resting on his belt. James Elway's parents were sound asleep on a couch in the waiting room. They were totally exhausted, but refused to leave until their son gained consciousness.

As a result of Gangsta Jake's hospital visit, Elway's chances of regaining consciousness would not be possible. He was now history. His limp body laid across the hospital bed, one arm on the bed, the other dangling inches above from the floor.

Without consulting with James Elway's doctors, Detective Freeman waltzed inside the room where Gangsta Jake hid behind the door. His eyes turned toward the patient he was hoping to interview, but he sensed something was terribly wrong, however. Before he was able to adjust his thoughts on what had just taken place, he found himself the prey of a killer. Gangsta Jake leaped from behind the door and placed Freeman in a full nelson.

"Wha, wha, what the hell is going on?" Detective Freeman struggled to get the words out of his mouth.

With ease, Gangsta Jake rammed Detective Freeman's head first into Elway's body over on the bed. Everything was occurring so fast, the detective could not believe what was taking place. He tried his best to break free from his assailant, but was having an awfully hard time doing so. Gangsta Jake fully understood that not only did his freedom rely on him bumping his victim off and getting away with it, but ending the detective's life as well. Detective Freeman would be eager to gun him down in a heartbeat, provided he was afforded the opportunity.

As Gangsta Jake released him from the full nelson, he then grabbed his victim around the neck and choked him to death. Well, at least Gangsta Jake thought he did, but Detective Freeman was still alive. He played possum by allowing his body to go limp and keeping his eyes shut.

As he laid motionless on the floor, Gangsta Jake stripped him of his gun, wallet, and a few pieces of gold attached to his body. His hatred for the police was so severe, that before leaving the room, he hauled off and kicked the detective square in the ass. It took everything Detective Freeman had not to respond to the pain of the swift kick as well as the vicious assault he had endured. But realizing how much his life depended on it was enough incentive for him not to make a single move. Satisfied with his performance, Gangsta Jake made his way over to the door, opened it quietly, and walked out with only a mild sweat on his forehead.

Once outside the room, the first thing he did was take off his plastic gloves and lower the surgical mask from his face. If one did not know any better, you would suspect he had just performed a major surgery. James Elway's parents continued snoozing in the waiting room as he vacated the premises.

*   *   *

Michelle was beginning to worry about his safe return when she looked up and noticed him heading straight for her.

"Get us the fuck out of here!" he commanded while closing the car door behind himself.

"Honey, what took you so long? Did everything go okay? Is Elway dead?"

"Hold on, Michelle. Let me catch my breath." He flipped on the air conditioner and turned the vent directly on his face. Minutes later, he filled her in on all the details. "Girl, you'll never believe what just went down," he said, exhaling and relaxing his head on the back of the car seat.

"What happened?"

"A cop walked in on me as I was leaving the room." Without saying another word, he reached in his pocket and flipped Freeman's badge to Michelle. To make himself look even better, he also pulled out the gun he took from Detective Freeman.

"I caught him slipping and choked his bitch ass out."

"What? You did that to a cop?"

"Now, Michelle, you already know I can't stand the police. Any chance I get, I'm having at their asses."

"As long as you made it out safe, it's all good. What about Elway?"

"Oh, there ain't no use in talking about him. He' a done deal. I handled him before that clown came inside the room."

"Nobody saw you leaving the room, did they?"

"Naw, I had my face covered up anyway."

"Good, baby. I'm so happy everything went okay."

In the meantime, Hardiman walked inside the room and discovered his partner in some serious pain. "Bill! Are you okay?" he asked his partner after pulling out his gun and looking around in all directions. Detective Hardiman was scared shitless, but managed to make sure the room was secure. Then he lifted his partner off the floor before summoning additional officers to assist with the situation.

"Are you sure you did not get a description of this guy, Freeman?" Detective Hardiman asked.

"Goddamn it, Mark, for the fifth time, I didn't see the fucker. I want this son-of-a-bitch just as bad as you do. The only description I have on him was his arms. He was definitely a black guy, a muscular black guy. His arms were strong as an ox. I was able to see them during the struggle. I believe he had on black shoes. No, I think they were blue." He paused long enough to rub his neck, "Aw, for Christ's sake, will you give me a minute to pull myself together, Mark?"

Detective Freeman was abused and confused. The vicious assault he sustained took a toll on his fifty-six-year-old body. Only twenty minutes had elapsed since his encounter, and he was still red in the face. His head was pounding, along with his rear end from the swift kick Gangsta Jake put on him. Detective Freeman could not believe what had taken place. He felt violated in every aspect, but was relieved to still be alive.

By now, police and security guards were running back and forth throughout the building in an effort to locate the perpetrator of Elway's murder and Detective Freeman's attempted murder. The officers' presence caused panic inside the hospital. No one was allowed to leave or enter the building. One woman claimed to have seen a guy walking out of the victim's room with a doctor's outfit on, which caused a few real doctors to be treated like common criminals. Once

Detective Freeman confirmed neither of the detained doctors' arms fitted the killer's, they were free to move about the immediate area. Elway's parents both nearly had heart attacks when the news finally reached them that their son was strangled to death in his hospital bed. By then, SWAT team members were summoned to the crime scene.

Hours of searching the inner and outer buildings came up fruitless for the scores of detectives. Detectives Freeman and Hardiman personally felt offended that a killer managed to commit a murder right under their noses and escape without a trace.

While other detectives and uniformed officers stood in huddles, discussing what had taken place, detectives Freeman and Hardiman conducted their own private conversation off to one side. Detective Freeman was nicely built for a guy his age. Five eleven and one hundred and ninety-eighty pounds described his height and weight. His bald head and white skin made him resemble Mr. Clean, the white guy on the disinfectant bottle. Mark Hardiman, his partner, had salt-and-pepper hair, which he wore neatly trimmed. His mustache also matched his hair. His normal attire was a two-piece suit, and today was no exception.

"Don't worry, Freeman, we're going to catch this worthless bastard." Detective Hardiman attempted to pep up his partner and friend of twenty years.

"You're damn right we will," Freeman responded as he twisted his neck and massaged his hand over it. He was still mentally and physically in great pain.

"James Elway's nephew described a black female leaving his uncle's apartment following the shooting. And now we have a black male over here finishing up the job. I'm sure the two are connected, Freeman."

"You bet your ass they are. We also need to find out more about the other security guard that was murdered, the one that the guy, Randy, told us about yesterday here at the hospital. I believe he said the other guard's name was Pistol Pee or something to that effect. I have his name written down in my notes back at the office."

"Oh, yeah, I forgot to tell you that I did check up on the other guard that was killed. His real name was Terry Armstrong, but everyone knew him as Pistol Pete. A gunshot wound to the head was his cause of death. The killer did leave a few footprints that were lifted and booked into evidence. Detective Burns will be handling that investigation over at the 77th Street Division.

"Come on, Freeman, let me take you home. I think these young buck detectives can handle the crime scene from here."

17

First Taste

*R*ing... *ring*... *ring*...

"Criminal court building, how may I help you?"

"Bitch, where is my damn money?" Michelle played around with her best friend in a man's voice.

"Michelle, shut the hell up, girl. You can't disguise your voice from me," Robin blushed, happy to finally be hearing from her best friend.

"Damn, Robin, you act like you can't call your girl anymore. We are still girls, aren't we?"

"Of course we are. Only death could separate us. Michelle, I've been really busy lately. So what's new? Are you still with you-know-who?" Robin looked away from the judge who she sat next to and turned her nose up.

"Don't even start with that. You already know the deal with me and 'you-know-who' as you refer to him."

"Anyway," Robin said while looking over some court files, "okay, we won't even go there. But you're only sprung because you want to be."

"I thought we wasn't going there."

"Okay, Michelle, I'll be nice. So is everything fine with you and your family?"

"I'm cool, but I haven't really heard from my family in a while."

"I can't imagine why," Robin sarcastically slid out the side of her mouth.

"What did you say, Robin?"

"Oh, nothing, girl."

During the girls' conversation, Gangsta Jake slept next to Michelle in their Inglewood apartment. His body flinched a few times from a bad dream he was experiencing. He could not picture any particular face in his dream, but someone had their hands around his neck as he strangled him violently. His dream suddenly developed into a nightmare that was interrupted by the palms of Michelle's hand.

"Ah!" he howled out from the shock of his imagination.

"Rohan! Rohan!" Michelle shook him by his shoulders, "Are you okay?"

"Yeah, yeah," he responded, still in a daze on his way back to sleep.

Michelle decided to call Robin later. Gangsta Jake jumping around in his sleep caused her to drop the phone and become very attentive to him. When she was convinced that all was well with him, she placed the phone back in her hand.

"What's wrong? Is everything okay?" Robin asked.

"Oh, yeah, everything is fine. Let me call you back a little later, though."

"Are you *sure* you're okay? You're acting a little strange."

"Bitch, I'm cool. Now stop worrying. No really, I'm okay." Michelle became serious for a moment.

"Okay, call me later then." Just as Michelle was about to hang the phone up, Robin called out her name.

"What girl?"

"Michelle, you know you're always welcome to come home if you choose."

"I know, Robin. And you are a sweetheart for constantly reminding me of that. I love you, girl."

"I know you do. Just be careful out there. And, Michelle, don't be nobody's fool."

"Okay, already. I'll talk to you later."

The last words Robin spoke sunk into her friend's mind. Michelle knew she was out of character for the way she was behaving, but felt she was in too deep to stop now. A tear rolled down her left cheek as she leaned over and kissed Gangsta Jake's sleeping face.

"She just don't understand," Michelle cried out in a low voice, still hanging over his face. Her tears fell, so much that it interrupted his sleep.

"Michelle, why are you crying?" he reached his arms out and wrapped them around her neck.

"I'm okay. I'm just thinking about some things."

"What things? If it have you crying like that, you need to start thinking about something different."

"Baby," Michelle said as she looked deep inside Gangsta Jake's eyes, "why don't we stop why we're ahead?"

"What are you talking about?"

"The killings. The snitches. You know what I'm talking about."

"Oh, is that what you're talking about?" He immediately went into a defensive mode. "Fuck that! I'm not giving them rats no passes for what they did. I told you from the beginning how I felt about the situation. If you're scared, go to church. I'm not stopping! I'm knocking them off every chance I get! As a matter of fact, who the hell you been talking to?"

"Okay, baby. You don't have to get so upset. I was only giving you an option."

"Don't forget, I went to that hospital and killed Elway to protect yo ass. He had your description in his memory, not mine." He flipped the script on her.

"Rohan, I still have your back 100 percent. I'm not suggesting that you abandon your mission totally. All I'm saying is, maybe you should take a break for a little while."

"Michelle, I feel you, baby, but I don't feel you. I know what I'm doing. Trust me; we're cool. I tell you what. Why don't you let me deal with this gangsta shit, because I don't think you're cut out for it. I'm not mad at you. I understand your position."

"It's not like that. I have no problem with helping you. I just don't want us to be locked down for the rest of our lives when we can walk away scot-free at this point."

Without saying a word, Gangsta Jake stood up and walked to the restroom. He grabbed his toothbrush and toothpaste and brushed his teeth as he stuck his hand in the split of his boxer's to take a leak.

"Don't pee on the seat," Michelle yelled out from the bedroom, purposely breaking the silence. She wanted to see how upset he had become, however, he was reluctant to express his emotions. His silence caused her to tiptoe up from behind and place her cold hand on his back, which still did not cause him to respond.

"Baby, I'm sorry." Her arms now caressed his upper body from the back up until he finished urinating. At the sink, she continued her conversation.

"Rohan, are you listening to me?"

He stopped brushing his grill for a few seconds to respond. "Yeah, how could I not hear you? You're all in my damn ear!"

"Dang, why are you being so mean? Rohan, sometimes you can be so damn insensitive."

"What do you want, Michelle?" His smooth, calm, and collective attitude suddenly kicked in. He did not want her to start crying. He was a sucker when it came to protecting Michelle's feelings.

"Rohan, I don't want to argue with you. Whatever you say is cool with me. If you want to jump out there, it's fine with me. I guess I was out of line for questioning your authority." She stood on her tippy toes and kissed the back of his head.

In an attempt to assess her sincerity or lack thereof, he checked her eyes out through the mirror he stood in front of. Ultimately, he believed her.

"Girl, you don't know what you want to do, do you?"

"I guess I do get confused at times. But it's all out of love. Baby, you know I don't mean no harm. I only want what's best for us."

"That's all to the good. However, from here on out, the only thing I want you to worry about is following instructions. Let me call all the shots from here on out. Do you understand me?" They made eye contact.

"Yes, daddy," Michelle responded looking very sincere.

* * *

One week later, the couple found themselves scanning the city for their next victim.

"Are you sure Tony don't live there any longer?" Gangsta Jake asked Michelle.

"That's what they told me at the front door."

"Damn it!" He clenched his teeth. "Get in; let's go."

Gangsta Jake was starting to become frustrated with the fact that finding his victims was such a challenge. The time lapse between their trial testimony and the present was a matter of years. In some cases, up to twenty years had passed since witnesses found themselves on the stand, spilling their guts. What he decided to do was further his research via the Internet.

Before attempting to locate his next snitch to die, he visited a local computer store. Michelle, along with a young black guy, introduced Gangsta Jake to the latest search engine technology. He was fascinated with how he could obtain personal information on people from a computer screen. He was under the impression law enforcement were the only ones authorized to gain such information. When he learned of what he could do with a simple laptop, he immediately purchased one. Instead of continuing with his research at the computer store, he decided to finish what he had to do at home.

Recent home addresses, photographs, and job sites are what he came up with after nine straight hours of diligent research. Gangsta Jake fell in love with the Internet after playing around with it all day.

"That's right. This is definitely what you're looking for, baby boy," he told himself, praising his work. "International superhighway, I'm at yo ass. Michelle!" he called from his room.

"What, baby?" She walked through the door brushing her long hair and wearing a black and red two-piece lingerie set.

"Roll me up one of those blunts you love so much. I have some real shit to celebrate." He was so caught up in the Internet, he did not pay attention to the attire she wore. Michelle's round butt cheeks hung out of her silk bottoms, while her firm breasts stood fluffy in the top piece. When he did look up and recognized her sexiness, he was instantly turned on.

"Here." She gave him a blunt that was rolled earlier, turned around in the opposite direction, and walked off, switching her butt cheeks. This was done on purpose to get a response from him.

"Where are you going? Come here, big booty."

"You don't want none of this. What you want is on that Internet you been playing with all day." She switched even harder before closing the door behind her. Due to the door now between the two, her voice could barely be heard.

"What did you say?" he shouted out before cutting off the computer and heading in her direction. She knew he would be coming and decided to play cat-and-mouse games with him. Inside the closet she went. When he made it inside the room, he was puzzled over where she could have gone so quickly. He looked over at the window and ruled out that exit since their apartment was on the third floor. When he heard some movement in the closet, he walked straight for it.

"I know where you are at now," he grinned as he walked toward it. He thought her game playing was kind of cute. In the same motion, he pulled his shirt over his head in preparation for the sex he planned on engaging in. She saw him coming through the slits in the door and ran out right past him. Gangsta Jake extended his arm out with his shirt over his head, but was not able to fish her into his arm. When he finally caught up with her, she was in the kitchen with something hidden behind her back.

"What do you have back there?" he asked with his arms crossed in front of him.

Without hesitation, she held up the contents of her right hand as if she was advertising a new product.

"Whipped cream! What do you plan on doing with that?"

"Put it on this," she said as she rubbed her right hand over her kitty cat.

"Is that right?" he frowned, displaying a dislike for what she had in mind.

"Come on, baby, do it for me. Please?" she batted her eyelashes seductively.

"I thought we crossed this road before."

"We did, but, baby, that don't mean we can't talk about it again. Come on, baby, you're spoiling the moment."

"That's just not my thing."

"Honey, it's not going to kill you; I promise. Let's go in the bedroom and talk about it." She held him by the hand and led him to the room.

Inside their bedroom, they began to kiss passionately. Michelle unbuttoned her lingerie top and completely took it off. Her hand slowly moved down the center of his body until it reached a hard spot. "Um-hum," she said.

Gangsta Jake was enjoying the touch of her soft, tender hand. She stopped kissing him long enough to lubricate her strokes up and down his shaft. The cold whipped cream Michelle sprayed him with tensed his nerves, but not enough to curb his pleasure. He knew where she was heading and laid back to gain more pleasure. A few minutes went by and all of sudden, Michelle cut short what she was doing. He assumed she paused to position her body, but this was not the case.

"You like the way that feels, don't you, baby?" she asked in a cute voice before licking whipped cream off her lips with her tongue.

"Hell, yeah; finish now," he requested, horny as a toad.

"No, not until you do me too. We can even do each other at the same time," she smiled in a manipulative manner.

"What? Aww, ain't that a bitch."

"Ain't it."

"So what do you call yourself doing, blackmailing me or what?"

"You can call it what you want to call it."

"You know what, Michelle?"

"What?"

"You got that coming. I'm not even going to front. I been thinking about breaking you off some ever since I was in the pen, but you know how it is. That's not something gangstas just come out and volunteer. The average one of us ain't into that."

She blushed from ear to ear. "Boy, probably 99 percent of your homeboys done ate some, but they'll never tell for one reason or another. Y'all need to quit lying to each other."

"Regardless of all that, don't you go around running your mouth about what we do in our bedroom. This is our business and strictly between us."

"Who do I deal with, but you?"

"You have plenty of friends."

"Not since you've been home. Anyway, boy, don't even worry about all that. Come here and satisfy your woman." While sitting on her bed, Michelle sprayed herself with whipped cream and became horny at the sight of Gangsta Jake headed downtown. Like a professional, he leaned his face over Michelle's body and brought her to ecstasy nine minutes after his first lick. He was surprised to see how easy it was and how excited his girl became once his lips touched hers. Afterward, they reclined on the bed and smoked a blunt together. He actually enjoyed the experience and looked forward to their next session. She started to tease him for refusing to give in at her first request, but instead, only giggled and left it as an inside joke.

18

By Accident

Summer of 2005 arrived and Gangsta Jake found himself driving down Crenshaw Boulevard in a clean sixty-one, ragtop Chevy he purchased from his homeboy, Gangsta Rat. The sixty-one was sprayed with the original Chevy metallic blue paint with two gallons of clear. All the emblems were dipped in chrome, including his thirteen-inch Daytons with the two-prong knockoffs. He was on his way to a pick up a few parts from the hydraulic shop, and then over to a barbeque at the park in his neighborhood. When he pulled up to the park, a group of females and his homeboys were mingling around four giant barbeque pits.

May 3rd is the day that the Five Trays all came together in order to celebrate the fifth month and third day of the year. Michelle went to hang out at her grandma's house while Gangsta Jake spent some time with his extended family on their hood day. Three of his homeboys noticed him parking his car next to several other low riders and decided to walk over and check out his ride. The parking lot was filled with some of the tightest low riders Los Angeles had to offer. Some 1962-63 Chevies, glass houses, luxury sports, and a couple of Lincoln Continentals were on hand.

"What's popping, loved ones?" Gangsta Jake greeted his three homies who made their way over to him.

"That rider is clean as the Board of Health, but do it got any hops in it?" Lil' Cisco asked with a smile. He had recently been released from the state prison after serving three years and had never seen the car perform. Up until he opened his mouth, Gangsta Jake did not recognize who he actually was. The two were real tight back in the days, but somehow lost contact during Gangsta Jake's incarceration.

"No, that ain't my nigga Lil' Cisco. Come here and give your folks a hug. When did you get out, loco?"

"Last week. I asked around for you, but nobody had a way to get in contact with you."

"Yeah, homey, lately I been trying to stay under the radar."

"I figured you would show up at Five Tray Day, if nothing else."

"You know I couldn't miss this. Look around. All the homies are here. How could I miss it?"

"Are you gonna let us see this vehicle dance or what?" Horsehead said, walking up out of nowhere with a hand-held video camera filming the scene.

"Damn, nigga, what is this candid camera?" Gangsta Jake mentioned right before placing his hand over his face.

"Don't be shy. This ain't the movie *Menace to Society*, where the dude sent the video of his homeboy committing a crime to the police station. Uncover your face, homeboy, so your big homey can get an exclusive of you."

"I'm cool."

"All right, nigga. You got that. I won't film you if you're not trying to be filmed."

Gangsta Jake dropped his hand and followed up with a smile. Then he walked over and placed his right arm inside his low rider window and hopped the front end four times until the back bumper scraped the ground, indicating its maximum height.

His actions caused several of his homeboys to show off their hydraulic systems as well. They hopped their cars against one another like they were in a hopping contest. The two dice games and people dancing nearby stopped so that the people could see the low riders jump up-and-down and move side-to-side. When all six cars stopped hopping, everyone began to cheer, then went back to what they were doing.

"I told you, couldn't none of them other low riders fuck with that sixty-one Gangsta Jake purchased from Gangsta Rat," Papa Gee told his homeboy, Criminal, who was hyped up from seeing so many cars hop at one time.

"Nigga, give me my fifty dollars," Papa Gee further stated.

As much as Criminal did not want to pay him, he reached in his pocket and gave Papa Gee two twenties and a ten dollar bill. "That's small shit. If you're that hungry, all you had to do was ask and I would have gave you fifty bucks," Criminal said, bitter about losing the bet.

"Hungry? Where did all that come from? Cuzz, you don't have to get in your feelings about losing," Papa Gee responded while turning his face up. "Nigga, don't bet if you can't afford to lose."

"Can't afford to lose? What are you saying, Gee? That I'm some broke-ass nigga or something?" Criminal attempted to walk up on Papa Gee, but was cut short by Gangsta Jake and Horsehead.

"Y'all need to kill that drama because I'll be damned if I let you fools mess up our celebration over some dumb shit," Horsehead stepped up and announced.

"Yeah, you better slow him down before he get some hands put on him," Papa Gee, confident with his fighting skills, spoke up.

"You ain't trying to see me. All that shit sound slick standing between two homies," Criminal replied.

"You know what, Criminal?" Papa Gee said after weighing out the situation. "This is a day of celebration. Let's turn the page on the drama like the big homey said. As a matter of fact, nigga, drinks and weed is on me. I got the smoke already. What you drinking, cuzz?" Papa Gee asked his younger homey as he placed his arm around his shoulder and walked him toward the liquor store near the corner of the park.

Before Five Tray Day, Papa Gee and Lil' Doc hit a decent lick for eighty thousand, which had him in a good mood. Any other day, Papa Gee would probably have fired on Criminal and turned the barbeque out.

"Come on, Gangsta. Let's go break up the dice game now that the homies kissed and made up," Horsehead told Gangsta Jake in a joking manner.

"Bet I hit that four for a hundred." Gangsta Jake was referring to the point he rolled on the dice.

"Bet you don't, Gangsta," Tiki hollered out as he stopped Gangsta Jake's roll of the dice. Tiki had the original fade for two hundred dollars and reserved the right to stop the dice from rolling as many times as he pleased.

"Cuzz, bet you don't hit for another hundred," Liver Brown tossed two fifty-dollar bills next to Gangsta Jake's foot.

"Any other betters?" he looked up and asked the huddle of his homeboys that circled around him.

"I got five hundred that say you don't hit it," Jimbo boasted, which made the whole crowd respond to the amount of the bet.

"Oooohhhhh," Lil' Man in the back of the crowd hollered out over the rest of his gangbanging buddies. "You ain't said nothing but a word. Drop it like it's hot."

"You sound like Snoop Dog with all that 'drop it like it's hot' shit. Bet!" Jimbo said as he set down five one hundred dollar bills on the concrete.

Gangsta Jake continued to roll after the last bet was made. "Four dice," he yelled out as he looked at the dice and snapped his middle finger and thumb. The dice rolled an eight.

"Come on, baby; back door little Joe." Tiki caught the dice, disturbing his roll. Everyone clearly saw that Tiki caught a five duce, which would have cost Gangsta Jake eight hundred had he not interfered with his roll of the dice.

"If you didn't have hands, you'd have money," Gangsta Jake pointed his finger at Tiki, making the crowd burst out in laughter.

"Damn, Tiki! If you scared, go to church. Let the dice roll. Whatever is going to happen is going to happen anyway," Jimbo yelled out, mad at Tiki for catching the craps while he had a five hundred dollar bet on the line.

"Here, cuzz, take your fade money. Let me have him." Jimbo tried to cover the original bet Tiki put up, but Tiki was not trying to off his bet.

"I'm cool, Jimbo. I got him. The dice run in pairs. Seven is coming back," Tiki told Jimbo, but he was really mad at himself for catching the dice that would have made him two hundred dollars richer. Gangsta Jake continued to shoot for his point.

"Tray and a freckle," Gangsta Jake shouted out as a three and a one popped up on the dice when they came to a halt. "See there? That's what all that catching do for you. Two hundred I shoot," Gangsta Jake spoke out while picking up the money he won from the four he just made.

Gangsta Jake was having a ball hanging out with his homies and doing some of the things they used to do back in the days. Shooting dice, drinking, and blowing plenty of weed, all while talking trash to one another.

*   *   *

What he did not know was, at the exact time he was having fun with his homeboys, detectives Hardiman and Freeman were investigating the many murders that occurred in recent months. Thus far, with the help of Michelle, thirteen people on his list of informants had been gunned down in cold blood. After knocking off Pistol Pete and Elway, he and Michelle stepped up their hunt. On one occasion, they managed to commit two murders in the same day. The more killings they committed, the more secure they felt about doing them and getting away.

Because Los Angeles was so accustomed to having scores of unsolved murders throughout the city, at first the detectives were not able to make a connection. However, when Detective Hardiman went through several unsolved murder cases and discovered the same .44 caliber might have been involved, he got a chill up his spine.

"Bill?" he looked up and over to his partner, who sat across from him at a long table. He also had stacks of unsolved case files in front of him. "I believe we have a serial killer running loose in our city."

"Beg your pardon?"

"I said, I believe we have a fucking serial killer on our hands. We already know that these two were killed with the same gun." He pointed at the photos of Elway and Pistol Pete. "But as I went through six additional files, I came to realize all these other victims were shot," he paused and took his glasses off, "in most of the cases in the face with a .44 caliber."

"So you're telling me that there were .44 caliber slugs retrieved from each of the victims or at the crime scenes?" Detective Freeman quizzed his partner.

"Well, yes. That's what led me to—"

Freeman abruptly cut him off. "Before we jump the gun, why don't we have forensics match the slugs to see if they were fired from the same weapon?"

"Okay, we can do that. But I have a hunch these cases are connected," Detective Hardiman stated while he checked the files closely, looking for other similarities.

*   *   *

"Well, cuzz, I had fun, but I have to run. It was all good hanging out with you fools," Gangsta Jake told a few of his homeboys before driving off, leaning to one side. He was feeling good from the food stuffed in his stomach and the weed and alcohol circulating throughout his system. Normally, he would smoke a joint or two, enjoy a swig of alcohol, and be done with it, but by it being Five Tray Day, he maxed himself out on weed and drink. A couple of his homeboys tried to drive him home, but he insisted he could handle his liquor. The way he drove off told another story.

As he pulled out in traffic and through a red light on Fifty-first and San Pedro, a big, black truck slammed into his side door, which ultimately caused him to run into a telephone pole. The loud crash caused almost everyone at the park to swing their heads in the direction of the wreck. The impact was devastating. Shattered glass, hot tire tracks, and various fluids from Gangsta Jake's engine marked the crash sight.

The driver of the big black truck suffered some minor injuries, but nothing compared to the ones Gangsta Jake sustained. Outside of a few cuts and bruises, he was okay. Gangsta Jake, on the other hand, was knocked unconscious. His body lay jackknifed across his front seat with a blanket of glass on top of him.

One hundred or so bodies came running toward him to assess the damage. Fifty-first and San Pedro was in the rear of the park, half a block away from the barbeque. Therefore, getting to the crash site took only a matter of seconds, one minute tops. Once they reached him, they could not believe how he looked. Still trapped in the wreckage, his legs could barely be seen. Blood was visible as a result of his head hitting the windshield. For Gangsta Jake, it was all bad. A fun day suddenly turned into a rescue mission.

"Gangsta! Gangsta!" Cool Boo yelled out as he tried to release his friend's legs from underneath the steering wheel. "Don't move him, cuzz!" Horsehead hollered out in a serious manner.

Lunatic ran over to the driver of the truck and gave him a hard time. The twenty-six-year-old correction officer could not believe how his daily routine had switched so rapidly. When he first noticed all the gang members running toward the accident, he started to make a dash for it, but did not want to leave his truck with all his personal belongings behind.

"Fool, you ran into the homey!" Lunatic yelled out at the Chinese guy before yanking the gold chain he wore off his neck. He then followed up with a right jab that the Chinese guy ducked by moving his body. When Cee-rag looked up and saw Lunatic's unsuccessful assault take place, he made his way over to help Lunatic in his efforts. The Chinese guy saw him coming and broke out running. Luckily for him, he had a little rabbit in his blood and was able to outrun his original attacker and the other five gangbangers who thought they could catch him.

"Someone call 911!" shouted Horsehead as he placed his ear up against Gangsta Jake's chest. Gangsta Jake was out cold, but still breathing. Tip-Toe, one of Gangsta Jake's homeboys that he beat up on his third day out of prison, enjoyed seeing him laid out, clinging to his life. While everyone else did something to help the situation like call 911, hold back the crowd, or say a prayer, he stood, silently hoping Gangsta Jake would not pull through.

Within five minutes of someone calling 911, an ambulance came rolling up with its overhead sirens on. Before it arrived, Horsehead put away Gangsta Jake's gun that fell to the floor, emptied his pocket of the five twenty sacks of chronic he possessed, and removed all his jewelry. For safe keeping, he also took from his left sock the six thousand in one hundred dollar bills and left him the chump change of thirty-seven dollars. When the ambulance placed him on the stretcher and drove off, his fate was unknown.

Horsehead was sick to see his little homeboy banged up and hauled off to the hospital. The Chinese man who ran into Gangsta Jake eventually called the police and was escorted back to the accident. He was so upset about Lunatic's performance, in spite of Lunatic not being there when he returned, he identified someone else as the perpetrator of the crime. No matter how much Evil Dee denied snatching the chain off the Chinese neck and stealing his personal possessions from his truck, he ultimately was carried off to jail.

Bay-Bay and her crew of eight females jumped in her brother's 454 Chevy truck and followed the ambulance to the hospital. Three girls, including Bay-Bay, sat in the front seat, while the others made themselves comfortable in the back of the truck.

"Bay-Bay, why are they driving this way? Martin Luther King Hospital is in the other direction. They have the best trauma center to deal with his injuries," My-My said.

"Girl, don't you look at the news? The trauma center at killer King is closed and has been for a while now," Bay-Bay informed her younger sister.

Once the paramedics arrived at the hospital, Gangsta Jake was taken out the ambulance and placed inside the emergency room. The hospital personnel worked on him while hospital security dealt with the flock of gang members that filled the lobby area in a matter of minutes. On the way to the hospital, Horsehead called Michelle and briefly filled her in on the situation.

After receiving the news, she immediately jumped in the car with her sister, Rachel. Rachel was high yellow with a short, blond haircut, who stood approximately five feet seven inches. She hated the fact that her little sister was in love with a guy she considered a loser. The hurt in Michelle's face after receiving the phone call, coupled with the tears in her eyes, were the only reasons she agreed to drive Michelle to the hospital.

Rachel was baffled at the scene when she and Michelle drove inside the hospital parking lot. Gangsta Jake's homeboys and homegirls were hanging out in the parking lot, drinking forty ounces and smoking cigarettes and blunts. The party basically continued at the hospital. One little guy no older than fifteen leaned up against Lord knows whose parked car and released his bladder. Most of them had on black or blue khakis with white tee shirts. The hospital lobby was not big enough to hold all of them, which caused the remainder to hang outside in the parking lot. They huddled outside like a pack of hound dogs. Half of his homies stayed in the neighborhood partying, while the rest went to check on their comrade.

"Michelle, look at all these niggas," Rachel told her as she tried to locate a parking spot. "Where in the hell am I suppose to park with all these gangbangers taking up all the spaces?"

"Rachel, stop complaining and find a place to park while I run in here and see what's going on with Rohan."

"Michelle, wait! Don't leave me out here with all these crazy-looking niggas."

"Girl, these are all Rohan's friends. They're not going to do nothing to you," Michelle told her big sister before jumping out the car and dashing toward the receptionist's desk. When she finally made it inside the building, Lil' Boss Hog noticed Michelle and made his way toward her.

"Michelle!" he yelled.

When Horsehead heard her name, he looked up and also walked in Michelle's direction.

"How did it happen?" she asked Horsehead.

"He was on full, ran through a red light, and a truck mashed him."

"What? How could you let him drive?"

"Hell, I tried to stop him, but you know how he is."

"He listens to you for everything else. Why the fuck didn't you—"

Horsehead cut her short when he recognized the blame game coming about. "Listen, little mama, there ain't no use in us going through all that. Blaming me is not going to change the price of butter. The situation hurts me just as much as it hurts you. You think I want to see my little partner fucked off like that?"

Michelle quickly came to her senses in order to find out more about his condition. She did not like the way it sounded so far. "How did he look? Did it seem like he would live?" she pressed.

Horsehead did not have a true answer to her questions, but managed to give her one she wanted to hear. "Of course, he's gonna to live. Gangsta Jake is a soldier. You know he ain't going out like that," he optimistically stated, hoping there was some validity to his statement.

Rachel eventually parked her car and made her way past the huddle of thugs, but not before being confronted, however.

"Say, cutie pie, slow your roll before you get a traffic ticket," Baby Face, from the 116th chapter of the Avalon Gangster Crips, told her. "It looks like you need a personal escort," he further stated with a smile.

"Thanks, but I'm okay."

"Oh, what you think? You're too good to holler at a gangsta or what?" He continued to look at her with his sleepy eyes.

"It's not like that. I just have to go," she told him as she turned around and kept walking.

"Fuck you, then, you pretty-ass bitch!" he screamed out, embarrassing her in front of everyone.

When Rachel caught up with Michelle, she immediately told her how Baby Face disrespected her. Horsehead was standing next to Michelle and did not like what he heard.

"Who talked to you like that, Miss Lady?" Horsehead asked Rachel, also infatuated with her beauty. By coming to her defense, he figured he could gain some brownie points and perhaps get to know her a little better himself.

Rachel refused to be the center of a brawl between two strangers, especially gangbangers, who she considered, the scum of the earth. Instead of pointing out who the guy was, she convinced him that she was not trying to press the issue. In the middle of their conversation, a doctor walked in the lobby area with some news on Gangsta Jake's condition. Due to all the unwanted guests, he requested to be escorted by two armed security guards.

"Excuse me!" he spoke loudly over the thirty-five gang members who packed the inside of the lobby area. The only reason he came out was to try and talk part of the crowd into dispersing. "Excuse me! Pardon me!" the doctor said to no avail.

No one heard a word he said due to all the back-and-forth chatter. A black guard standing next to the doctor noticed no one paying him any attention and stepped in to assist the situation. He stood on a chair, placed his two middle fingers between his pink lips, and whistled three times loud enough for any corpse in the morgue to hear.

"Can I have your attention, please!" the dark-skinned, slightly overweight security guard yelled. The nicks at the top and back of his head were clear indicators he had a rough time shaving his bald head. "This is the doctor that will be caring for your friend. His name is Doctor Parondo, and he's here to update you folks on his condition."

Hearing the news caused everyone in the lobby area to stop what they were doing, close their mouths, and pay close attention. Michelle held her hands in a praying position and prayed that the doctor would deliver some good news. Up until that point, she never imagined what life would be like without him. Ever since they met over the telephone, he had made her feel like a queen. In spite of all the drama, she still loved him with all her heart and would be lost without him.

"Ladies and gentlemen, as the guard just mentioned, my name is Dr. Parondo. As of now, Mr. Lemon is in stable, but critical condition." Aws could be heard throughout the lobby when he mentioned the word "critical." Michelle almost passed out. "He suffered some trauma to the head area as a result of his head banging up against the windshield," he continued.

Michelle's eyes filled with tears. She only wished she could have been there to drive him home safely. "God, please let him live," she told herself as her nose began running.

"If—*when* he regains consciousness," Dr. Parondo quickly changed his statement to sound more optimistic, "my staff and I can better assess the extent of his injuries."

"Is the homey going to live or what?" Bogart candidly asked.

"To be totally honest," the doctor looked around at the size of the crowd as a slight sweat built up on his forehead and his face turned red as he answered the question, "it's hard to say at this point. I've seen people in worse condition turn around and fully recover, and I've seen people in better shape than him not make it. Hopefully, he'll be in the first category. As of now, there is nothing any of you can do for him at this time. I advise that someone come back and check on him in a few days. Now if you all will excuse me, I have to get back to him," Dr. Parondo told the entire crowd, knowing he was really on his way out the back door and off to his beautiful home in Beverly Hills.

*   *   *

Four days following Gangsta Jake's accident, he regained some type of consciousness. Michelle happened to be in the room praying over him when all of a sudden, he began mumbling something. His head slowly rocked side-to-side as his body movement gained momentum.

"Mi, Michelle," he grunted out, his mind blurry from the dream he was experiencing. "Kill him, Michelle. Watch out!" he screamed, slightly raising the top of his body and then flopping back on the bed.

"Baby! Rohan! Are you okay?" she looked him in the face and discovered his eyes had closed back up.

"Help!" she screamed loudly, turning her head toward the door. Her hands remained planted on his face. A black, female nurse heard Michelle's cries for help and ran inside the room. She promptly notified a nearby doctor, who responded in a matter of seconds.

"What's the problem?" Dr. Williams asked as he quickly made his way toward Gangsta Jake, Michelle, and the nurse who was in the process of checking his vital signs. The black doctor was five minutes into his shift and was already earning his take.

"His wife told me he woke up and said a few words. His blood pressure is normal at 120 over 83, but his heart rate is a little rapid."

"What did he say, Miss?" Dr. Williams asked Michelle as he opened Gangsta Jake's right eye with his left thumb and flashed a light over his eyeball.

She thought about what he said, and then the doctor's question. "He said he loved me. He called out my name and then told me he loved me. That's what he said." She felt her answer would suffice for the purpose he was looking for.

"Michelle," Gangsta Jake mumbled in a very sleepy voice. Michelle hoped he did not repeat his previous comments.

Doctor Williams checked his heart, pulse, and temperature. After his examination, he determined he definitely was not 100 percent, but did seem to be making a swifter than expected recovery. The doctor recommended Michelle patiently allow him sufficient time to fully gain his awareness. She had no problem with allowing him some time to recuperate. As long as she knew he would be okay, she was fine with that.

On her way home, Michelle called over to Horsehead's apartment and gave him the update on Gangsta Jake's condition. Horsehead was thrilled to hear the good news and looked forward to paying him a visit later on that evening. He told Michelle to swing by his apartment in order to pick up the money and other possessions he retrieved from Gangsta Jake after the accident.

Unfortunately, Gangsta Jake's sixty-one Chevy was totaled. However, Horsehead did manage to save part of his hydraulic system and two of his rear Dayton wires. Michelle obviously did not care about those material factors. Her concern was only focused on assisting in the recovery of her man, the man that she had, on numerous occasions, placed her very own life on the line for. Her love for Gangsta Jake was so strong that if she could have possibly taken the pain off of him and place it on her, she certainly would have.

19

Michelle's World

Three weeks following his accident, Gangsta Jake was allowed to return home. Dr. Parondo told him he was very lucky to have survived his ordeal. If it wasn't for the fast emergency response, chances were that he would not have pulled through. His loss of blood was massive. Minutes after arriving at the hospital, Dr. Parondo contemplated amputation of his left leg. It suffered the most damage. The few broken ribs and his head injury were minor compared to his crushed leg. The doctor estimated the cast running up his thigh would have to stay in place for at least six months. The news was heartbreaking to Gangsta Jake. The extra load would hamper his mission, he thought, as the doctor delivered the bad news. His car or leg being destroyed did not piss him off more than his inability to pull a trigger and get away without a trace. Michelle would have to fill the void. It was time she stepped her game up, he selfishly pondered before speaking his thought.

"Michelle," he called in a low, weak voice.

She was in the kitchen cooking them a meal. "Yes, honey, is everything okay?"

"Yeah, it's all good. I just wanted to holler at you about something important."

"What is it, baby?"

"Look at my leg. I can barely move this big-ass cast around." He found himself at a loss for words and decided to do like he'd always done: be straight-up with her. "Baby, I need some work put in on this clown right here." He showed her the list of thirty informants, thirteen of whom had been crossed out with a blue or black ink pen.

"Baby, why don't you wait until you get better? Six months is a nice period of time to let things cool off."

"Cool off? What do you mean, cool off? We're straight. As long as we're free, we're cool. Baby, come here." He looked at Michelle with his eyes low from a combination of his body aches and the joint he smoked ten minutes earlier. She walked over to the couch where he was resting.

"What?" she asked, pouting like a little girl instead of the cold-blooded killer she had become.

"Michelle, you already know that I can't do much in this condition. But you, on the other hand—" he coughed, and sipped on a glass of water which sat next to him, "you can do it with no problem."

"I don't know if I can do it without you, Rohan."

"Girl, you have this thing down pat. I got a lot of confidence in my girl. Don't let daddy down." He searched her eyes, looking for confirmation.

"I don't know, Rohan," she said, thinking about shooting someone and getting away with it. "I'm so use to you assisting me whenever I do it. I'm not sure I can do it by myself."

"Baby, sure you can. All you have to do is what you've basically been doing all the time. It don't get no easier. Once you've done it a few times, it's just like taking candy from a baby. You even told me yourself, it's easier to get away with murder than you thought." He went on and on about the subject for at least an hour.

The longer he talked, the more Michelle felt she could handle it. At first, she wasn't too confident about continuing on with his plan, but after nearly an hour and a half of talking back and forth, she conceded to his request. The look in his eyes, the love for him in her heart, or perhaps the way he dicked her down since his release helped to influence her decision. Whatever the reason was, her mind was made up that she could pick up where he left off.

Gangsta Jake was a vicious individual who would stop at nothing to clear his list of informants. He took advantage of Michelle's passion for him. Sure he loved her, but obviously not enough to lead her in the right direction. Killing informants was his direction, which ultimately became hers. Had she refused his request, he would have certainly come up with other remedies to execute his agenda. Maybe sending bombs through the mail or something. Until his list was clear, he would not be satisfied.

*   *   *

Back at LAPD headquarters, Detective Freeman was on the phone with forensic lab personnel, who revealed that the .44 slugs he had requested to be matched up to several of the victims came back positive. Furthermore, the technician informed Detective Freeman that the same footprint had been discovered at more than one crime scene.

This was all the fuel Detective Freeman needed to begin a bigger investigation. He called his partner, Detective Hardiman, into his office for an emergency meeting that laid the groundwork for a larger investigation among detectives from other divisions. At the end of their short meeting, the two shook hands and joked about how solving the case would lead them both to big promotions.

Inside a conference room sat ten detectives. Their agenda consisted of comparing evidence in reference to the many execution-style murders that took place throughout their divisions of the Los Angeles Police Department. Detective Hardiman sat at the head of a long wooden table, while the other homicide detectives sat on both sides of it. Now that some connections were established to tie several of the murders together, the group of detectives worked diligently to discover more tie-ins and bring the killer or killers to justice.

"Ladies and gentlemen, first and foremost, I'd like to thank you all for agreeing to join me in this investigation of the person or persons who are responsible for committing these scores of murders throughout our county. Our initial investigation has revealed that the shooter's primary weapon is a .44 caliber. Most of his victims have been males, but a couple of females were killed as well," said Detective Hardiman.

"Have you and Detective Freeman come up with a motive as of yet?" asked Detective Stone from the Rampart Division. He held an ink pen between his index and middle finger.

Detective Hardiman promptly answered his question. "I'm afraid we have not, but I'm certain as this investigation moves forward, we will. We do have a size twelve footprint that was discovered at a few of the crime scenes. On one occasion, a female was seen leaving the scene of the homicide. Our details are sketchy as of now, but we do believe the perpetrator or perpetrators are African-Americans, or at least one of them is."

"Why do you say that?" a black detective with dark skin and full lips spoke up.

"Because of my partner," he said, looking at Detective Freeman and giving him a quick nod. His partner nodded in return. "Detective Freeman was personally assaulted by someone we believe is our man. Detective, if you will, please inform the others of your encounter with the man I am referring to."

"Yes, of course. My partner and I were in the process of conducting an investigation into the shooting of one our victims. As I walked into the victim's hospital room, a man named James Elway, I was attacked from the rear by an unknown assailant. When I first entered Mr. Elway's room, I noticed something was not right from the awkward position of Mr. Elway's body on the bed. But before I could investigate, someone attacked me from the back. Unfortunately, I was unable to see the attacker's face."

Every detective in the room imagined himself in Detective Freeman's position and felt personally connected to his experience. He had every person's undivided attention.

"During the assault," he continued, "the scumbag was able to retrieve my weapon and badge. I want this asshole to die in the gas chamber!" His neck and face began turning red, then he hit the table displaying his raw emotions. "I'm confident we, as a team, will bring him to justice."

Before the meeting was adjourned, the detectives all agreed that since they did not have much to go on, they would turn to the public for help. The little evidence they now obtained was not enough to come up with a suspect on their own. Detective Burns suggested they wait a few days in order to compile the evidence already in their possession. That way, all the facts would be lined up once the media began to ask questions.

*   *   *

All that was fine and dandy—but not enough to avoid another informant from becoming the next victim of Gangsta Jake's scheme. Michelle knocked off poor Tom Carpenter like she was a professional hitman. When Tom walked outside his home to pick up the morning newspaper, there stood Michelle with Gangsta Jake's .44 snuggled in the palm of her right hand. The first shot went to his chest, the second to his neck, and the third is the shot that ended his life. The white, thirty-five-year-old father of three had made a bad choice when he took the stand against one of Gangsta Jake's allies, Big Al Capone, from the Five Duce Broadway Gangsta Crips.

After gunning Tom Carpenter down, Michelle ran up the street to their van. Gangsta Jake waited there for her. In spite of his injuries, he still wanted to be close by when the action went down.

Carpenter's youngest daughter, who was only five years old, waited patiently for him to return in order to finish giving her a bath. When he didn't, she began crying at the top of her lungs. Her cries went on and on until an officer from the LAPD responded to the call of a shooting. What the officer discovered was Tom Carpenter lying in his own blood on the ground. His life was over by the time the officer arrived. The only thing the officer could do at that point was to make sure his little daughter was okay.

When Detective Hill arrived at Tom Carpenter's house, he noticed the murder fit the description of what Detective Hardiman talked about days earlier. Detective Hardiman had e-mailed every division in the LAPD, requesting that he be notified immediately if this type of homicide occurred.

"Do you have any witnesses?" Detective Hardiman asked Detective Hill after emerging through the yellow tape and introducing himself. Because of the rain, Detective Hardiman wore a long trench coat and a hat. He then walked over to the corpse and began asking the examiner a few questions. His primary concern was whether or not the victim was shot with a .44 caliber, which was often used by the assailant.

When it was unofficially confirmed that a .44 was the weapon used, Hardiman's adrenaline began flowing. That discovery caused him to stop what he was doing and place his two index fingertips between his lips, whistling loudly. That stopped the other investigators in their tracks.

"Ladies and gentlemen," he shouted to seven detectives and six uniform LAPD officers. "My name is Detective Hardiman and I'm from LAPD main headquarters. I'm the lead detective in the investigation of a string of murders in the Los Angeles County area. Yes, people, I'm on the hunt for a serial killer and as of now, so is each and every one of you. There may possibly be more than one killer connected to this case. Little is known about the suspect, or suspects involved in these homicides.

"The reason I stopped everyone," he looked around the room, "is to make sure you guys do your best detective work in gathering the evidence at this crime scene. No mistakes allowed people. This man," he pointed at the dead body that had not yet been covered with a white sheet. The body still had blood oozing out of it. Thick blood and brains was splattered all over the immediate area. "may very well be the fourteenth victim to fall prey to the vicious animal that our department is hunting."

"My God," said a young, sixteen-year-old, freckled-faced police explorer who rode along side a seasoned LAPD uniformed officer.

Detective Hardman continued, "So again, I caution you all to do a good job and avoid destroying or looking over any potential or crucial evidence."

Only twenty minutes had elapsed since the detective began investigating the murder and like all the other homicides Gangsta Jake was responsible for, Michelle did not leave the investigators many clues to work with. However, the detectives were able to determine that possibly the same caliber gun was used as with the other victims, which established the connection Detective Hardiman sought. With that information in mind, he wrote a report and met Detective Freeman over at headquarters.

*　　*　　*

"Michelle, why are you driving so fast? Slow your roll, baby, before—" just as he was giving her a warning, a highway patrol officer came out of nowhere and pulled her over.

"Damn, baby!" Michelle smacked her lips together. "We have company. The police are pulling us over. What should I do?" she asked.

He was still sitting in the rear of the van and planned on staying there. Without hesitation, he made his way to the back window in order to see what type of police was pulling them over.

Michelle was beginning to panic. She was sure the officer was pulling her over as a result of what happened to her last victim twenty-two minutes ago. "Should I keep driving or what, baby?" Her heart began to pound even more than at the actual time of the shooting.

"No, pull over. It's only the highway patrol. They may only be pulling you over for speeding. Hand me the gun, though, just in case he has something else on his mind." She eased it to him and pulled off to the side of the highway.

"What do I do if you have to shoot him?"

"Drive the fuck off! What kind of question is that?"

Moments later, the highway patrolman walked up to the rental van. Gangsta Jake rocked his body back and forth as he held his pistol underneath a jacket being used as a makeshift blanket. Michelle was instructed, if asked, to tell the officer he had recently been in a car accident, and furthermore, was mentally retarded. That would explain why he was in the backseat and rocking back and forth.

"Hello, Miss," the black officer said with a straight look. The dark glasses he wore hid his eyes, and his rigid posture reminded Michelle of a robot. "You do understand why I pulled you over, don't you?"

"Because I was driving too fast," she said with a calm, but slight nervousness registering on her face.

"What's your hurry, Miss?" he asked while looking in the back of the van. He noticed Gangsta Jake and wondered why he was rocking back and forth while looking deranged. After a second, he assumed the obvious, that he must be mentally ill.

"I'm holding my pee. I was driving fast so I could hurry up and use the bathroom," she told the highway patrolman while swaying her thighs side-to-side in an attempt to hold the pee that really was causing her discomfort. Fortunately for Michelle, he believed her and allowed her to go her way without receiving a speeding ticket. Gangsta Jake's fabricated condition influenced his decision to allow Michelle to continue on without a ticket. After a verbal warning, the two were back on their escape route.

"Thank God," she said to Gangsta Jake while looking over her shoulders and out the back window.

At that point, he uncocked his gun and stopped rocking. "Good job, baby girl. Now get us to the house."

20

Press Conference

Four days went by and then Detective Hardiman instructed Detective Freeman to notify the local media of their investigation into the unsolved murders. The five o'clock news told it all. People from the desert to the sea and all throughout Southern California received the news that a serial killer was on the loose. The LAPD had reason to believe two people may be involved, but voted against revealing that piece of information. They wanted to see what the public may know about a second suspect. Detective Freeman promised to deliver a press conference the following day to clarify their findings.

Phones immediately began ringing off the hook at LAPD stations throughout Los Angeles County. Communities were afraid and were willing to do anything possible to bring whoever may be responsible to justice. Folks began locking their doors and windows at the thought of someone invading their homes and gunning them down in cold blood. Several citizens went out and purchased handguns for their protection. Ninety-nine percent of the phone calls received by LAPD personnel would not prove to be useful in their investigation. The calls were mainly out of fear and concern for their safety. Many of the callers were interested in how close the department was to solving the case. The other 1 percent did, in fact, have information about the case, but their statements were already recorded by homicide detectives following the murders. When the news about the unsolved murders reached Gangsta Jake, he felt like a silent celebrity. He enjoyed the fact that his doings were finally receiving the media attention he craved.

"See, baby! I told you they were sleep on us!" he said excitedly. She walked over to him and rubbed the back of his head as if he was a kitty cat, Michelle then smiled in a supportive manner without saying a word. "Snitch muthafuckas!

That's what the fuck y'all get," he yelled, pointing at the news segment while hitting himself in the chest like King Kong. He wanted to stand up and crip walk, but the cast on his leg interfered with that form of celebration.

*   *   *

The following day, Detective Hardiman and his partner addressed the media as promised. Gangsta Jake was five minutes late tuning into the news conference, but nevertheless, right on time. When Hardiman turned the microphone over to Detective Freeman, Gangsta Jake thought he had seen a ghost. "What the fuck?" slowly came to his lips as his mouth gaped open.

"What's wrong, baby?" Michelle asked as she sat next to him, eating popcorn and drinking soda. She looked more like a person watching a movie as opposed to someone awaiting her fate.

"That's the police from the hospital. The one I choked. I thought I killed that clown."

"Wait, baby, hold on for a minute. Let's see what he's talking about."

Fifteen microphones from various news stations sat on a podium before him. Detective Freeman adjusted his notes, which also rested on the podium. After clearing his throat, he spoke.

"Over the course of a year or so, LAPD detectives were called to several unsolved murder scenes. We have reason to believe fourteen of the murders are related. We at the Los Angeles Police Department are turning to the citizens of this community for information about these homicides. We are asking the public to contact their local police department if they have any information that may possibly lead to the capture of the perpetrator of these senseless execution-style murders."

"That's what the fucking problem is, right there. Why do you stupid muthafuckas think you're on the news right now?" Gangsta Jake hollered out at the comment Detective Freeman made in reference to having people provide information on criminals.

Detective Freeman continued, "Whoever is responsible for committing these crimes does not deserve to be among our communities. The suspect is considered to be armed and extremely dangerous. Please, do not attempt to apprehend this suspect if you discover who he or she might be."

Detective Hardiman interjected, "We at the Los Angeles Police Department are asking anyone who comes across this person, or persons," he slipped, causing Michelle's eyebrows to quickly raise, "to please notify us at once. Do not attempt to approach the person on your own. Call us at our hotline below," he stressed, realizing how dangerous the killer or killers were. As far as he was concerned, enough people had been killed already.

"Baby, they know it was me. You heard him mention the part about a female." Michelle could not hold back her words any longer. The fears she overcame a while ago were starting to come back.

"Shhhhhhh. Be quiet for a minute!" he insisted with his index finger up to his lip.

Detective Hardiman placed the pictures of all fourteen victims on the easel to the right side of the podium. "Here are the pictures of victims who, we believe, were murdered by the person our department is seeking. Our goal is first, to place a face to the unknown person who is responsible for committing these brutal crimes, and second, to see to it that the victims and their families receive justice."

*   *   *

"Damn, Blood! Look at this," Half-dead, from the Bounty Hunters, said to his celly of seven years, Lil' Bee. They were also watching the press conference from their prison cell. "That looks like the fool who snitched on me at my trial."

Half-dead jumped off his bunk bed and hurried over to the television to confirm his assumption. "That's him, homey, that's him!" he told his celly with exhilaration. He felt happier than a million-dollar lottery winner once he realized his accuser was one of the faces being displayed on television.

"Warlock!" he screamed down the tier to his Crip buddy, who happened to be from Gangsta Jake's neighborhood. Blood and Crip issues were not relevant on the row. However, out of respect, their gang affiliations were reserved for their own kind. Half-dead and Lil' Bee both represented Blood gangs, which made it okay for them to talk with each other the way they did.

"Turn your tube to the news, dawg. Somebody is on one out there in the city. They killed the rat who got down on me in trial."

Is that right? Young Lad thought to himself as he turned from his regular program on the portable television in the tiny cell.

"Half-dead," Young Lad yelled down the tier after flipping through a few television channels, "what station is it on?"

"Eyewitness News. Hurry up and turn to it," Half-dead said, not wanting him to miss a moment of what was being televised. Crazy Mike and several other guys on the tier heard the conversation, like so many other ones they've heard throughout the years. And within seconds, everyone on the tier was tuned into the broadcast.

Young Lad observed each victim's photo with Gangsta Jake in mind. He and Gangsta Jake spoke about killing a bunch of snitches if one or the other were released, but he never imagined their conversation becoming a reality. As he scanned through the photo display and discovered the two security guards who took the stand against him, he came to realize his main man, Gangsta Jake, was, in fact, responsible for the killing spree being described. Unlike Half-dead, who wore his emotions on his face, Young Lad chose to celebrate within his own temple. Furthermore, he did not want to bring too much attention to his partner, who, he believed, was doing the right thing. Had the shoe been on the other foot, he would have taken the same action as Gangsta Jake. Young Lad also could not stand snitches and felt honored that someone was finally taking a stand.

Crazy Mike recalled all the conversations he overheard Gangsta Jake and Young Lad venting about over the years and also had a pretty good idea who was responsible for the killings. *I'll be damn*, Crazy Mike pondered in amazement while looking at the fuzzy television set he owned for the past twenty-five years. "I knew the youngster would not be satisfied with sitting still somewhere out of the way. That boy had a habit of always craving attention," he mumbled to himself in disappointment.

* * *

"Michelle, don't even trip off of him referring to a second person being involved. Like I told you, they're sleep on us. They don't know too much of anything; if they did, why would they turn to the public for help?" He waved his hand at the crystal-clear television set as Detective Hardiman began wrapping up the press conference. "Fuck what them lames are talking about. They haven't seen nothing yet! It's gonna be some more snitches resting in their graves as long as I'm alive. They better not piss me off, because I will switch my focus on their bitch asses. Coward-ass police, I can't stand them son-of-a-bitches. Baby, don't get beside yourself. Let's just stick to the script."

She knew he was serious as a tsunami and would possibly send her at the police. To avoid being placed in a high-risk situation, she downplayed his radical theories.

The press conference did not scare Gangsta Jake one bit. If anything, it fueled his desire to kill additional snitches. As a result of the many murders the two of them had already gotten away with, Michelle was no longer afraid to pull a trigger. Eventually, she became comfortable with what was being asked of her. To demonstrate how much he did not care about what the LAPD had to say, Gangsta Jake sent her on an execution three days following the press conference. He became so cocky and secure with Michelle's performance, he allowed her to go at it alone.

* * *

As Michelle stood in the mirror and put on her lipstick, the mailman dropped four pieces of mail inside their mailbox. Three bills and one letter from Young

Lad fell through the slot of their front door. Michelle stopped what she was doing for a second and walked over to retrieve the mail. "Bills, bills, a letter from Lemuel, and another bill. Here you go, baby." She handed Gangsta Jake the letter from Young Lad and sat the three bills next to a letter opener on the kitchen table.

"It's about time this fool wrote me." He peeled the letter open and began to read it while picturing Young Lad in his mind.

Greetings, loved one,

I'm not even going to ask you what you're up to because I put two and two together and figured out what was cracking on your end. Me and the homies watched a little television the other day, and the news seemed to be the best thing to look at. Stay down for your crown, baby boy.

Gangsta Jake broke a half smile while thumbing the side of his nose. He knew exactly what his partner was referring to without him actually saying it. He relished the fact that Young Lad knew what he was up to since his release. Their conversations and dreams were finally in play, he imagined, as he continued to read the letter he held with both hands in front of his face.

You're a soldier, baby boy. I got a lot of love and respect for you for keeping your word, cuzz. You're one of the few who were freed from the belly of the beast and honestly did what you said you would do. Stay having a ball. Whatever you do, make sure to watch your back and your front. Me and the homies need you out there.

Most of us haven't had it this good in prison since we've been locked down. We appreciate all the packages and money you blasted our way. Crazy Mike sends his love too. The government granted him a 90-day stay of execution, but the prosecutor was hot about it. Rumor has it that his bitch ass is planning on retiring from being a prosecutor and flipping over to politics. So he's basically trying to get all the stripes he can get off of us. An execution would be big for that fag's career, but I ain't letting it happen though.

So what's been going on in the neighborhood? I hope you been taking care of your leg. Horsehead sent me some flicks last week. That's all he fucks with is hoodrats. Tell that nigga to send pictures of some fly females up in here. I like jacking off to cuties with big asses, not these ghetto rats who look like they can knock niggas out. O yeah, cuzz, all kind of little homies have been getting at me and Warlock with money, flicks, and magazines. I guess the ass beating you put down when you first got out paid off.

The homey Black Dog sent me a kite from Folsom Penitentiary telling me the same thing was happening with him and some of the homies on that end. Nigga, it's been a good year for prison since you left, especially with the latest news.

All right, cuzz, I guess I'll lay on back and talk shit to Dre. This fool still thinks he can beat me in chess. Let me serve him real quick, loved one. Stay smashing on them bustas out there. A's up, my nigga. Tell all the real Avalons I said, Avalon's up as well.

Gangsta Jake folded the letter back up and placed it in the envelope with a smile on his face. Things were looking up for him and his folks, which had him feeling pretty good about his freedom. Every homey he dealt with inside the penitentiary books were on fat; he contributed to over a dozen snitches resting in their graves; and on top of all that, he remained a free man with a beautiful killer by his side. He was in such a good mood that he cut Michelle's mission short for the night.

"Say, cuteness, come over here for a minute," he told Michelle as she groomed herself in their door-size mirror.

"What, honey?" she asked while pulling a baseball hat down over her head and walking toward him in her usual, seductive manner. He leaned his body back in his cushy chair and asked her to sit next to him.

"I changed my mind. You're staying home with daddy tonight. Cancel what I told you earlier."

She smiled. "Whaaaat? Let me check you out." Playing with him, she removed the black leather glove on her right hand and placed her soft hand against his forehead, checking his temperature. "This is something new. I never saw you hesitate to have a rat killed."

"Yeah, I'm cool. I just don't want my sweetheart out of my sight tonight," he said smoothly, like a movie star. Looking at the ruby-red lipstick on her shiny lips was causing him to have an erection. Beating her pussy up the way he wanted to had become a challenge with the heavy cast running all the way up his thigh; therefore, he choose not to hit it lately. However, that night he had to have some, and it was written all over his face.

The look he gave her said enough. Before she hopped on top and rode him like he was a wild bull, Michelle unzipped his pants with her gloveless hand, reached inside his fly, and whipped out his nearly erect shaft. Once she fully exposed him, her lips gravitated to his shaft like a starving hostage to a barbeque rib. The bill of her hat was slowing down her flow. After ten strokes, instead of tossing her blue baseball cap to the floor, she flipped it in the opposite direction like a back catcher. Michelle's groove was now creamy from the warm, hard pipe she took inside her mouth. Seconds before he came, she took it out and jacked him off. Gangsta Jake placed his head on the headrest and closed his eyes. He was not ready to ejaculate, but could not help himself. Once Michelle realized he was coming, she reconnected her lips and swallowed every drop he produced.

"Damn, baby," was all he said and the last words he remembered stating the following day. The dim lights, combined with the weed and alcohol in his system, put him straight to sleep five minutes after telling her to hold on while he took a quick break. She was not upset one bit. Besides, her middle finger substituted just fine while Gangsta Jake slept like a newborn baby.

The following day, Michelle woke up to the sound of her cell phone. It was Robin calling to discuss what she and her sister talked about the previous night. Robin's sister, Evelyn, had called out to New York from her apartment in Los Angeles and filled her in on the news of the killings.

Robin knew how Gangsta Jake operated and assumed he was probably the one responsible. The stutter in Michelle's voice after mentioning it confirmed her belief.

"Who is that?" Gangsta Jake asked Michelle as he came to from a good night's sleep.

She covered up the bottom of the phone with her hand and quietly told him it was Robin.

"You don't say. I wonder what the fuck she wants," he whispered under his breath.

Robin continued, "Girl, I sure hope you don't let him get you in any trouble. I know he's the one who's out their killing those people."

Based on Michelle's facial expression, Gangsta Jake grabbed the phone out of her hand. He was only able to catch the last three words Robin spoke. "Haaaaay!" he screamed into the telephone. He was attempting to drown out what Robin was saying. He assumed the police might possibly be tapping his phone.

"Bitch, what did you say? What the fuck are you talking about? Killing what people?" He continued to play dumb and pump fear in her heart. He was furious about her statement and demanded a response. Robin kept him in suspense by not saying a word. She was fed up and scared at the same time. But this time, however, no matter how afraid Robin was, she refused to be intimidated by him any longer. Her initial fears caused her to hang up in his face, but within seconds, she built up enough courage to call back and give him a piece of her mind. Robin understood going off on him may cost her life, but at that moment, she was smoking hot and did not give a fuck about him, herself, or anything. The distance between the two also influenced her outburst.

"Rohan, I've been real patient putting up with your bullshit. From this day forward, I refuse to accept your disrespectful ass coming at me any type of way you please."

"What the fuck are you going to do—tell the police on me about nothing? Make up some kind of lie?" He waited for an answer.

"You act like you want me to set your ass out or something. Every time I talk to you, you're constantly tossing the subject up in my face. If I wanted your stupid ass in jail, don't you think you would have been there a long time ago? You need to leave me the fuck alone; me and Michelle. You act like I don't have family who got my back. Punk-ass nigga, I got cousins that are Bloods, from the Pueblos. I could have had them get you if I was into that type of shit. But I'm not going to stoop to your level."

"Yeah, and if you do . . ." Gangsta Jake quickly thought about what he would do to them if they were to try and get at him and decided not to fall into what she was screaming. "Girl, I know more niggas from the Pueblos than you can imagine. I probably even know your cousins if they ain't no bustas. Being that you never spoke on them beforehand, they probably are."

"Fool, you're a buster. You don't know nothing about my family."

"I know about you and your parents, though," he reminded her. "As a matter of fact, bitch, don't be calling over to my spot, threatening me with no bullshit. I'm not worried about no nigga doing nothing to me. Hoe, I'm smoking yo punk ass for even coming at me like that. Watch what I tell you, you little, big-booty bitch."

Robin had him irate and unfocused on what he was saying. The police possibly tapping his phone line totally escaped his mind.

"Baby, give me the phone." Michelle reached for it. "Rohan, please don't talk to my friend like that. Why can't you get along with her?" She retreated, realizing he was not giving up the phone.

"Kick back, Michelle. I don't like the way this little hoe is coming at me."

"I got your fucking hoe between my legs, you trick, no good nigga."

Robin was very upset at the way he was referring to her. She considered herself to be a lady and did not appreciate his repeated insults. "I'm not going to sit up here and argue with your sorry ass. You're nothing but a loser, and as much as I hate to say it, you turned my girl into one as well. All you ever did was take advantage of her vulnerability, you bastard!" Her anger grew more intense. "All you know how to do is destroy people's lives. Sorry-ass nigga, I pray to God you burn in hell. I'll bet money, your stupid ass will not have any good luck. God don't like ugly."

"Check this out, you punk bitch. Before you start talking—" *click*. This time, Gangsta Jake was the recipient of a dial tone, and he was hot about it. He hated not being the one who got the last word in. With a magnifying glass, you probably could have seen the steam coming off his forehead. That was the straw that broke the camel's back. The shit had truly hit the fan, and hard. Not only did he forbid Michelle from being friends with Robin, but he wanted her dead!

"Michelle, I know she's your partner and all, but that bitch has got to leave this earth. I gave her all the chances she's going to get. She got her fucking nerve to talk to a gangsta like that! I done killed muthafuckas for less. I'll be damn if that goat-smelling, ass hoe gets away with carrying me like a sucka!"

"Rohan, don't get so upset. Calm down and think about what you're saying."

"I don't have to think about nothing! She should have thought about that shit before she called over here with that foolishness. As far as I'm concern, that bitch is about to be pushing up daisies. She acts like she don't know who the fuck she was talking to."

"Baby, please, relax for a minute." Michelle tried placing her hand on his shoulders and reasoning with him, but he was not trying to hear it.

"Michelle, what part do you not understand? The girl witnessed me kill three people and she knows how much I hate snitches and want them dead. That bitch could place me back on death row. Can you understand that much of what I'm saying? It's really nothing to talk about other than how we are going to go about doing it." He looked her square in the eyes with a serious attitude.

Michelle returned the stare as if he was going too far this time. She knew he was for real, but was not willing to accept it. "Wha—what do you mean?" she asked with puzzled, puppy-dog eyes. Michelle already knew what he was thinking, which is why he came straight out with it.

"I want you to kill her for me, 'chell."

"What?" Her mouth nearly dropped to the ground. "I'm not doing shit like that to my best friend," she began to protest at the thought of Robin being murdered, especially by her.

*   *   *

Meanwhile, Robin was not taking any chances on Gangsta Jake coming out to Brooklyn, knocking her off or her parents. The following day, she arranged for her family and her to temporarily relocate. She knew Gangsta Jake would hunt them down if they did not make a move. She fully understood he meant business and took all safety precautions to save the lives of her parents and herself.

It took a little white lie to convince her parents to leave their home of forty years, but eventually they agreed. Robin led them to believe their house had been selected for a free home makeover, which required them to evacuate immediately. They both were surprised and went along with Robin's tall tale. Since they owned a vacation home in Miami, once they decided to leave, the move was easily done.

That very same day, Robin and her parents packed their bags and were on their way to Miami. Every mile she drove away from Brooklyn made her feel that much better. Somehow, she had to tell her parents the truth about their sudden departure, but she did not have the courage at the moment. She prayed to herself that she was making the right move and chose to deal with the situation at a later date.

* * *

Gangsta Jake explored the possibility of Robin telling on him and concluded that no matter what, she had to die. Two hours of talking to Michelle assured him that she would not have the audacity to kill her longtime friend. Michelle was head over heels for him and up until that point, had done everything he asked of her. But she drew the line when it came to Robin's well-being.

"Rohan, don't be coming at me like that! That's just like me asking you to do that to your homeboy, Horsehead, or Young Lad, or someone you love. I ain't doing nothing like that for you or nobody else."

"You right, baby. I don't know what came over me." Another plan flashed in his mind. "My bad for coming at you like that. Come here."

They hugged, and she forgave him once again. But little did she know, he was not letting Robin off the hook that easy. He did not take her verbal assault lightly. He viewed it as a breaking point in her decision to go to the authorities and point a finger at him. He regretted not killing her back when he killed Lil' Papa, Terra, and their housekeeper. He did not feel safe with her having the key to his freedom.

He slipped his cell phone inside his pocket and went into the restroom. Gangsta Jake was starting to become paranoid. So much, that he did not feel comfortable with staying at the apartment he and Michelle called home. He constantly thoughts of the police rushing inside their apartment and gunning both of them down. To avoid his irrational feelings, he and Michelle checked into a motel near Venice Beach.

"We'll have our furniture moved to storage in a couple of days," Michelle said, sitting on the hotel bed with a slight pout attached to her face. "Why do we have to move? I like our little apartment. Robin is not going to tell on us. I know her. She wouldn't do that to us."

"Well, I'm not taking any chances," he stubbornly stated.

"So how long are we going to stay here?"

"Not forever; just long enough to find another apartment. The next spot we find, I don't want nobody knowing where it is. Do you understand?"

She nodded her head indicating she did.

"What about your homeboys in prison and the ones on the street?" she sarcastically asked. "How are they going to get in contact with you?"

"Go to the post office and get us a P.O. box. They can write me like that, or hit me on my cell phone. Besides your girl, Robin, no telling who might be willing to sell me out for that $100,000 reward on my head. We have to start playing this thing extra careful now."

21

The Chase Is On

Four days after the press conference and less than twenty-four hours following his decision to abandon their apartment, the LAPD, ATF, and a team of FBI agents raided their Inglewood apartment trying to apprehend him. Gangsta Jake's hunch was correct. Someone had spilled the beans on him.

The team of twenty-five officers showed up at 6:45 a.m., fully prepared to take down the person who they believed was the vicious serial killer. The crew of mostly white officers wore all black, ninja-style jump suits, armed with pistols on their sides and submachine guns in their hands. A few team members made wagers on which officer would kill their suspect. They were awfully upset when they discovered that no one was inside the apartment. After interviewing several of Gangsta Jake's neighbors, they realized that a female also stayed at the apartment with the suspect. All the neighbors were very shocked to find out a possible serial killer had lived among them.

"Oh, my God," said a 26-year-old white girl with freckles on her face and who thought that Gangsta Jake was the most handsome and articulate black man she had ever spoken to. She could not believe the allegations against him.

"He and I engaged in a two or three-minute conversation just the other day," she told a news reporter who was covering the story. "He stopped to talk to me in this very spot," Sally continued as she pointed at the ground below her. "At that time, he explained to me how he busted his leg up in a bad car accident. I am really amazed," she said, looking the reporter in the eyes, totally flabbergasted.

Detective Hardiman and Detective Freeman walked outside of Gangsta Jake's apartment with frustration written on their faces. The detectives were hoping the tip they received the day before would have put an end to their murder investigation. The person who called in on Gangsta Jake was not all that concerned with the reward money. That person was more interested in personal gratification.

The detectives' investigation was starting to become fruitful as the days went by. Although they did not arrest their prime suspect, thanks to their informant, they were able to gain a positive identification of the person they had reason to believe was their killer. At the couple's apartment, they discovered several shoes that matched the footprint left behind by the perpetrator. They also found several boxes of .44 bullets, the same caliber of weapon used by the serial killer. Furthermore, photographs of Gangsta Jake and Michelle could be found throughout the one-bedroom apartment. The day turned out to be bittersweet for the homicide detectives. Although they did not have their killer/killers in custody, they were convinced that they were on the right track.

As Gangsta Jake and Michelle laid up in a motel room on La Brea and Jefferson, the police were shaking down their apartment like a prison cell. Little did they know, they had been exposed and were in some deep shit. Before the detectives went to their residence, they were well aware of Gangsta Jake's killing spree and his motive for doing so.

Before the raid took place, they parked down the street near the couple's apartment and flipped through LAPD files. The information obtained confirmed that the victims had all testified in the trials of some of Los Angeles' most hardcore gangbangers. The information given to them turned out to be credible, which made them feel so relieved. Since no information was given on Michelle connecting her to the murders, she was only sought for questioning in the investigation of her boyfriend's whereabouts.

*　　*　　*

"Michelle, hand me that remote control on the table."

"What channel do you want it on?" she asked. Instead of handing the remote to him, she flipped the channel on her own.

"Turn to the news," he said as he slowly stood himself up and hopped on one leg to the nearby bathroom.

Michelle slowly flipped from channel to channel before finally stopping on the news at noon. The two photos depicted on the television screen made her rub her eyes and question whether or not she was having a bad dream. After pinching her arm, she was satisfied that she was not. The next thing she did was run to the restroom and inform Gangsta Jake of the broadcast.

He immediately cut short picking at a bump on his face and with the help of Michelle, made his way to the television. Once there, he saw the TV camera pointed at the front entrance of their apartment. The previously recorded broadcast showed SWAT officers walking to and from their apartment, accompanied by several detectives. Two of them held several bags of evidence linking Gangsta Jake to several murders. All he could think about was Robin selling him out.

"I told you about that hoe, didn't I?" he pointed his index finger at Michelle's face. "I knew that scandalous bitch would drop a dime on us. So I guess you still don't want to go out there and smoke that snitch bitch, do you?"

Michelle looked befuddled. She didn't know what to say; therefore, she did not say a word.

A news anchor spoke to Detective Freeman, who explained that Rohan J. Lemon, also known as Gangster Jake, was wanted for the execution-style murders of at least thirteen informants throughout the Los Angeles area.

Every snitch in the city had chills going up their spines when it was revealed that someone was going around slaying their kind. A few informants even called the prosecutor for whom they testified and requested to be placed under protective custody.

"Here," Gangsta Jake gave Michelle the phone. "Call Robin and see what she has to say for herself."

Curious to know as well, Michelle dialed Robin's home phone with the tip of one of her freshly polished fingernails. The phone rang twice before a recording came on, requesting that the caller leave a message at the tone.

"Her answering service is on."

"Call over to her mother house."

"Rohan, let's not involve her parents in this."

"Just do what the hell I said." His lips turned up. Gangsta Jake was not trying to hear what she was saying. He did not have any pity for anyone who, he felt, played games with his freedom. Against her judgment, she reluctantly did as he asked of her.

"The answering service came on also," she turned to him and said.

They're on the run, came to his head without concluding anything else. *The homies could not have made it out there that quick and handled their business,* he thought.

One hour after hanging up the phone with Robin, Gangsta Jake had called Horsehead and arranged that he and Lil' Too Cool drive out to Brooklyn and kill Robin and her parents. He had enough trust in the two to put them on that type of mission. They both were given five thousand apiece and an all-expense paid trip to put an end to what he viewed as a threat to his freedom. As much love as the two had for him, they would have killed the three for nothing.

"What are you thinking about, honey?" Michelle wondered and finally asked him.

"My next move."

In the meantime, Rachel called Michelle's cell phone after receiving a call from her boyfriend, telling her that Michelle's picture was on the news only minutes ago. Rachel was worried to death after hearing the news. Two seconds after hanging up the phone with Eddie, Rachel made the fastest call she ever made in her life.

"Hello."

"Michelle! Eddie told me you were on the news! Girl, what's going on with you? Is everything okay? Where are you?" Rachel was very afraid for her little sister and that fear could be heard in her voice.

"I'm okay."

Gangsta Jake looked at her in the eyes as if he were coaching her through something.

"Yeah, I saw my picture on the news too. I don't know what they are referring to. It's a bunch of lies."

"He said your boyfriend is wanted for killing some people, and they also want to talk to you about finding him or something like that."

"It's all a lie," are the only words Michelle was able to muster up.

"So where are you? Let me come and get you, so we can go to the police station and straighten this thing out. Grandma is sitting right here, worried to death about you. The police came to your apartment, but you were not there. Michelle, I'll be right there. Give me the address where you are."

"Rachel, I'm not going to no police station. They might try to do something to me." The guilt from committing the murders was starting to kick in.

A young detective by the name of Detective Steven Small listened in on the conversation between Michelle and Rachel. Once Michelle's identity was known, Detective Hardiman had gone to Judge Taylor and requested to set up a wiretap at her last known residence. He was just as eager to know the whereabouts of Michelle as Rachel was.

"Rachel, me and Rohan are going to work things out on our own." Hearing the name Rohan caused a sense of alertness. Both Rachel and Detective Small keyed in closer to her conversation.

"Rohan and I are going to lay low for a couple of days. Tell Grandma not to worry and that everything is okay."

"She and I can't help but to worry about you with your picture all over the news."

Gangsta Jake gave her the "cut her off signal" by waving his hand underneath his throat.

"Rachel, I have to go. I'll give you a call later," Michelle quickly said before hanging up the phone in her sister's face. She did not permit Rachel the opportunity to say goodbye, nor allow her granny to speak to her. Michelle clearly heard her grandma's request in the background. Michelle was at the point of no return.

Gangsta Jake had her under his command and in an extremely dangerous situation. He was definitely not the type of guy you would take home to meet your parents. Had Michelle listened to Robin back when she decided to stay in Los Angeles and leave her life in Brooklyn behind, she would not have the problems she was faced with today. If she could turn back the hands of time, she would have. But since she could not, she thought about the situation, cried for a little while, and decided that all she could do was go with the flow. Michelle understood that she was too deep in the game to walk away like nothing had ever happened. Too many people's lives were lost due to her bad choices. Chasing a piece of dick turned out to be a costly mistake.

Robin had called over to Michelle's grandma's house and had a long conversation with Rachel about Michelle, of course.

"Rachel, I've tried talking to her over and over, but she's like a brick wall when it comes to being with him. She will not listen to a word I have to say."

"Do you think he's really responsible for what the police are suggesting? They claim he killed more than a dozen people."

"I wouldn't doubt it. You know he served twelve years for killing some little girl in a drive-by shooting. I assure you that that nigga is capable of doing that and more."

"He went to prison for killing a child?" Rachel asked with emphasis on the word "child."

"Yeah, and Michelle stayed down with that low-life ass nigga for most of the time he was there."

"How could she be with someone like that?"

"I can't call it, Rachel. I don't see what's so great about him that would have her so caught up like this. Good looks come a dime a dozen."

"She seemed to be afraid when I talked to her. Do you think she's being held against her will?"

"I doubt it. As stupid as he is, I don't believe he would harm her like that. He did slap Michelle once before, though. Just to be totally honest, I don't put nothing past a person like him. One minute he seems to be okay, and the next he's doing something stupid. I don't trust him as far as I can see his scandalous ass."

"When I spoke to her this afternoon, she would not tell me where she was. So, do you have any idea where they are? I want her ass home. Me and grandma are going to have a nervous breakdown if we don't get her away from that crazy man."

The young detective homed in, hoping to get a location, but came up short.

"I'll give her a call and see if I can talk her into going home where she needs to be."

Seconds after hanging up with Rachel, Robin made an attempt to call Michelle's cell phone. But at Gangsta Jake's request, Michelle had changed her phone number and trimmed down her hair into a short, Halle Berry-style haircut.

He and Michelle went under the radar. From then on, only certain people would be able to contact them.

*   *   *

As expected, Horsehead came back from Brooklyn and notified Gangsta Jake that Robin and her parents were nowhere to be found. Thanks to Robin not having an inch of trust in Gangsta Jake, she and her folks were blessed to survive what he had in store for them.

"Damn, young homey, I sure hate to see you in the mix like this," Horsehead told Gangsta Jake as he drove the two of them down the 91 Freeway.

"Get on the Harbor Freeway," Gangsta Jake told Horsehead as they approached the Harbor Freeway interchange. Gangsta Jake did not seem to be worried about the police on his tracks at that moment.

"Where are we heading? To the hood?" Horsehead asked since they were heading in the direction of their neighborhood.

"Yeah."

"For what? You need to be lying low and out of the way."

"I am."

"Well, why are we heading to the hood?"

"To get some weed. I been out for a couple days."

"Some weed? Fuck some weed. I got a wet one right here. Are you trying to get high or what? This shit will have you feeling like you smoked twenty joints, especially after the little pinheads you smoke."

"I haven't smoked PCP since back in the days."

"I damn sure can't tell, crazy as you are."

"Hand me that shit." Gangsta Jake grabbed the sherm stick and placed it up to the car lighter, then to his lips. After hitting it once, he leaned out the window and spit a wad of saliva out of his mouth. The mixture of chemicals tasted so bad, he only hit it two times.

"Now I remember why I stopped smoking this bullshit. This shit is nasty as fuck," he spit again and gave the sherm stick to Horsehead.

"Let me show you how to hit this wet daddy, baby boy." Horsehead hit it once, inhaled it, and blew the smoke out real quick. He then repeated the same thing two more times.

Sixty seconds was all it took for the PCP to circulate throughout Gangsta Jake's body and affect his brain. The two hitter-quitter had him off balance. He did not know whether he was going or coming. His speech became slurred and the thought of killing people filled his mind.

Horsehead was also high out of his mind, but by being a seasoned PCP smoker, he was able to control his high much better.

"Nigga, what the fuck are you doing?" Horsehead asked when he turned to his right and saw Gangsta Jake cocking and uncocking the hammer of his .44 over and over again in slow motion.

"Damn, nigga, you only hit that shit two times," dragged out of Horsehead's mouth also in slow motion. Every word being said and action being taken was perceived to be slower than it actually was.

"Give me the pistol," Horsehead said, grabbing it out of Gangsta Jake's hand before he did something crazy like shoot at someone on the freeway—or worse—shoot Horsehead on an accident.

"Cuzz, give me my strap," Gangsta Jake requested in a low pitch.

When Horsehead refused, he attempted to grab the steering wheel while they were driving at fifty-five miles an hour. Luckily, Horsehead anticipated him doing something stupid like that and was able to fight off the attack.

Horsehead pulled off the freeway shoulder as fast as he could. With his foot on the brake, he and Gangsta Jake tussled with one another for a few minutes. "Stop tripping, homeboy!" said Horsehead as he tried to restrain Gangsta Jake's incredible strength. Once he realized he could not do so, he managed to slip out of the headlock he was twisted in.

Gangsta Jake was so high, he had no control or knowledge of his actions. Horsehead realized the PCP had taken over his homey's mind and decided to wrestle with him for a few minutes. When Gangsta Jake's grip started to get too tight around him, he found a way to free himself and jumped out of the car. People driving by saw the commotion and blew their horns in disapproval. To display his sentiments, he gave up the middle finger to every car that passed as he walked over to Gangsta Jake on the passenger side of the vehicle. Tired and gasping for air (now that the door was between the two), he was able to communicate his thoughts more effectively.

"Dawg, you need to calm the fuck down before we both go to jail." He caught his breath and continued, "I know you hear all these damn people blowing their horns at us. If you keep messing around, the police are eventually going to roll up and wonder what the hell is going on."

Gangsta Jake looked at him and turned back around like some type of animal with a brain the size of a peanut. His thought patterns were on pause as Horsehead tried to talk some sense into him. "Homey, you're wanted for murders up the ass, and this is how you're carrying it. We have to get the hell away from here. When I jump back in the car, don't come at me with that bullshit." Still Gangsta Jake did not say a word.

"Do you hear me, cuzz?" Horsehead pushed him by his shoulders. "Gangsta! Gangsta! I'm serious as fuck! Homeboy?"

"What?" His level of high dropped a notch, enough to, at least, think for himself and say a word or two.

"Are you ready to stop playing these games?" Horsehead was getting fed up. Gangsta Jake started laughing at the sight of seeing him upset, which was a rare occasion for his big homey. He is normally full of laughs, but due to all the trouble Gangsta Jake was in, he did not lose sight of the possibility of the police driving up and ending his career in the free world.

"Let's roll, big homey," Gangsta Jake told him as he laid his head back and realized how dumb he was behaving. His high temporarily faded his problems away, but they were obviously not gone forever.

Once Horsehead exited the freeway at the Slauson off-ramp and made his way over to the park in their neighborhood, the police presence could be felt. Three cars of the gang unit task force were parked next to one another. They were conducting a search on six of Gangsta Jake's homeboys. Before the police arrived, all six of them were enjoying three forty-ounce bottles of cold beer; once the police arrived, the cops spitefully poured the drink onto the concrete.

"Where in the fuck is Gangsta Jake?" one of the CRASH officers asked Bad Luck, as he stood directly behind him and squeezed Bad Luck's fingers that were interlocked together over his head.

"Ouch! I don't know, man. He hasn't been around here in months."

"I'm not your fucking man! You refer to me as officer or sir, do you understand me?" the black, slightly heavyset officer said as he squeezed his fingers harder.

"Oucchhh! Yes, I understand you, sir," Bad Luck let the officers know as he twisted up his boyish, freckled face. He was hot and pictured himself blasting on the cop who was causing his discomfort.

"Look at that shit. The hell with some weed. I'm getting you the fuck out of here," Horsehead said, pointing at what he saw as they drove by the liquor store from a distance. "They're sweating the shit out the homies. I already knew the hood would be hot as July by them looking for you."

"Fuck them mark-ass police. I'll bust on their bitch asses. Hand me my heat. I'll show you what I'm made of."

"Yeah, right! You must be crazier than a bag of baldhead, basehead bitches, if you think you're going to be doing that foolishness out of my hooptie. I see that you're still too high. Let's swing by the supermarket and get you some milk to drink. The milk will bring your high down a little more, because you got to be on one if you think I'm about to be in the mix of that episode. Ten years ago, I would have been down for the cause, but this ain't ten years ago."

Slouched down low in his car seat, Gangsta Jake looked at Horsehead, then toward the police they were driving away from. As the two gained distance from the law, Gangsta Jake held his extended arm out the window as if he was shooting a gun at the team of officers.

"Aw, yeah, let me hurry up and get you back to your motel, chief. I see you done went plum crazy. You lucky none of them tobacco-chewing rednecks saw you doing that dumb shit. I'm not with drawing myself into a shootout with police and getting killed. I enjoy being among the living, and free, I might add. I don't know about you, but I don't have time to be sitting in a jail cell, kicking war stories about back in the days, while drinking on some hot coffee and sharing a cigarette with two or three of the homies. Nigga, I got kids to raise. I ain't got time for this bullshit you're taking me through."

"Fuck the one time! I can't stand their police asses," Gangsta Jake told Horsehead, gaining back some more of his faculties.

"Yeah, I'm with all that too. I can't stand them either, but I'm not stupid enough to think I can win a gun battle with them."

"Cuzz, you done got soft in your old age," Gangsta Jake said.

"Yeah, I'll go for all that. I'll be soft, square, or whatever you want me to be. You know what they say, 'sticks and stones can break my bones, but names will never hurt me.' Go ahead and call me what you want to call me. Just call me a free man when you get through."

"You wasn't talking like this when I gave you and the homey that money to go to Brooklyn and kill that hoe and her folks," he sarcastically shot at Horsehead, who could care less about what Gangsta Jake was saying.

"That was light shit. They wasn't going to be shooting back like the police would," replied Horsehead.

"So what are you saying? You ain't a gunslinger anymore? I thought you were a rider for life."

"For life? All that shit sounded slick when I was a youngster, but now that I'm a little older and wiser, I don't think like that."

"Whatever! It's on like Donkey Kong with me. This shit don't stop until the casket drop. I'ma be a rider 'til I die."

"Go on with yo bad self. You seem to have it all figured out," Horsehead joked sarcastically.

"Cuzz, take me back to my bitch!"

"Fasten your seat belt, nigga. We're on our way."

22

A Bad Feeling

A few months went by and Gangsta Jake determined it was time to remove the cast from his leg on his own. He certainly was not going to a doctor's office and take the chance of being recognized by someone who was familiar with his situation. Every move he made was a calculated step to maintain his freedom.

He and Michelle rarely went outside during the day. Often, they would stay in their apartment for days without considering stepping one foot outdoors. No matter how much shit he and Horsehead talked to one another, they had too much love to let anything or any situation come between them. To demonstrate his continuous loyalty toward Horsehead, he and Michelle moved into a one-bedroom apartment only one building away from Horsehead so they would have someone to aid them.

Unlike the first apartment they lived in, which felt more like a home because of all the nice furniture and cozy accommodations, this apartment looked more like an insurgent's hideout. They slept in a sleeping bag, stored food in a portable ice box, and their television sat on the carpet next a new HK assault rifle.

With a pair of wire cutters, Gangsta Jake was able to chip at the cast until he accomplished his mission. Once it was removed, he stood on both feet to assess his recovery. The first step he took caused some discomfort to his right hip. His straight walk was no longer the same. He now depended on a slight limp to complete his every motion. As he walked back and forth throughout his small apartment, he turned his right cheek up to subside some of his pain.

"How does it feel, baby?" Michelle asked with a happy, but cautious look. She actually had the look of a parent happy to see her kid walk for the first time, praying he took another step before he fell.

"I'm, I'm straight." She could see the hurt in his face, but the thrill as well. He was ready to get back in the mix of things. He had a mission to complete and felt good to be taking a step toward that direction. A few minutes on his feet placed a full smile on his face.

"Yeah!" Both of his hands went into the air in a victory position. The first thing he walked to after his initial steps was the list of informants. He stashed the list inside the tape deck of a ghetto blaster. "It ain't over," he spoke to the paper as he bopped his head to the music from the tape deck he just turned on. "I can't wait to kill another one of you fags. Y'all thought the police were going to scare me off, didn't y'all?"

"There you go. Boy, you can barely walk and you're already talking about killing someone."

"Don't be complaining too much. You're the one who's about to take on my position."

"What? Baby, why can't we just chill out for a little while longer?"

"We've already wasted enough time as it is."

"You always win our arguments. Can I win one for a change?"

"Yeah, you can, but not this one. I've already let these cowards live long enough," he pointed at the list, which had over a dozen names crossed out as a result his unyielding hatred toward stoolpigeons.

After a long conversation, Michelle, as usual, put her defenses down and focused her mind on doing what he asked of her. Her adrenalin flowed the way it always did prior to committing a murder. However, by her not killing anyone in over three months, she was more nervous than normal. Her insides felt the same way they did when she committed her first murder, and she did not like the feeling. As she got dressed, she attempted to talk herself out of the situation once again.

"Baby, I'm going to be honest with you," she looked at him in the eyes. Michelle was literally dressed to kill. She had on her makeup, Gangsta Jake's gun secured in her handbag, and a large hat covering her head and part of her face. To accompany her sophisticated but casual look, Michelle had on some of the nicest smelling perfume Gangsta Jake had ever smelled.

"Damn, you smell good, baby. What is that you have on?" He smelled and kissed her on the neck, ignoring her statement of being honest with him.

"Rohan, did you not hear me?"

"Yeah, I heard you, baby, but as you can see, I'm trying to smell your sweet self." He tickled her in an attempt to change the subject. She laughed for a few seconds, but still had the same feeling inside. He knew something was bothering her, but his mind was set on dealing with it once they returned. His agenda was set, and he did not want to interrupt it.

"Quit it, baby, I'm serious." Michelle withdrew her body away from his.

"All right, what is it?" he finally gave in enough to at least hear her out.

"I don't want to do this today. I'm not feeling it."

"Come on, baby. How many times have you felt like this before and felt better after the fact?"

"It's not like that. I have a different feeling this time. I feel sick. I threw up two times last night while you were sleeping like a baby."

"Sick?"

"Yeah, sick."

"Aw, come on, Michelle. You're really stunting now. Vamonos!"

"What? What does that mean?"

"That means, 'lets's go' in Spanish, and 'let's do it moving' in our language. So let's do it moving."

Against her inner feelings, Michelle grabbed her handbag with the .44 stuffed inside, put on a quarter-length leather jacket, and walked toward the front door following Gangsta Jake's lead.

Their victim was very familiar with the fact that someone was going around killing people who had the same profile as he. Ever since Ernest Fuller viewed the news and came to realize the killer's motive, he maintained a low-profile lifestyle. No one from his neighborhood was aware of the fact that he testified at the trial of Young Charley from the Thirty Pirus, a Blood set on the eastside. By Charley being a Blood and Ernest Fuller being a Crip, he felt his actions were justified. In actuality, he knew he was going against the code of the street when he let the homicide detectives cross him into taking the stand against Young Charley in exchange for immunity in the case of a simple possession of cocaine charge. When he witnessed Charley kill his homeboy in a gang rivalry shooting, he did not retaliate like most gangbangers did when their opposition got out on them. Instead, he decided to work with the homicide detectives, who sweated him a few times for information about the murder.

Ernest Fuller caved in to the interrogation of the detectives after a few visits, and Gangsta Jake did not plan on letting him slide with that. He did not care about the circumstances of the case, or the fact that Charley was a Blood. His primary concern was the fact that Ernest Fuller went against the grain and snitched on someone he came to have a lot of love and respect for throughout the years of their incarceration together. Ernest Fuller was a dead man walking as far as Gangsta Jake was concerned. How hard or soft he may have been as a gangbanger was irrelevant. Once he crossed the line and became a snitch, he was open game for a killing.

"Michelle, there he goes right there," Gangsta Jake told her as they sat three houses away from Ernest Fuller's house. The two had barely pulled up and parked the van they were in when he noticed Ernest. He had planned on having Michelle walk up, knock on the door, and spray Ernest Fuller with bullets to the face like most of his other victims. However, due to Ernest walking out of his house and jumping inside his car so fast, Gangsta Jake was forced to change his plan of execution.

"What's next, Rohan?"

"We're going to follow him and catch him slipping in traffic."

"Are you sure that's him?"

"I told you, he and I went to school together back in the days. I know that busta's walk a mile away. Trust me, that's him."

Michelle had a bad headache and was hoping he would just call the whole thing off, but Gangsta Jake was not into putting things off very often. His motto was, if it's going down, let's get it over with. If he had anything to do with it, Ernest Fuller's days on this earth would be limited to minutes, not years.

Gangsta Jake trailed him around like a groupie on a rap superstar. Every corner he turned, they turned. The two drove so close to Ernest Fuller that he eventually looked through his rearview mirror and noticed someone following him. His impulse caused him to swing his neck around to confirm his suspicions. When he looked back and recognized the two as being the same couple on television, he damn near pissed in his pants. Ernest Fuller swung his head back straight and pretended he was not being trailed.

"Rohan, I told you, we're too close to him. He looked back and saw us."

By Gangsta Jake looking through his own rearview at the same time as the intended victim, he did not get to see Ernest Fuller's sudden movement.

"He didn't look back at us! You're scared and tripping!"

"Baby, I'm not tripping! He did look back. You were looking somewhere else at the time."

"Are you sure?"

"Yes, I'm sure. The muthafucka turned around, facing us, then turned back around real quick, like he noticed us trailing him."

Ernest Fuller continued to drive down Sunset Boulevard, hoping that his mind was playing tricks on him. In case it was not, he reached under his jacket and pulled out a chrome 9mm handgun.

"Jump in the back of the van and hand me that assault rifle. Something told me to bring my HK. I'm not about to be playing no games with this rat!" he told Michelle as he looked out his side and rearview mirrors going 35mph.

"So what do you plan on doing, driving up and shooting him with this?" Michelle gave him the assault rifle. He then sat it across his lap.

"When I pull up on the side of him, all I want you to do is lean back in your seat. I'll handle it from there."

At the very next red light, Gangsta Jake drove up alongside the Caprice Classic Ernest Fuller was driving and aimed the HK directly at him. As instructed, Michelle leaned back in her seat. To bring herself some comfort, she gripped the .44 in her hand.

Pow! Pow! Gangsta Jake got off only two shots before the HK, which he continued to squeeze the trigger, jammed on him. Had Ernest Fuller not seen the attack coming, he wouldn't have had time to react and probably would have experienced his life flashing before him as his assailants sped off in traffic. Luckily for him, the first shot missed, and the second only grazed the tip of his nose.

Without thinking, Michelle and Ernest Fuller raised their guns and began letting off shots at the exact same time. Neither bowed down until their last shot was fired. The sudden exchange of gunfire caused everyone in sight to hit the ground and mind the concrete before them. Bullets flying in several directions evoked panic and fear among the people, who took refuge on the ground and behind parked cars. A thirty-two-year-old woman shielded her two children that lay beneath her oversized body. After the gunshots ended, the two kids were fine, but their mother took a stray bullet to the back of the head.

"Oh, my God! Someone call an ambulance!" a sixty-two-year-old woman screamed out at the sight of seeing the short, Mexican lady's lifeless body on top of her two beautiful children, with blood running out the back of her head. A tear came to the old black lady's right eye when she thought about the two kids growing up without a mother, the same way she did.

Gangsta Jake looked over at Michelle, and then punched the gas pedal running through the red light before him. Ernest Fuller was dead as a doorknob, thanks to Michelle's quick reaction. However, his death did not come without a cost. Michelle had also been hit, and bad. Blood was running out of her ear due to the bullet that caught her in the neck.

"Michelle! Michelle!" Gangsta Jake raised her slumped body while driving away from the crime scene. "Damn!" he banged the dashboard with the right side of his fist. "'chell, say something to me, goddamn it!" His face turned up, expressing his anger and fear of losing her.

Michelle struggled with her words from being so weak. "Rohan . . ." she mumbled in a feeble voice.

"Save your energy, baby. We're on our way to the hospital. You'll be fine," he told her as he put his arms around her neck and pulled her closer to him.

Michelle managed to muster up enough strength to place her left hand over the other gunshot wound in her right side. "I told you . . ." she choked over her words. "I told you I had a bad feeling about today . . ." her words came out slow, but meaningful. "Baby . . ." Michelle whispered.

"What, Michelle?" he responded, full of energy and hatred in his heart from the way things turned out.

"Please, don't let me die," she said as she closed her eyes and tried to relax. Michelle began to cry and go into shock as Gangsta Jake pulled up to the emergency room entrance. Her blood dripped on the van floor as he lifted her body and made his way through the parking lot.

Two ambulance workers who had just dropped off a patient saw Gangsta Jake fast approaching with Michelle in his arms. They volunteered to help transport her from the parking lot to the emergency room.

The operating room door was as far as he was allowed to enter. Two doctors made sure Michelle was breathing before hooking her up to an IV and a heart monitor. A bright, overhead light made it possible for the operating crew to assess her wounds. Her chest had to be cut open in order to remove the bullet that lodged inches away from her heart. As the doctors worked feverishly to save Michelle's life, Gangsta Jake paced the lobby area, hoping they would revive her before the police showed up asking questions.

Moments after entering the operating room, Michelle's blood pressure began to drop and the doctors found themselves losing her. She fought death like any other person in her position would have. Every time her consciousness faded out, she tried hard as she as she could to fade it back in. Michelle was in the biggest fight of her life, and knew it. All the battles she's ever been in were no comparison to the one she faced at this very moment. If she was blessed to make it through her situation alive, the warnings Robin and Rachel gave her would not be taken lightly. She prayed to God as she tried to focus on her breathing and opening her eyes. The word "Help" went through her mind, but not through her mouth, based on the small amount of strength she had in her body. Her flinching was a clear indicator that she was trying to hang onto the little life she possessed.

Seeing her efforts caused the doctors to fight even harder for her. They did everything possible to save her; however, no matter how much Michelle or the doctors believed she could survive, it just was not going to happen. Five minutes after placing her limp body onto the operating table, Michelle was dead. She realized the way she was living would ultimately lead to her own destruction, but never did anything to change her ways.

Gangsta Jake knew what time it was when he looked up and saw the hospital chaplin walking directly toward him. His emotions overcame him when he was officially notified that she did not pull through. He now regretted putting her on the line the way he did. If he could do it all over, he would, but since he could not, all he could do is move forward with a vengeance.

"Muthafucka!" he told himself as his right fist tightened up at the thought of Michelle being out of his world forever. As much as he hated to leave her, he had to or else it would be too late.

Before making his departure, he quickly made his way to the back of the hospital and said goodbye to the love of his life. The one security guard on hand tried to stop him, but Gangsta Jake was not having it. He ran by him like he was nowhere in sight.

"Hey, what's going on? Who let him in here?" Doctor Dash looked up and asked the security guard trailing behind Gangsta Jake.

"I tried to stop him, but he would not listen to me, doctor."

Gangsta Jake did not say one word. His undivided attention was on Michelle, whose body laid on the operating table.

"Damn, baby, I'm sorry," came out of his mouth moments after leaning over her body and placing her face in the palm of his hands. Blood was everywhere, but it did not bother him.

The white security guard did not like the scene, which caused him to walk in the direction of the telephone in order to call for backup. When Gangsta Jake recognized his intentions, he swiftly made his way to the guard, who was not armed.

"What the fuck are you about to do?" he asked the guard with a cold look in his eye.

Since the guard was not armed, there was little he could do to control the situation. The guard, along with the two doctors on hand, became very frightened at his threatening voice. Instead of making his call for help, the security guard stopped in his tracks.

"Well, if you're not going to do it, I will. I'm calling the authorities to get this man removed from here," Doctor Dash stated as he attempted to snatch the receiver out of the guard's hand.

As far as Gangsta Jake was concerned, enough warnings were given. He walked over to the physician, grabbed him by the collar, and bitched-slapped him twice. The others present were thoroughly intimidated.

"Don't you see I'm trying to say goodbye to my girl before I leave? Shut the hell up, and don't fuck with me right now!" he fiercely stated while locking eyes with the doctor and everyone else, all, of whom, had suddenly huddled up against one another. Doctor Dash silently cried, while holding his busted nose and looking in a big mirror on the wall. The security guard recognized Gangsta Jake from the local news and became scared five times over.

"Yes, sir, Mr. Lemon," slipped out of the security guard's mouth, a man who looked like he was barely old enough to be out of high school.

"Who the fuck did you call me? How the hell do you know my name?" he pressed. It only took him a few seconds to realize the guard had to know him from watching the news. The two doctors and nurse also wondered where the guard knew the strange intruder from.

"Punk-ass security guard! You just talked yourself into some drama. As I'm sure you already know, I don't like your kind anyway." Since Gangsta Jake was not armed with his gun due to Michelle dropping it during the shooting, he grabbed the same scalpel the doctors used to cut Michelle open. The sight of her blood on the tip of it really pissed him off and led him to going berserk.

Slash. The scalpel slit open the white kid's jugular vein. Blood went everywhere! The two doctors and nurse screamed at the sight of the violent attack that was taking place.

Gangsta Jake had to cut his visit short based on all the commotion he created. He looked over at Michelle's body one last, quick time, and then quickly dashed through the same double doors in which he entered the operating room. Judging by the loud screams behind him and the pep in Gangsta Jake's step as he exited the room, everyone outside the door knew something dramatic had occurred. Two hospital workers ran inside the room to put an end to the suspense.

"The guy who ran out of here just stabbed this guard. Call the police! Hurry! I think this guy is going to die, and we don't want to allow the murderer to get away!" Doctor Dash ordered one of his co-workers as he and the others hoisted the security guard's body onto the emergency table next to Michelle's. Their professional duties as physicians overrode any fears they may have had. Their primary concern was to save the life of their patient before them.

"Have someone from the morgue come up here and take this body down to the basement!" the other white doctor wearing round glasses and a white doctor's coat looked over his shoulder and told a nurse who ran inside the room trying to make sense of what had taken place.

"Yes, sir, Doctor Clarkson!" The nurse was frightened as hell, but complied with his demand.

When the police finally arrived, the security guard was dead, and Gangsta Jake was in traffic driving a new BMW he carjacked from a hospital employee. The flat tire on his van was the reason he abandoned his vehicle at the hospital. Thanks to Gangsta Jake, the homicide detectives had a very busy day ahead of them. The evidence found inside the van was helpful, but fruitless without the suspect.

After examining the two bodies left at the original crime scene, Detective Hardiman and Detective Freeman made their way over to the second crime scene at the hospital. Recovering the .44 at the first crime scene was a big development for the detectives. With a smoking gun, they would be able to positively tie several of the murders together by comparing bullets left at the various homicides.

A couple walking by during the shooting described the events to Detective Freeman as a scene from a violent movie. The detective tried to fully imagine the events unfolding as the witnesses relayed it to him. However, as beautiful as Michelle was, he had a hard time imagining her hanging out the window of a van, pumping slugs back and forth with Ernest Fuller.

As he examined her body at the hospital, all he could think about was putting an end to her boyfriend's killing spree. "What a wasted life," he said to himself. Michelle's beauty and age reminded him of his very own twenty-six-year-old daughter.

"You say something, Bill?" Detective Hardiman asked his partner as he looked through Michelle's pants pockets in search of some type of identification.

"No, no. Just an inside thought; nothing important."

23

Bad News Travels Fast

News reporters were all over the place once the police scanner told them that one of the possible serial killers might be dead. Reporters with their cameras were lined up at both the hospital and the original crime scene, where two bodies still lay lifeless on the ground. A young detective could be seen tracing one of the corpses with a white piece of chalk.

Mary Garcia's family was notified immediately of her death. While the media waited for the detectives to give a press conference, one reporter interviewed members of her family.

"Tears always make a good story" was the motto of the reporter who decided to give the interview.

"My name is Judy Hays from Channel 7 *Eyewitness News*. I am live at the corner of Sunset and Highland with the sister of Mary Garcia, who was caught in the crossfire of another senseless shooting that has left two people dead and possibly two more dead at a nearby hospital. Information as of now is sketchy, but we will update you as we learn more about this situation. However, in the meantime, I have with me the sister of one of the victims who were killed in this shooting.

"Silvia, I know this a difficult time for you and your family, so I really appreciate you taking time to talk to us. If you will, could you please tell us a little about your sister and why she was walking down this street during the time of incident?"

"She was one of the kindest people in the world, who would do anything for anybody." The tears that the reporter wanted to see suddenly rolled down Silvia's face. Her husband and brother-in-law both placed their arms around her for comfort. "She did not deserve to die like that. My sister was a wonderful mother of two. When Mary was shot, all she was doing was walking her two children to school. It's not safe even to walk your kids to school these days. I hope the person who killed her burns in hell!"

"Have the police told your family any details regarding who may be responsible for her death?"

"No, they haven't said anything yet, but they promised to fill in some of the blanks here shortly," her brother-in-law, José, interjected when he saw how emotional his sister-in-law had become. Even he could not hold back the tears. He started off okay, but after awhile, he also started to cry.

Over at the hospital, detectives Hardiman and Freeman were making sure all the evidence was properly preserved. Once Michelle's identity was confirmed, Detective Freeman ordered a young detective to contact someone in her family and notify them of her death.

Since their phone taps yielded nothing, he was hoping someone from Michelle's family might be mad enough to make known the whereabouts of the man they so desperately wanted to catch.

"Hello, this is Detective Jones with the Los Angeles Police Department Homicide Division. Do you know someone by the name of Michelle Williams, ma'am?"

"Yes, she's my sister. What's the problem?" Rachel's heart began to race when the person on the phone mentioned he was from the homicide division.

"Miss, I'm sorry to be the one to inform you of this, but Michelle was killed in a shooting this morning."

"Noooooo! Noooooo!" Rachel screamed out in disbelief. "Michelle's not dead! Tell me this is a crank call. Please, don't play with me like this."

At first, Rachel did not believe the young detective. She was hoping and praying someone was playing a terrible joke on her. She knew Michelle was in bad company and understood that eventually, something bad could happen to her, but not so suddenly. She figured Michelle was smart enough to ultimately wing herself away from the bad relationship she got herself into. Unfortunately, she did not realize how much influence Gangsta Jake had over her little sister until it was too late.

"I'm very sorry about what happened to your sister. She died a little over four hours ago at a hospital in Hollywood."

"Oh, my God. I can't believe this has happened." She paused and cried for a few seconds. "I tried to convince her to come home, but she would not listen to me. Oh, my God. How am I going to tell my grandmother about this?" she wondered to herself as she calmly gasped for air.

"Miss, what did you say your name was again?"

"Rachel," she told Detective Jones in between sobs like a little girl who was left by her mom on the first day of kindergarten.

"Rachel, are you familiar with a man by the name of Rohan J. Lemon, better know as Gangster Jake, from a street gang called the Five Tray Avalons?" he asked her while looking at a photograph of Gangsta Jake inside a folder. Detectives Hardiman and Freeman compiled a file of information that consisted of photos of all the victims Gangsta Jake was suspected of killing, along with his entire criminal history and possible hideouts.

"The only thing I know about him is the fact that he was my sister's boyfriend. I only met him once."

"Do you know where they were living?"

"The place they had in Inglewood was the only place I've ever known them to live. It was the place the police raided, looking for him. After seeing the two pictured on television, I called Michelle and like I just told you, I tried to talk her into leaving him and coming home."

"What's the phone number you called her at, ma'am?"

"It's not going to do you any good. She turned the number off the very same day I talked to her."

"Rachel, as difficult as it may be, I'm going to need you or another family member to come down to the coroner's office and positively identify the body as your sister."

"Who are you talking to child? Why are you crying?" Rachel's grandma asked, very concerned about the tears running out of her eyes.

"I'll be there within the hour," she told Detective Jones before hanging up the phone.

"Granny, I have something to tell you."

"What's wrong, baby?"

Instead of beating around the bush, Rachel hit her straight with it. "Granny, Michelle is gone," she bowed her head in sadness.

"What do you mean gone? Where did she go?"

"She's dead. Someone killed her, Granny. I just hung up the phone with a detective from the LAPD. He told me she was in a gunfight with some guy."

"What?! A gunfight? Oh, Lord," Granny said before grabbing her heart like Red Foxx often did on the *Sanford & Son Show* back in the days.

"Granny, sit down," Rachel said while grabbing ahold of her arm and sitting her granny's fragile body on her plastic-covered sofa.

"Are you okay, Grandma? Wait right here while I run and get you a glass of water."

Miss Helen was sad about what happened, but up until that point, took the news very well. While she waited on Rachel to return with the glass of water, she flipped her television onto the local news. Detective Hardiman and several members of the LAPD and other law enforcement officers were conducting a press conference at the hospital. They announced to the pubic that the suspect whom they believed was responsible for killing over a dozen people had struck again.

"This time, unfortunately, not only was the serial killer's victim killed, but a mother of two as well. It is unclear as of now, but we have reason to believe the girlfriend of the killer, whom we previously sought for questioning, was also killed. Furthermore, a security guard who tried to apprehend the man we are looking for was also killed. He truly will be remembered as a hero. Before I conclude this press conference, I'll be happy to answer a few questions," Detective Hardiman said, pointing at a news reporter like he was the secretary of defense.

The cameras and all the media attention were starting to stroke his ego. He enjoyed being in the limelight, and it showed.

"What's the name of the suspect's girlfriend, and was she having a shootout with the latest victim? I am referring to the informant, not the parent of the two children or the security guard. And the man that was murdered was an informant, wasn't he?" the reporter slid in before waiting on a response.

"You said two questions and that was three," Detective Hardiman joked with the red-haired female reporter who gave him a fake smile. "Starting with the first question, her identity has not yet been confirmed, so I'll have to get back to you on that one. Regarding the next question, according to two pedestrians who witnessed the shooting, the girlfriend of the suspect did exchange gunfire with the victim. The victim has been identified as Ernest Fuller, an informant for the district attorney's office in a murder conviction. We do believe the man who was driving the van that the young woman was shooting out of is the person we all know as Rohan Lemon, a.k.a. Gangsta Jake."

"That's a damn lie. My baby ain't had no shootout. She's not that type of person," Grandma Helen shouted at the television. "Child, do hear this nonsense this man is saying about my granddaughter?" she asked Rachel as Rachel handed her a cold glass of water and wiped the sweat off of her forehead.

"Girl, this fool is breaking your grand mama's heart with this madness he's saying," she said as tears began to roll down her cheeks.

"Granny, try to stay calm."

In Grandma Helen's eyes, Michelle was not capable of doing any of the above. She was a saint in her sight. She would never fix her mind to believe that Michelle would do the things that were being said about her; nonetheless, it hurt her so much to even hear those words.

* * *

"Open cell block eight," Lieutenant Harris ordered back at San Quentin Prison. At his request, Crazy Mike's cell opened. To everyone's surprise, Crazy Mike was being escorted down the tier and on his way to an attorney's visit.

"Crazy Mike, where are you going, old head?" Warlock yelled down the tier, looking through a mirror he held in the palm of his hand.

"I'm not sure, youngster!" he yelled back in his deep, scratchy voice.

"You have an attorney visit, sir," a regular guard walking in the rear of Crazy Mike stated.

"Attorney?" Dre said to Young Lad, as the two lay in their bunk beds. "He don't have no lawyer. Hell, I'm his lawyer," Young Lad spoke out, facing the wall his bed was mounted to. Young Lad thought about the sudden move Crazy Mike was making and abruptly drew back the blankets on his body while hopping out of his rack.

"Crazy Mike!" he yelled out standing at his cell gate, hoping to catch him before he and the guards exited the tier. "Somebody probably plugged him up with a lawyer," Dre told Young Lad with his eyes closed as he snuggled his body underneath the three white-knitted blankets on his bed.

"Yeah, you might be right. Maybe even Gangsta Jake paid for an attorney for him. I did write to him and put him up on Crazy Mike's situation with the courts. He knows they're trying to fry Crazy Mike."

"That does sound like something he would do," Avalon Blue said after burglarizing their conversation from two cells down.

"He's a good nigga. You would think after all he's been through lately, he wouldn't have time to reach back and see to it that we're straight on this end," Half-dead told his celly 4-Ball.

"That's just how real niggas carry it. If I ever get the fuck out of this death trap, I'm looking out for all the homies too," 4-Ball said while tapping a fresh pack of non-filtered cigarettes up against the palm of his hand. It was the same pack Gangsta Jake sent to him in a package weeks earlier.

"I'll be glad when this rainstorm leaves this area. I already missed six hours of videos."

"Fuck some videos. I'm trying to see the news," Young Lad replied to Avalon Blue's remarks.

"Aw, nigga, you wasn't watching the news on the streets, were you?" Avalon Blue shot back at him.

*　　*　　*

While his homies were on death row, popping off at the mouth to one another, Gangsta Jake and Horsehead were lounging in Horsehead's apartment, smoking on a blunt Michelle rolled the day before she was killed.

"Damn, cuzz, I can't believe my girl is gone." He imagined Michelle in his mind and reflected on their past relationship.

"Young homey, I don't mean to throw it up in your face, but you drove her too hard. You should've known as hard as you were going, anything was capable of happening."

"I know, dawg, but it still hurts to lose my girl like that. If that fucking gun wouldn't have jammed, she would still be alive. She was a down-ass female. Somebody got to die behind my girl getting fucked off like that!" he said angrily. "I'm killing that nigga's mama and kids if I can get my hands on them!"

"Slow your roll, dawg! Think about what the fuck you're saying! You can't just keep going around killing people because you're upset at the world."

"Fuck that! I'm not trying to hear none of that! My bitch is dead! Somebody got to die for that! I'm not letting that shit slide." He held back a tear as he thought about what might have been going through Michelle's mind as she took her last breath.

"Young homey, you don't have nothing to prove to nobody."

"I'm not trying to prove nothing to nobody! I'm just being myself."

"And what is yourself? Who are you?"

"I'm a killer!" he shouted, in an attempt to subside his somberness.

Horsehead saw the hurt in his face and decided to fuck around with his young homey to change up the monotony "So what are you saying? You act like you get some type of charge out of killing folks. You aren't turned out on this killing shit, are you?" Horsehead laughed to himself.

"You got damn skippy I am. I get a thrill out of seeing dead snitches on the front of newspapers and the evening news."

"I feel you on the knocking off snitches part because I can't stand them either. I'm talking about smoking innocent people like the dude you just mentioned, mom and kids. Are you going to enjoy killing them?"

"What's your point, cuzz? Where are you going with this? Can I mourn my girl without hearing all this soft-ass shit, because just to keep it one hundred, I'm not trying to hear it," he told Horsehead before placing the forty ounces of beer in his hand up against his lips.

"See there, that's your problem right there. You never want to listen to nobody. You're just like an alligator—all mouth and no ears. Nigga, pass the drink! I see you ain't feeling me no way, so I'm through talking about it."

"Good! You should be. You already know I don't have good sense anyway. My girl is dead, every police in the city is looking for me, and frankly, I don't give a damn," he joked around with Horsehead while keeping his emotions in check.

"All right, clown around if you want to. That's going to be your ass in the gas chamber. I done told you that you need to get a fake passport and get the hell out the country while you have a chance."

"I thought you were finished talking."

"Yeah, you right, you right, you allllllllllways right," Horsehead put extras on the word, attempting to be funny. "And I'm always wrong."

"So what the hell are you going to do with that gee-ride in the parking stall?" was Horsehead reply to his sarcastic statement.

"What gee-ride?" Gangsta Jake said, standing up and almost falling backwards from being so intoxicated from the beer and weed in his system.

"The BMW you carjacked at the hospital."

"Fuck! I almost forgot about that car I took from that Asian lady."

"Let me have it," Horsehead suggested with the thought of selling it on the black market for five or six thousand.

"Take it, dawg. The keys should be under the mat."

"Good lookin', baby boy, I knew your wild ass was good for something."

24

The End of the Road

One week went by and the time arrived to lay Michelle's body to rest. After confirming her identity, Rachel phoned Robin and broke the bad news to her. Robin was saddened to learn what happened to her best friend. But she was even sadder to learn that not only did Michelle manage to get herself killed, but also the seven-week-old twins she held inside her stomach. The coroner's officer notified Rachel and the rest of her family that Michelle was, in fact, pregnant with twins. That discovery fully explained why Michelle had been so sick lately. If only Robin could have gotten through to Michelle, she would still have a best friend who would have been the proud parent of two kids. She thought about how the babies could have gotten Michelle on the right track.

Michelle's death hurt Robin so badly, she literally cried herself to sleep the night she was informed about what had happened. Her fears of Gangsta Jake creeping up on her at the funeral nearly stopped Robin from attending the service. However, she eventually talked herself into facing the situation head-on. Knowing that most of her and Michelle's family would be there also influenced her decision to attend. Rick wanted to tag along with Robin, but he was unable to get out of his work detail.

*   *   *

"The Lord giveth and the Lord taketh away," the heavyset preacher spoke out in a high-pitched voice as sweat ran from underneath his double chin. "This day is a somber one for us all as we celebrate the life of our little sister," he paused long enough to adjust the glasses on his face. "Let us not forget that God loves each and every one of us. He would never close one door and refuse to open another. I can see the excitement in your eyes. How many people want to talk about the Lord?" Hands raised and the crowd began to cheer him on.

"Folk always going around speaking on this and that person, gossiping about things that are not important to them, and forgetting to gossip about the Lord, the one they really need to be gossiping about. He's the one who holds your admission to heaven. Oh, you all thought I was going to stand up here with these tight gators on my feet and talk about Michelle. Michelle is cool!" the preacher jacked his slacks up like a pimp, bragging to another pimp about a new prostitute he recently came up on.

"Her destination is determined! Wherever she's going is up to her and God! We have no control over her destiny," his voice lowered as he thought out his punch line.

"But yours, yours, and yours," he pointed at several people in the audience, "you have a choice whether or not you are going to heaven or hell. Now what are *you* going to do, young brother?" Rev. Wooten said, looking at Michelle's cousin Tee Baby, from 107 Hoover Crip, straight in the eyes as he smoothly picked up his Bible and turned the podium over to one of Michelle's family members, who was about to read from the obituary. But not before saying a quick prayer.

Let us bow our heads. Heavenly Father, all praise is due to You and Your Son, Jesus Christ, our Lord and Savior. We come together today in prayer and holy reverence to praise Your holy name. Lord, I am requesting graciously for You to extend Your blessings upon all of us here today as this service goes forward. Our main focus is to comfort the family of this dearly beloved child, Michelle, who was taken away from us at such an early age. Michelle, we will all miss you for you were truly an angel and a breath of fresh air to each and every one of us here today. Lord, we thank You for the time You allowed us to spend with her. And as we move forward, we ask that You give us the strength to continue on. In Jesus' name,

Amen.

When Rev. Wooten walked away from the podium, the organ player pumped the volume up a little louder, allowing the reverend's message to sink into the souls of the audience. The funeral home on Crenshaw and Coliseum was packed with at least two hundred and fifty people. Michelle had a lot of family and friends who thought the world of her.

Once Gangsta Jake came home, she grew distant from most of them, but that did not change the love they had for her. She was an angel in all of their hearts. And that could be seen by the tears in everyone's eyes around the chapel. Seconds after the minister walked away from the podium, one of Michelle's cousins read part of her obituary.

"Michelle was born March 25, 1977, in Los Angeles, California, to James and Artess Williams," read her seventeen-year-old cousin, Karmilah, who had on a black-and-white trimmed dress. "Michelle was the second born of three kids. She received her education at Crenshaw High, Compton Community College, and later obtained her B.A. at the University of Southern California."

A few drawn-out, but quiet "What?" could be heard throughout the audience when it was said that Michelle had a bachelor's degree under her belt. A lot of people were amazed with her level of education compared to the route she chose to take in life. Mostly everyone attending her service saw her on television and knew the type of lifestyle she ultimately chose to live, based on her infatuation with a thug. At the end of the obituary reading, Robin was called to the podium to say a few words. She stood up, took a deep breath to relax, and spoke what was on her heart.

"Michelle, words cannot express what I'm feeling at this moment. Girl, I wrote you a poem, but my stupid self spilled coffee all over it this morning. You already know how clumsy I can be at times." Laughter could be heard from several people in the audience, which was a lot of comfort for Robin, who held so much pain inside her heart. "When I first heard what had happened to you, I thought it was just another bad dream I sometimes have. But after being convinced that it was not, I couldn't help but to cry the whole night through. After crying my eyes out the night before, God woke me up the following day and told me everything was under His control. He told me not to worry and that one day, it will all make sense. As much as I trust in God, it still hurts so bad to know that you're gone."

Robin paused and began to cry while a few people from the audience gave her some strength by shouting for her to be strong. The tears running down Robin's face demonstrated her pain and anger. She was very upset at Michelle for not listening to her when she constantly tried to warn her about her bad relationship. With the crowd's encouragement, Robin tried to hold back her tears and continue.

"The fun we had as kids and adults will remain in my memory forever. You taught me a lot about life, and I'll never forget you, Michelle. I love you, girl, and no matter what, you will always be in my heart."

When the funeral director noticed Robin's eulogy coming to an end, he began playing the song "Stairway to Heaven," by the O'Jays. In the middle of her last line to Michelle, Robin's heart nearly jumped out of her chest, not from the shock of losing Michelle, but from gaining a good look at the man who slid through the back door of the chapel. He was decked out in a black suit with dark sunglasses to match. Several people in the audience recognized him as well, which caused whispers throughout the building.

"We'll now begin the viewing of the body," Rev. Wooten announced, while two ushers directed the first two rows of people to have their last look at Michelle before her body was laid to rest. Robin walked off the podium, and out of fear, made her way over to her two gangbanging cousins.

"Bobby, Bobby," she grabbed hold of Fila Bob from the Pueblos Bishops.

"What's wrong, girl?"

"That nigga is here." She embraced him closer, trying to hide her entire body as if she could. Robin was so shook up, at first, she could not properly explain herself.

"Who, Robin?" Bobby asked his cousin while looking at her with a twisted face. "What are you trying to say?"

"Michelle's boyfriend. He's here, right now," she whispered loudly over the music.

Her cousin looked around to locate her fear, but could not find him. By the time his stare met eye to eye with Gangsta Jake, their turn had arrived to view Michelle's body. A thin, salt-and-pepper-haired black woman wearing white gloves placed her left hand on Robin's elbow and steered her toward the golden casket with chrome rails that would be Michelle's final resting place.

Michelle looked even more beautiful than the last time Robin saw her in Brooklyn. Her hair was absolutely gorgeous in the new Halle Berry-cut that Gangsta Jake made her get. Her dress was dark blue with gold buttons running down the middle of it. Seeing her best friend's body laying in a casket and having her worst nightmare at the top of her head was too much for Robin to bear. The pressure of the two caused her to faint.

"Look at that punk bitch," Gangsta Jake leaned over and whispered in Horsehead's ear.

"That's the female on the picture you gave me? The one you wanted knocked off in Brooklyn? Damn, baby boy, fine as she is, it would've been hard to take her down without running up in her guts first," he joked.

"I wouldn't have cared what you did to that snitch bitch as long as you killed her once you were finished."

"Nigga, I'm only bullshitting with you. I get too much pussy to be taking it."

Robin's people scooped her up and tried to bring her limp body back to consciousness. Realizing she was halfway out of her daze, her two male cousins stepped back and engaged in a conversation.

"Blood, do you have your heat outside in the car?" Fila Bob asked his cousin B-Rat, who looked like a younger version of Mike Tyson. Fila Bob's face was dark and he had a round head with big eyes.

"You know I don't leave home without my pistol," B-Rat answered him.

"Slide out there and get it. We might have to serve that nigga and his homeboy," he looked over at Gangsta Jake and Horsehead. "We already know how dangerous that fool is."

"We can't disrespect Michelle's funeral like that," B-Rat advised him.

"Any disrespect will be on him. He's the one who showed up after coming at our relative like that. I don't plan on running up on him and dumping or nothing like that for the foul way he got at Robin, but if he gets out of line, I'm peeling his cap, simple as that."

"Ain't he wanted for a gang of murders?" B-Rat asked.

"Yeah, so hurry back with that thang. There ain't no telling what that fool's motive is."

Bold as an Iraqi insurgent in a car bombing, Gangsta Jake walked up to Michelle's casket and placed both hands on her chest. He did not care what the people in the crowd thought about him. Half of them knew exactly who he was minutes after he walked inside the door. They all wanted a piece of him, but based on knowing his reputation, refused to confront him.

Horsehead stood behind him, strapped with a concealed Mac 10 like his personal bodyguard. Gangsta Jake was also heated with a blue steel Colt .45. They both understood everyone would hate their presence, but that did not stop Gangsta Jake from seeing his girl for the very last time. A few minutes of paying respect to Michelle's body was satisfying enough to send him and Horsehead on their way. After kissing her on the lips, the two made their way toward the exit. People in the crowd could be heard expressing their hatred for him as the two put some distance between them and the crowd.

Neither said a word as they walked outside. The two were suited and booted in fifteen hundred dollar fits. After saying his goodbyes, Robin came to the top of Gangsta Jake's mind. He thought about what he wanted to do to her, but did not verbally express it. His lips stayed shut tight while he held back the hurt of losing his girl inside his heart. His hardcore mentality could not match up to the fact that he was crushed about what happened to Michelle.

A group of people saw him and Horsehead walking their way and made a hole for the men to walk through. Gangsta Jake looked at the crowd up and down like they had shit on them. He was tired of hearing the sarcastic remarks being said under their breath. While mean-mugging everyone in sight, he scanned the crowd looking for Robin, who had ducked into a limousine.

"Blood, fuck this fool," Fila Bob told his cousin who sat in the limousine with him and Robin. They could see Gangsta Jake and Horsehead through the one-way tinted windows.

"No!" Robin grabbed Fila Bob by his shirt. "Just let that nigga leave. I know what he's capable of doing. That boy is out of his mind and extremely dangerous! Let God deal with that fool!" she said as she looked at her cousin with fear registering in her eyes.

Fila Bob wanted to step out of the limousine and pump hot slugs in Gangsta Jake for showing up at a funeral where he was not welcomed. He wanted to show him that his disrespect was not appreciated, but the way Robin was speaking about Gangsta Jake had Fila Bob kind of shook up and not wanting to engage in a confrontation with him. A handful of his aunts and other family members present also detoured his decision not to step from out of the limo and start acting the fool he really could be.

Once word finally reached Michelle's grandma that her granddaughter's boyfriend was on the scene, she wanted to meet him for the purpose of cussing him out. Her chance came soon after being told of his presence. The guy Grandma Helen had so much hate for almost bumped into her while making his way through the crowds. Miss Helen's thirteen-year-old great-granddaughter pulled her by the sleeves and told her who he was. And when she did, Grandma Helen made sure her presence was known.

"You no-good bastard! You're responsible for my grandbaby being taken away from me," Grandma Helen yelled out, kicking off the drama that ensued.

"What did that old bitch say?" Gangsta Jake turned to Horsehead and asked, knowing good and well he heard her loud and clear.

"I didn't stutter. You heard exactly what I said."

Gangsta Jake turned his face up at her remarks. Granny continued. "Boy, I'm not scared of you," she responded while balling her wrinkled fists up and holding them by her sides.

"Somebody come and get this old lady because I don't know what she's talking about."

"You know what the hell I'm talking about." Granny's blood pressure was rising. She was as hot as a volcano and ready to run up on Gangsta Jake and bust him in his mouth. However, before doing so, Michelle's Uncle Joe and cousin Too Tall stepped up. They refused to sit back and let anything happen to their family, especially a senior member.

Too Tall was six-seven with a dark complexion. He had mad squabbles for a guy tall and skinny as he was. His thirty-three-year-old body was in good shape. He actually knocked out a guy two sizes wider than him the other day and felt he could handle Gangsta Jake. Joe was almost fifty and really not looking for any type of misunderstanding, but he never ran when it came to assisting a family member.

"Fool, you better back the fuck off my grandmother," Too Tall told Gangsta Jake as his fist went into the air. His reaction caused several of his family members to also come to his aid. No blows were exchanged yet, but Too Tall, Uncle Joe, Michelle's brother-in-law, Ray Ray, and her female cousin, Tangy, were posted and ready to destroy something behind their grandmother. They were not playing around when it came to their grandmother. Their family did not give a damn who Gangsta Jake was. Once Too Tall's fists went in the air, so did Gangsta Jake's and Horsehead's.

"I'm calling the damn police. I'm not having this mess at my baby sister's funeral!" Rachel yelled out while reaching for her cell phone deep inside her purse.

Fila Bob suddenly hopped out of the limousine, holding his cousin B-Rat's 9mm inside his pants pocket. Even with everyone at the funeral on her side, Robin was still too afraid to step from behind the tinted windows of the limo. Enough chaos was already occurring without her presence. She figured if she were to surface, the situation could only get worse.

After viewing Michelle's body, Gangsta Jake's mind was on Robin. He planned on laying in the cut and popping her off when the time permitted. That would have been a perfect plan for him if it wasn't for the drama that unfolded. Now, instead of speeding off with a smile on his face, he and Horsehead were caught in a situation that could potentially turn a lot more deadly than he planned. Someone from the rear of the crowd tossed a bottle of water at Gangsta Jake and Horsehead, who both were in the middle of a crowd of people that had grown.

"Punk-ass niggas!" said another unknown person in the pack as someone else tossed a disposable camera at them. The crowd's hostility was starting to grow.

"Don't get knocked the fuck out trying to be tough, homeboy," Gangsta told Too Tall as the two squared off with one another. When the fight appeared to be a head-up battle, Horsehead put down his fist and shifted the Mac 10 in his pants. His previous movements almost caused the Mac 10 to fall to the ground.

Too Tall was seconds away from throwing the first blow when Fila Bob jumped in the middle of the situation. The gun he possessed was not drawn, but the way he held it in his pocket let everyone know he was strapped. By now, everyone heard about the drama taking place outside and made their way to the center of attraction.

"Hold up, Too Tall," Fila Bob lightly shoved him to one side. "We don't have to put up with this bullshit from him!"

Horsehead did not like the way the situation was unfolding, which is why he grabbed Gangsta Jake and attempted to cut him short from what he was doing.

"Nigga, get the fuck away from here," Fila Bob demanded. As he continued to grip the gun in his right pocket, Gangsta Jake's response to Fila Bob's comment was, "Shut the fuck up, you bitch-ass nigga."

Horsehead, leaning up against Gangsta Jake, was the only reason he did not knock fire from his opponents and deal with the consequences like he was used to doing.

"I'm not trying to be disrespectful at my girl's funeral, but you cowards are making it real hard for me not to." Gangsta Jake looked up and down at Fila Bob and a few other people, male and female, and stated, "Don't let that little pea shooter you're holding in your pocket get you and your family shot the fuck up."

People in the crowd became scared at what he had to say. Once he turned to Horsehead and made sure his words held some validity, he was ready to rumble with the closest guy to him. "Fools, what's cracking?" Gangsta Jake shouted out as he balled his fist up and threw his knuckles in the air.

"Here comes the police right now!" Michelle's sixteen-year-old niece yelled out and pointed at the officers who were responding to a disturbance call. Everyone in the crowd of people was thrilled about the arrival of the police—except Gangsta Jake and Horsehead, who never left his little homey's side.

When Gangsta Jake looked up and saw the police coming, he cut short what he planned on doing. He and Horsehead swiftly made it through the crowd and inside a new rental car parked on a side street facing Crenshaw Boulevard. The way the two were moving caused one officer to look in their direction while the other officer spoke to the people standing before him.

"What's the problem?" the officer asked as he noticed the distressed looks on the crowd's faces.

Robin finally hopped out of the limo, believing the coast was clear.

Grandma Helen took center stage when she pointed her index finger at the vehicle Gangsta Jake and Horsehead were getting away in. "That son-of-a-bitch right there is the problem. He's the fugitive your department is looking for."

"I beg your pardon, ma'am?"

"That heathen is wanted for killing a bunch of folks." Her Southern accent made it difficult for the two white officers to fully understand her.

"Excuse me, ma'am, what did you say?"

"What she's saying is, the guy that's driving off in that black Thunderbird is the person your department is looking for. He's the person labeled as 'The Informant Killer,'" Rachel told the officers with exhilaration.

"Look, he's about to get away!" she continued to point at the rental car they were driving off in. Gangsta Jake, sitting in the passenger seat, looked back and saw Rachel pointing at them.

"Look at that punk bitch snitching on us. Punch it, big homey!"

"Are you sure that's who he is?" one officer asked Rachel as his heart rate sped up.

"Of course, I'm sure. This is his girlfriend's funeral." She showed the officers Michelle's obituary. "That's why he showed up here today, to attend her funeral."

Once he was satisfied with the statement that Rachel and everyone else standing at his car window made, the officer's eyes lit up like a Christmas tree. He and his partner knew exactly who the Informant Killer was and what he was capable of doing.

"Wait here. I'll send someone back to get a statement from all of you. We have a criminal to catch." The officers realized they had already wasted enough time and took off in pursuit of the black Thunderbird Horsehead was driving. One of them radioed the situation into the dispatcher and requested all units available. They were not taking any chances on apprehending a criminal alone as dangerous as the Informant Killer.

"Be advised that One Adam Sixteen is in pursuit of a black Thunderbird headed northbound on Crenshaw Boulevard. We have reason to believe we are in pursuit of a one eighty-seven suspect and backup is requested."

"10-4. Unit One Adam Twelve is within a few minutes of your location. I'll notify One Adam Twelve and all other available units in the vicinity."

"Copy that."

"They're about to try and get with us. I can tell by the way they're speeding up," Gangsta Jake told Horsehead as he looked back and saw the police approaching them a block and a half away.

"Damn! What the fuck have I gotten myself into fucking around with your crazy ass?"

"We're straight. I got a plan to get them out of our business!"

THE END